RIVERS BETWEEN US

A SMALL-TOWN WESTERN ROMANCE

Greta Rose West

PUNK ROSE
PRESS

COPYRIGHT

Rivers Between Us: A Small-town Western Romance
Original Copyright © 2022 by Punk Rose Press
Rivers cover by Sarah Kil of Sarah Kil Creative Studio
Cover photography by Rob Lang
Release date: September 2022
All Rights Reserved
This book is licensed for your personal enjoyment only and may not be re-sold, copied, or given away to others. Thank you for respecting the hard work of this author.
Names, places, characters and events are the product of the author's imagination or are fictionally used. Any resemblance to actual events, places, or persons alive or not is coincidental.

Ebook ISBN 978-1-955633-10-9
Print ISBN 978-1-955633-11-6

ALSO BY GRETA ROSE WEST

Wild Heart: Welcome to Wisper A Short Story

Join the newsletter for this short introduction into the Cade Ranch world and for extra goodies and scenes. Sign up on my website.

gretarosewest.com

THE CADE RANCH SERIES

Book 1 - BURNED: A Cade Ranch Novel

Book 2 - BROKEN: A Cade Ranch Novel

Book 3 - BUSTED: A Cade Ranch Novel

Book 4 - BRAVED: A Cade Ranch Novel

Book 5 - BLINDED: A Cade Ranch Novel

THE WISPER DREAMS SERIES

RIVERS BETWEEN US

STORMS INSIDE US

ACKNOWLEDGMENTS

How the heck did we get here? A new series? Whoa.

To Tracy: the bravest woman I know. Love you, Sistah! Thanks for reading, and rereading, and rereading…

Stephie, my sisser: Thank you for Nashville! The drive home made this book what it is. Love you. #alabamahaint

Mama Terre, thanks for letting me use your love story in my book. I know Dad is proud of this one, and he's up there, pumping his fist and wishing he could hug us.

To my editor, Peter: I'll be forever thankful to you for every time you make me blush with your margin comments, but more importantly for how you always make me dig deeper and try harder. I'm not sure if I've ever told you, but the work you do to guide me to develop my characters has helped me in my personal life too. I've processed a lot of grief through these characters' stories. Thank you for that. Ik hou van je.

To my indie romance writing community at TIRAA, thank you for being a place where I can gain help and guidance when I need it and for being a place where I can occasionally give it, which feels good too. I love you all, and I'm proud to be "flamazing!"

Thanks again to Rob Lang for his beautiful cowboys, and to Calum Winsor, the cover model featured on Rivers Between Us. I've never received so many emails about a cover!

Which leads me to Sarah Kil, my cover designer. This one made me squeal. Thank you!

A Twinsie shout-out goes to my counterpart across the pond, GH Brookhorn. We have to be related. There's just no other explanation. Thanks for BETA reading and pumping me up about this book when I was at my usual point before release of doubting every single word I write. <3 You didn't know it, but you saved the day.

Joanne, Boba queen, I'm not sure I've ever thanked you for making my Style Guide/Series Bible. I check that thing A LOT! And thanks for making my words sound gooder. ;)

To my ARC and Street teams. You guys make me smile every day. I appreciate y'all so very much. Any success I've found with my books is partly due to your efforts and support, and there's nothing I can offer besides THANK YOU! I <3 you all.

I know they'll never see this, but I've gotta thank Shane Smith and the Saints for their song "All I See is You". That song was the foundation for Carey's book's playlist, and it fueled me throughout writing this book. Seriously, I can't even say how many times I listened to it in my car. I'd be embarrassed. Check your Spotify plays. I swear, in the first part of 2022, they have to have skyrocketed.

To Wyatt and Hannie Banani, thank you for indulging my Stranger Things addiction. It helped to clear my head, vegging out and watching again, trying to apply your theories when I was in a writing slump. Eddie Munson 4eva!

And to Sean for helping me redo my office, for listening to endless pointless rants about mailing lists and bookseller rankings, and for feeding me when I forgot to eat cuz the words just wouldn't stop. I'm half spicy teriyaki sauce, half shrimp burrito now.

Lastly, thank you to coffee.

Words.
Heavy things.
They hurt and mock and taunt.
But they build, and they deliver and flow.
And breathe and rise.
And breathe and rise,
like a river.

PROLOGUE

Carey – Thirteen years ago

Famous last words: "He's a good guy. You'll see."

Frannie swore to me. She promised me she knew what she was doing, dropping out of high school to elope with Doug Morris, Dipshit #1 in the long lineup of teenage dipshits in our little town. It was a mistake. I knew it in my bones, but she wouldn't listen to me. She'd made up her mind. Frannie was like that—determined. When she made a decision, she stuck to it, every damn time.

"Carey, I told you," Frannie said. "You never listen. You can't dream anymore. You turned that part of yourself off, but it's all I do. I need to get outta here. I don't wanna be stuck in this stupid town. Will you ever leave it?"

Shrugging, I shook my head. I didn't have the answer to that question. But I had the answer to a more important one. "Frannie, he's not good for you. He makes promises he won't keep. You're gonna regret this, and your dad's gonna be so mad. Have you thought about that? What about your mama, your sister? You know the rodeo will most likely end in disaster. Didn't you learn anything when my ol' man died?"

Her face fell; she knew how hard it had been for my mama and me since my dad died, but she shook those thoughts away. "Carey, don't you understand? My daddy is the reason I want outta here. All he cares about is appearances. He doesn't care if I'm happy. He just wants me to look good for his stupid campaigns." Biting her bottom lip, digging her teeth into the skin hard, she took a deep breath, trying to avoid the truth, and finally said, "And my mama will be fine. She made her choice, stayin' with a man who cheats on her and treats her like garbage. Besides, once Doug makes it on the pro circuit, I'll have the money for school. I'll make somethin' of my life without my dad's help, and then he'll be proud of me. This'll all be water under the bridge. But if I don't go now, I'll never do it. I'll end up at UDub, studyin' pre-law, and I'll be miserable."

I'd loved Francesca McKinnon since the very first day I moved to Wisper, Wyoming.

It was a speck of dust on the map, but my mama and dad had moved us here when I was eleven, almost twelve, because it was closer to all the places my dad had needed to be for his rodeos. He was a bull rider till it killed him.

Frannie and me, we were next door neighbors, best friends, and, instantly from the moment we'd met, in my mind at least, soul mates.

And now, standing between our houses, me in my boxer shorts and T-shirt, and her in her tightest jeans, a long red sweater, and no shoes, she was saying goodbye. I always loved her in red, her fiery copper hair, same as mine, competing with the color. Maybe it was dumb, but it was the reason I loved her the moment I'd set eyes on her. Like we'd been made for each other. Like we matched. She had the most beautiful rosy hue to her skin under her millions of freckles, and I knew I'd miss that flush of color the second she was gone.

Frannie knew me inside and out. My every fear, every joy, the sadness I felt watching my mama's happiness bleed away slowly, more and more every day since my dad passed. She knew the frustration I felt at the loss of control over my own life. I'd been such a carefree kid, riding my bike around town, fishing on the weekends, and hanging out with my friends and Frannie every night. But that all came to a screeching halt.

She knew how my dad had treated my mama on his selfish and self-centered quest to be a rodeo star, and I was afraid Frannie would end up in the same kind of situation. Doug Morris wasn't known for his compassion or concern for others.

I couldn't stomach a life like that for Fran. She may not have loved me the way I loved her, but she was the person I confided in. The one who filled my arms at night when I shared every thought I'd ever had with her.

I had no clue why she'd decided to leave town with him. She wouldn't tell me, and it hurt, but at seventeen, I didn't have time for love anyway. I was still in high school, but my nights and weekends were spent working two jobs to help my mama with the bills. My dad's death had left us with a pile of medical debt and a mountain of regret. Mama blamed herself for never trying to talk him into working a normal job. She said she'd always known the risks he took rodeoing, but that she knew the joy it brought him, too, and she could never bring herself to ask him to give it up, even for me.

He'd put us both through a lot, her more than me, but still, she'd loved him.

So Frannie's plan to run away to "follow her dreams"

sounded like a pile of horseshit to me. It sounded like the same bullshit dreams my dad was always yammering on about, the bullshit that got him caught under a two-thousand-pound bull with a broken neck.

Her leaving now, though, it was confirmation to me that I wasn't what she wanted. I wasn't enough. She wanted a bigger life, something much grander than Wisper, but I was afraid a bigger life meant something completely different to Doug than it did to Frannie.

Life would quickly catch up to her. Hopefully, she'd come home when it did, minus her jackass boyfriend, but what if she didn't? What if she got stuck out in the world, stuck out in real life, and I wouldn't be there for her every day? Her family wouldn't be there. She'd be alone.

My heart ached to think on it.

I didn't want her to go.

I wanted her to stay with me where it was safe, where there was no chance of broken necks or broken promises. Maybe it wasn't the exciting life on the road or the fantastical call of the city and fancy culinary schools that could make her famous someday, but it was home. She was *my* home, and I'd never wanted anything more than to be hers.

There was a time when I thought she might have wanted that, too, but now I knew I couldn't have been more wrong. Somehow, she and I had gone from soul mates to barely friends, and I was forced to watch as she drifted away, metaphorically and, now, literally.

But even so, I had to at least *try* to talk her out of this stupid plan. "Can't you at least wait till after graduation?" I said. "Don't you want that? A high school diploma? To see all our friends graduate? Don't you want your parents to have that?"

"I already looked it up. I can get my GED. It won't take

long at all. And Mama'll get over it. She has Jilly for all that stuff anyway. You know she lives to be their perfect daughter." Squaring her shoulders, she said, "And my daddy can kiss my butt. I'm tired of bein' a prop to him. He won't let me go to culinary school. It's law school or it's nothin'." She shook her head. "You know this. We've talked about it enough times."

"I know but, Frannie, just wai—"

"I can't wait, Carey. You know I can't. You're the best friend I've ever had. You always will be, and I love you, but I'm almost eighteen. It's my decision, and I wanna live." She stepped closer to me, resting her hand on my cheek. "Please understand?" Her eyes lingered on my jaw while her fingers stroked the stubble I had yet to shave 'cause she was sneaking out at five in the morning. "Will you just trust me that this is what's best for the both of us?"

How could her leaving be good for me?

But where Frannie was concerned, I knew when I'd been defeated. Shaking my head, I sighed. Nothing I said would stop her.

"Promise you'll call me when things don't go the way you want? 'Cause they won't, Frannie. They ain't gonna go your way."

She pressed her forehead to mine softly, then kissed my cheek for the last time, whispering, "Isn't there one thing you dream about? Just one? You're so serious, but isn't there one thing that keeps you up at night 'cause you can't stop wishin' and hopin' and wantin' that thing?"

Yeah, there was one thing. Looking in her gray eyes, feeling all my hope leaking out with every blink, I tried so hard to show her the love I felt for her. I hoped, if she could see it in my eyes, maybe she'd stay. And there was a flicker. But then it was gone, and she looked away.

"This is how I get what I want from life, Carey. I don't see any other way. And I'm gonna prove you wrong. You'll see." She hugged me and that was it. She was really going, and as she walked away, she peeked back over her shoulder. "I promise I'll call, but it's gonna be to tell you when all my dreams come true. So get to workin' on your own dreams, you hear?"

But my dream had just walked away from me on a cold morning in March, not even three months till graduation.

And when she crossed the Wisper border with Dumbass Doug Morris behind the wheel of his old, beat-up pickup truck, that dream died.

CHAPTER ONE

CAREY

DREAMS. Yeah, screw that shit.

It was the Fourth of July, or almost, but the end of June was just as hot, and the ridiculous calls were already pouring in.

"Oh, Sheriff, thank God you're here." Mrs. Dubois practically gasped when she met me at her front door with her hand over her heart and a dish towel slung over her shoulder. "My sister stole my Crock-Pot on Easter, and I need it back to make my lil' smokies for the Fourth. I'd like to file a report."

Adjusting my hat a little higher on my forehead so she could see my smile, I said, "Now, Mrs. Dubois, you gotta know that doesn't qualify as aggravated theft. You probably loaned Myrna your Crock-Pot and just forgot. Why don't we call her and see if she'll drop it by?" Secretly, I was wondering if there was some way for me to get my hands on those delicious, bite-sized sausages drowned in sugary gravy. Maybe I could arrest her and take the Crock-Pot as evidence.

Then there were the fires and completely avoidable injuries. Teenagers were bored around these parts during summer break, and our little Fire and Rescue department was on high alert 24/7 till the end of July. We'd been in a drought for a while, so the fireworks were an extra worry this year, but now the humidity was ramping up. We'd had light rain several days this week, and it was unrelenting. Everyone was wishing for a big storm to come through and dump rain on us, and hopefully, it would clear that heavy, damp air away when it left.

But it wasn't just the kids. Last week, Vern Wexler almost lost a finger when he tried to set a Roman candle off in his hand. The whole thing exploded. That colossal idiot could've killed himself, but luckily, the paramedics got Vern and his damn finger to the ER in time. The doctors reattached it, and Vern spent the last week making a tour of Wisper, spinning his tale. In his version, somehow, he made out like a hero and the town bad boy all at the same time.

Fortunately, nobody bought his bull. Vern was an unemployed twenty-nine-year-old landscaper/cowboy and professional beer drinker who still lived in his childhood bedroom and screamed at his mama if she didn't cook him dinner. I knew 'cause I'd been called out to their house to haul his pathetic ass to the drunk tank when the neighbors reported shouting and banging noises 'cause Vern couldn't control his temper or treat his mama with respect. He was currently cradling his reattached finger in a cell in the Wisper sheriff's station.

And he was Dumbass Doug Morris's best friend.

Since Frannie had moved back to Wisper with her kid and her asshole husband, I saw more and more of that waste of skin, and if Doug was doing something illegal or just plain stupid, I could be sure Vern wouldn't be far behind. All of it served as a monthly, if not weekly, reminder of what I'd lost when Frannie left. She was back in town, but she wasn't the same Frannie McKinnon I'd fallen in love with all those years ago.

She'd gone and married the idiot, and sure enough, her light had been dimmed. She wasn't the determined young woman she used to be, the one who never shied away from fear or an obstacle. Now, she was scared of her own shadow, and she barely talked to anyone. Word around town was that Doug and Fran were separated. He was a loser of epic proportions and most likely a shit husband and father. He hadn't become the rodeo star he'd sworn up and down he'd be, he couldn't hold down a good job, and the added stress of having another hungry mouth to feed probably didn't help matters any when Frannie gave birth to a daughter. I had no idea what she'd been thinking—Doug Morris couldn't stay upright on a horse that was standing still, let alone a bucking stallion. He was charismatic back in high school, though, I had to give him that, and he'd lured her away with so many bullshit promises.

We'd barely spoken since she'd moved back to town, and when we did, it was awkward. I wanted her to talk to me the way she used to, like my best friend, but she wouldn't, and I always walked away from the exchange disappointed.

Whatever. She wasn't mine now, and she hadn't been mine back then either. I'd faced that fact a long time ago. She was just a failed dream.

I didn't need that headache, and I never let myself think about it if I could help it. Besides, I had enough on my plate as it was. This time of year, I spent my days dealing with all kinds of stupidity, like all the calls I got about the firework noises. Didn't people realize that I was the *actual* sheriff of Teton County and it wasn't my job to hand out tickets for noise ordinance violations?

Technically, I should've charged them all with false 911

complaints, but this was Wisper. We were a small town, only a few thousand people strong, and everybody knew everybody. You couldn't walk down Main Street without running into at least five people you knew. I'd grown up here. They knew my mama, and they still pinched my cheeks when they thought they could get away with it. They also knew every bit of news and gossip that went on around here, so alerting the sheriff was just a check on many to-do lists, not some kind of state emergency.

When Myrna had returned her sister's Crock-Pot and they'd gone inside for iced tea, I climbed back into my cruiser to check my messages, and I broke open the tin of cookies Mrs. Dubois had given me. She'd even decorated the people-shaped sugar cookies in brown sheriff's uniforms, which was more proof that she'd planned on calling me today, probably armed with a big ol' scheme to get her sister arrested or fined, at the very least, just to entertain herself and feed the rumor mill.

Biting the head off a cookie, I chewed while I thought about how goddamn hot it was. No one was outside attending to their lawns; there weren't even kids playing in the street like there normally would be. Everyone was holed up inside their homes, enjoying their AC. Even in my truck with the air on high, I was sweating through my shirt. How the hell did anybody bake cookies in this heat?

It made me think of Frannie. Like an idiot, I sat there, imagining how she'd look with her red hair twisted up into a sexy bun on the top of her head and sweat trickling down the back of her neck while she baked. She'd always loved it and could make anything. She'd made me a lemon soufflé when we were sixteen, and I still remembered how it had melted on my tongue.

I'd heard she was doing a pies-for-cash service since

she'd separated from her husband and he'd moved out. She had been working over at the Italian restaurant downtown as a line cook, but they'd closed and Frannie had found herself out of a job. Again. She hadn't had any kind of luck but the bad kind since they'd moved back to Wisper with their kid, and it seemed like bad had gone to worse if she was trying to sell pies out of her house for a living. It couldn't earn her much money.

But it wasn't any of my business. We barely spoke, even if we had the occasion to, which was rare, and it was strained between us, so it was better if I could put her out of my mind yet again.

Thankfully, a call came through on my dash radio, interrupting thoughts I shouldn't be having, and also thoughts of stripping down to my boxers, which probably wouldn't go very far to getting me reelected.

"Carey, you copy?"

"Yeah, Abey. Just finished up at the Dubois'."

"Did Myrna really steal the Crock-Pot? And did you ask Mrs. D to make us a batch of her lil' smokies?"

"No, I didn't ask, and no, she borrowed it. Good Lord, when will these ladies learn to just call each other? Last month it was Myrna's favorite knittin' needles. I mean, don't they know we have actual jobs to do? I'll feel like a heel, but next time I'm gonna have to charge 'em both or fine 'em or somethin'. This is gettin' outta hand."

Abey chuckled. "I hear you, boss. Alright, well, I think I got a legitimate case for you. Carl Aberforth called. He says he's had a real theft from his barn. Some campin' supplies, and he said he had a brand-new pair of muck boots go missin'. It doesn't add up to much money, but he reports the lock bein' busted open and there's blood on the floor."

"Blood?"

"Yeah. He said it's just a little puddle, but it's weird. He's a loner. He don't even have ranch hands anymore, so he can't figure out whose blood it could be. He was a real smartass when he called, too, 'cause I asked if he maybe coulda just misplaced his boots, or maybe it was one of his cows who broke the lock. His reply was, 'Well, missy, if I spot a heifer stompin' 'round my property, wearin' my new galoshes, I'll be sure to call back to apologize for wastin' your damn time.'"

I snorted. "Alright, I'm headed out to Cade Ranch for dinner, so I'll stop by to see Carl on my way. Thanks, Abey. You headed home soon?"

"Frank's on his way to relieve me, yeah, but I think I'll go for a beer at Manny's tonight. We been gettin' complaints about that new bartender. Thought I better check up on the situation. You wanna join me after your dinner?"

"Ah, thanks, but I think I'll make an early night of it. Things've been relatively quiet around here lately, which is ironic since fireworks are goin' off every five minutes. But I should use the opportunity to catch up on my sleep." I sighed. "Shit, I shouldn't have said that. I probably just jinxed us."

Abey laughed. "Don't worry, boss, I got your back. Have a good sleep."

"Thanks. And Abey, Dede ain't 'new' anymore. Just ask her out already, would ya? You been starin' at her ass now for two years."

She choked on her reply. "I-I, no. I don't… Ughhh."

"Mm hm. You think it's a secret?"

"Don't you have a crime to investigate, Sheriff?"

"10-4. I surely do."

Abey scoffed over the radio. "We ain't Smokey and the Bandit… but over and out."

Maybe my life was pretty boring compared to some, but at least I had constant entertainment. The townsfolk, my friends, and my deputies never had a shortage of quirks and problems to amuse me, and I loved 'em all for it.

/ CHAPTER TWO

FRANNIE

PHILOMENA BEASLEY, an old friend of my mama's, was on my front porch, waiting for her coconut cream pie. Thunder boomed when she knocked, and I almost didn't hear it. There wasn't a bakery in Wisper, so I'd started a homemade pies and cakes business out of my kitchen, and it earned me a little extra money. I made birthday cakes for kids' parties, and pies and tarts for weekly bridge games. It wasn't a booming pie corporation, and the fresh and non-processed ingredients cut into my profits, but still. Twenty dollars was twenty dollars. Baking was the one thing in my life I was good at, and Grace loved to help me.

"Hey, darlin'," Phil said when I opened my screen door, allowing her inside and out of the misting rain. "How you handlin' this heat?" She swiped her long salt-and-pepper gray braid away from her face and stepped forward to hug me.

Phil was known around Wisper for being the weird old mountain lady, but she was kind and had become one of my mama's best friends later in her life. Suffering from anorexia had been a debilitating and debasing experience for her, and it had weakened her heart and body, so I was glad for anyone who helped and supported her since I wasn't here for her.

"Bet it gets hot in here with the oven on," she said. "Man, I tell you, lately, it feels like we're livin' in the seventh circle of Hell."

"Hi, Phil. C'mon on in. Yes, it does get pretty warm, but I make my crusts at night, so that helps a little. The humidity makes it hard for certain pastries, but pie crusts do fine with the added moisture. Just need a little longer bake time. Wait," I said, remembering Phil was perfectly able to make pies on her own. "Why didn't you just make this pie yourself? You bake better than I do."

"Oh, hogwash. Besides, I'm a busy lady. I finally got my truck fixed, so now I got places to go and people to see. No time for bakin'."

"Sure." She was fibbing. Ordering pies from me gave her an excuse so I could think I was earning the money she wanted to give me instead of accepting a handout.

She followed me into the kitchen while I grabbed her pie from the fridge and placed it in a cardboard box. José at the diner downtown had added them to his weekly order for me, so now, I had something other than tin foil or plastic wrap to send the pies off in. He said I should get some stickers with my name or a business name printed on them to put on the boxes, but that was a little out of my budget at the moment. Besides, no one else in town sold homemade pastries that I was aware of, so people who knew I baked would know they were my pies, and people who didn't know—people I didn't want to know—wouldn't be any wiser.

He also said I could use his kitchen to bake the pies if I needed more space, but so far, making them at my house was working out fine. There was a slight chance that I'd pass out from the heat leaking from my old oven, but I'd live.

"Grace havin' a good summer? She playin' with her little friends today?"

"Uh, no," I said, blowing my hair out of my eyes, but I was sweating, so it stuck to my forehead. "She's readin' in her room in front of a box fan. She doesn't like this heat either." That was the truth, but it was more than that. Grace wasn't good at making friends, and even when every other ten-year-old neighborhood kid was outside, running through sprinklers and screeching and squealing as they played, Grace stayed inside. Part of it was my constant worry about her blood sugar dropping when I wasn't there, but it was also because she was shy.

Maybe shy didn't quite cover it. She was timid, that was true, but she was afraid. She never left my side if she didn't have to. And most days, I was the only person she talked to.

And all of that was because of her father.

So far, Doug hadn't discovered my side hustle, and I hid the money I made under a loose floorboard in the hall closet. I'd only saved a little so far. Cakes and pies hadn't made us rich yet, but that was the dream.

It wasn't a possible dream, but a dream nonetheless.

I remembered baking with my mama when I was Grace's age, and it was where my love for it had come from. It was the only time I remembered her lighting up, and it was the only thing either of my parents had ever praised me for. My father thought it was a waste of my time and intelligence, but he still ate the damn pies. Mama didn't. She stopped eating much of anything when the affairs started.

My father had wanted me to be a lawyer like he was and like my younger sister had become, but it was the last occupation I could ever see myself in, and I was pretty sure you had to go to college for that. The only diploma I had wasn't really even technically a diploma. It was a GED. Not very prestigious. At least, my father didn't think so.

"Fran, don't you have air conditionin'?" Phil asked, fanning her face with her hand, and a bead of sweat dropped from her hairline down the side of her face. She pulled a tissue from her pocket and patted it away, looking around at all the open windows. It was still raining, and the wind was blowing it in, but cleaning up rainwater was better than suffocating to death from heat and humidity if I closed them.

I lied. "We do, but it's on the fritz. I've got a technician comin' later."

We didn't have AC. We'd never had it. Grace's dad hadn't held a full-time job in years and had moved out of our house because a wife and kid interfered with his goal of getting high and drinking beer every night till he puked or passed out. Now, if I could just convince him to move out of the state… Although, even if he moved to another planet, it wouldn't be far enough.

My father paid for my little rental house using money from a small inheritance my mama had left me and Grace, but he didn't trust me enough to allow me to access it, and since my sister worked for him and basically managed his life, she dealt with the money and paid for Grace's medical insurance. Bradley McKinnon, State's Attorney for Wyoming, couldn't be bothered, it seemed. He'd never even been to our house, and that was a good thing. If he knew the state of it, with no AC, a barely working heater in the winter, and used, mismatched furniture, there wouldn't be anything to stop him from telling me how disappointed he was in my life choices. Again.

"Oh, good. I hate to think of y'all bein' stuck without some relief from this nasty weather. You know, I was thinkin' about your mama the other day. I sure do miss her," Phil said, and I smiled politely, but I didn't respond. If I didn't have to, I never talked about my mama. The guilt was too strong. "I said a quick hello when I went over to visit Rand's grave. You know, my husband's been gone now four years, and I swear, it still feels like yesterday."

When I turned and held the pie out to her, she said, "You ever feel like that about your mama?"

My breath hitched and a pit opened up in my stomach when she asked. I preferred not to feel *anything* about my mama at all. "Yeah, guess so."

"Well, you oughta go out to the cemetery, take her some flowers. I know she'd appreciate that."

Except she wouldn't, because she was dead.

"Sure. Yeah, I should do that."

Phil set two twenty-dollar bills on the counter next to her and took the pie from my hands, but then she cocked her head to the side. "You okay, Fran?"

"Yeah. What do you mean?" I looked down at myself. I was presentable. A little sweaty, but fully clothed and socially acceptable, but she was probably referring to the sadness that felt pasted over me like a second skin anytime I thought about Mama, or about the past in general.

I'd made so many mistakes. I knew I couldn't, but what I wouldn't have given to go back…

"Nothin'," she said, shaking her head. Everyone could see I was unhappy, but really, what could anyone say to that? Phil and I weren't that close. It was the usual reaction from all my neighbors. They knew I was separated from Doug and that he didn't live with Grace and me, and they could all probably guess what kind of a marriage we had, but no one ever *really* asked. They wanted to pretend everything was okay, and I couldn't blame them. My problems were not theirs to solve.

"You know I only charge twenty dollars, Phil," I said

when I stuck it in my back pocket 'cause I knew she wouldn't let me reject the extra cash.

"I know. It's a tip, so you can't give it back. That'd be rude." She smirked at me, the crafty devil. "Well, you and Grace plannin' to go to the Fourth of July festivities this year? The parade starts at ten. Oh, you should sell your pies afterwards. Bet you'd make a fortune if you set up a booth by all them food trucks before the fireworks." She lifted her box's lid. "Your pies sure are beautiful, and that's nothin' compared to how they taste. Is that fresh toasted coconut?"

"Thank you. Yes, it is. That's a great idea, but it's a little too late to do it this year. I don't have the space or time to bake all those pies before then, and besides, I think they rent those booths six months in advance, at least. Maybe next year," I said, trying to shut the conversation down. I would never be able to afford the booth rental, and Doug and his buddies hung out downtown getting drunk and causing trouble every weekend, so it was nonstarter anyway. We'd only been back in Wisper for three years, but he'd spent three of those Fourth of Julys in the drunk tank. I had no doubt this Fourth would end the same way, and I planned to stay far out of his way. "But Grace and I'll watch the parade. She likes the little cars the guys over at the VFW drive. They have those funny-soundin' horns, and she gets a kick out of 'em."

"Alright, I'll see you there. Oh, and if you talk to your daddy, give him a hello from me. He and your sister still in Cheyenne?"

"Yes, ma'am. They are. They're pretty busy with work these days, but I'll tell 'em you say hi."

"Well, I expect they would be busy. I still can't get over your daddy bein' appointed as State's Attorney. That is some accomplishment. And little Jillian is some big lawyer tycoon. I know your mama'd be proud."

"She would. Yeah."

"Okay, I've talked your ear off enough." Holding her pie in one hand, she popped her purple polka-dotted rain jacket's hood over her head. "I'll get outta your hair. See you on the Fourth."

"See you. And thank you."

"Welcome, dear. I'll call you in a few weeks with my next order. Next month I'll need at least two pies. I'm takin' 'em over to the retirement village for our annual Dog Days of Summer movie marathon. I know they'll be a hit."

I smiled again. "Great. Sounds good. Just let me know what kind you'd like."

"Will do. I'm thinking maybe lemon meringue or some-thin' light and summery," she said, and she gave a little wave before she headed to the door, but she turned back toward me when she got there. "Fran, smile. Whatever's eatin' at you, it can't be that bad. It might be rainin' right now, but the sun'll be out soon enough."

"I know." I smiled on cue. "Have a good night, Phil."

A mention here or there about my mama wasn't so bad. I was successfully able to steer my mind away from the regret landmines, but lately, it felt like they were exploding all around me, and it brought back so many memories…

"Daddy!" I hollered, running into my house and slam-ming the front door closed behind me after school. I was supposed to take my shoes off at the door, but that day I was too excited.

My mama was probably at the grocery or running errands for my dad, and my little sister, Jilly, was still walking home. I'd beaten her because I was pumped up about my test. I hadn't always been the best in school, but my sophomore year had gotten off to a good start, and I'd been trying really hard. Plus, I'd finally found a subject I liked. Regular classes bored me to tears. Math and English were the worst classes ever, and my B- and C+ weren't the greatest grades, but I'd finally gotten an A, and I knew it would make my dad happy. Grades were important to him, and I tried hard to please him. I did the best I could, but it never seemed to be enough for him, so this time, I was really proud of myself and so excited for his reaction.

Normally, I wasn't allowed in my dad's office, but I knew he'd want to hear my news, so I rushed toward it, calling for him the whole time. "Daddy! I got an A+ on my test, and—" But when I pushed the door open, he rushed forward to close it. There was a woman in there, and she was missing her shirt. My dad's collared shirt was open, his tie was on his desk, and his pants were unbuttoned. His office was paneled in dark wood, and with the blinds closed, it was hard to see much, but I saw that.

The woman was pretty and very professional looking, with straight, flowing dark hair. It was so long, it almost reached her butt, and she shot me an annoyed look over her shoulder when she noticed me watching her as she adjusted her miniskirt. Her lipstick was a shocking red color, even in the dark, and I remembered thinking it looked more like paint instead of makeup.

I looked up into my dad's eyes right before the door thudded shut in my face. "Daddy?"

Through the door, he scolded me, "Goddammit, Francesca. I told you never to come into my office."

"I know," I said to the door. "I didn't mean to interrupt your meetin', but I got an A+ on my cookin' exam in Home Ec today, and I ran all the way home to tell you."

I heard their voices behind the door. I couldn't make out what they were saying, but my dad sounded angry at the woman, but when she opened the door and stormed out, pushing past me at the end of the hallway, the look on my dad's face told me he was angry with me.

The woman's perfume was so strong, and my eyes were watering and I was blinking when I said again, "Daddy?"

Stepping out of his office, he pulled the door closed quietly. "Cooking is not a class, Francesca. It's a fun break in between your real classes. You'd better start applying your-self, or you'll go nowhere in life. Now," he said, turning his attention from the back of the woman, who was making a fast escape out our front door, to me. "Don't do this again. It's rude." The look on his face was disappointed, and it put a rock in my gut.

Once again, I'd failed.

He followed the woman out our front door, stepping around my mama when she appeared on the porch, like she wasn't even there.

"Brad?" Mama asked, adjusting the brown paper bag of groceries in her arms, and she looked over her shoulder at the woman climbing into a blue car parked at the curb. "Who was that?"

His lack of an answer made me feel sick to my stomach, and Mama's face fell.

When she turned around, she looked sick too. "Fran? Who is that woman?"

"I don't know who she is, Mama. I just got home from school. But look," I said, trying to cheer her up. Surely, she'd be proud of me. I held out my test for her to see. "I got an A+ on my Home Economics test, and Mrs. Kinny says I should look into culinary programs. They have 'em for kids my age in Jackson. Wouldn't that be—"

"That's wonderful, honey, but not now, okay?" she said, waving me away as she followed my father to his car parked in the driveway. Mama's floral housedress was pathetic

looking compared to the woman's clothing, and she tugged at it. She knew she didn't compare, not in my dad's eyes, and no amount of adjusting was going to fix that. "Brad! Where are you goin'? You said you'd be home for supper tonight. You promised."

He didn't stop. He climbed into his car and shut his door, then rolled down his window and scolded Mama, the business-sounding tone of his voice making him seem even colder than he was acting. "Get ahold of yourself, Sophia. You're whining again. I have work, and you know it's important."

Mama dared to ask again, "Who was that woman?"

"She's my new campaign manager. Go inside. We'll talk about this later. You're causing a commotion."

Mama looked up and down our block, and sure enough, several of our neighbors were peeking their heads out their front doors, and a few had congregated near their mailboxes to see what was going on. The street we lived on was a petri dish for town gossip. The whole town of Wisper was. They were judging Mama, pity all over their faces, and I watched as she realized what they must have thought of her.

She was embarrassed and red-faced when she turned back toward me standing in the doorway as my dad backed out of the driveway. I pretended to act confused, but I knew exactly what was going on. My dad was cheating on my mama, and she knew it too.

My A+ was forgotten then when Mama made me help her clean the house and prepare dinner for my dad. I had no clue why she bothered. He wouldn't be home till after midnight if his recent activities were anything to go by. And he wouldn't eat the food, not even the apple crumble pie she'd made just for him. He rarely did, usually telling Mama he'd eaten when he was out for his meetings.

I was pretty sure the other woman was cooking for him at

night, maybe more than one woman over in Jackson, where Daddy's campaign headquarters were, and now, as my mama rushed about the house, trying to make everything perfect, she was aware he was lying to her. Again. It had happened before, but no one talked about it. She didn't say it, but it was apparent from her shaking hands and the panic that was trapping her inside it like a straitjacket.

I hated my mama in that moment. I was so mad at my dad —furious actually—but my mama was weak, and it made me seethe inside. I never wanted to be treated the way my dad treated her. Like I was nothing. Like all I was good for was cooking and cleaning and raising children. Why didn't she ever speak up for herself or put her foot down?

That wasn't going to happen to me. No way.

CHAPTER THREE

CAREY

"SEE? You see that pile of blood there?" Carl demanded, pointing to the small pool of dark red, goopy liquid on his tack room floor at the back of his barn. "So don't you go tellin' me it was one of my cows who broke in. I've checked 'em all and ain't one injury on nary a cow."

"Yessir, I see it," I said, bending over to get a closer look at the four-inch-wide puddle. Looked like blood, all right. Straightening, I asked, "What was taken? Abey said you're missin' some campin' gear?"

"Damn right I am. This was all my son's crap from when he was in the Eagle Scouts. Now, you know Harold ain't been home in a long time, and the junk's just been takin' up space in here. It's probably fulla moth holes, but there was a one-man tent right there." He pointed to some dust in the corner surrounding an empty space on the floor where some kind of cylindrical shape used to be, like a tent roll. "And there was an old canteen hangin' above it. Now, that's an heirloom, that is. My daddy gave that to me when I was a boy. And my new boots are gone! What're you gonna do 'bout that?"

"Anything else missin'?" I asked, pulling my phone from my pocket to catalogue it.

"Yeah, all kinds of things I use around here every day."

"Like what?"

"Well, I dunno, but I'm sure the thief took somethin' valuable. Gimme some time, and I'll think of it."

"Carl, you can't make stuff up to get money from insurance. And you gotta have receipts to prove the worth of what's missin'. Insurance companies won't send you a check just 'cause you tell 'em to."

"Fine, but I still want you to look into this, Carey. I'm an old man. I don't have much, but if Harold comes home someday, I wanna be able to give him his things. He's a good boy."

"Yessir, I understand. I will. I'll see what I can find, okay?" The poor guy still had hope his family would come home, even though his wife had left him over a decade ago with some two-bit rock star wannabe, and his son was reported to be off somewhere in New Jersey, gambling and chasing tail.

"Alright then, s'pose that'll have to do."

I patted him on the back, and he led me outside.

"Dammit," he cursed, shielding his face with his hand from the misting rain. "I didn't know we were gettin' rain again tonight."

"Yeah, the forecast says a storm's buildin' up," I said, looking up at the evening sky, but the rain seemed only to be falling on Carl's property, and I could see the sun setting itself into pink and orange clouds behind the Tetons in the distance. It reminded me of the color of the flush in Frannie's cheeks.

I hadn't actually laid my eyes on that flush in over a year, at least not up close. I'd seen Frannie around town, but we weren't friends anymore, and for the second time in less than an hour, I was annoyed with myself for still thinking of her every day.

Carl groaned. "Great. Just more sludge to slip in. I've already had to call the vet out twice for twisted knees. You'd think it was a cow skatin' rink out here, the way these damn animals slip and slide. They're fat enough, they should just sink."

I laughed at the image in my head of one of his heifers roller skating on her hind legs with a pink scarf wrapped around her neck and a purple tutu around her waist. But the rain reminded me of something. "You didn't notice any foot-prints or tracks around your barn, did you? Before or after the break-in?"

"No, but we've had light rain three days this week, so I wouldn't have. I didn't notice any tire tracks either, 'fore you ask."

"Okay, so maybe your thief was careful. Good to know. I'll look into this and get back to you. Sound good?"

"It's sufficient, I guess. Don't you need to test the DNA of that blood or somethin'?"

"Yeah, don't touch anything. I'll call someone to come out and get a sample, but I don't expect too much from the results. I'll call you either way though," I hollered after him when he turned to walk away. "Happy Fourth of July!"

He waved his hand behind him to dismiss me. "It ain't July yet."

Carl's unique brand of hospitality had me shaking my head and laughing to myself while I texted my friend Dean: *I'm on my way. Don't you fuckers eat without me. I'm starving.*

His soon-to-be wife Oly texted back: *Do you really have*

to cuss in your texts, Carey? Jeez. Hurry up. Everybody's waiting. Oh, btw, this is Oly.

She yelled at me, even in texts. Since Dean would've told me to fuck off or to hurry my ass up, I laughed out loud and texted back: *I figured ;p*

"WHAT'S SHAKIN', Carey?" Finn Cade asked when I stomped the mud from my boots on his kitchen rug.

"Not much, Finn. How're you? How's Aislinn?"

"My woman is good. She's finishin' up in the office. She'll be in in a minute. Jack and Evvie are on their way. Jack said Junior was havin' a temper tantrum 'cause they took his pacifier away. And Dean and Oly are upstairs. The twins have colds, so they're tryin' to get 'em to lie down a bit."

Jesus. Just the mention of all that stuff had me stressed out. I wasn't sure how my friends were handling being parents. I couldn't imagine myself in their shoes *at all*. Just the thought of changing diapers and cleaning up baby snot was enough to make me shudder. It wasn't that I didn't like kids. I did. But I had enough to deal with corralling the local adults. Adding kids to the mix sounded like three times the work and a headache to boot.

But since my mama had retired and moved to Arizona, I was glad for the Cades and their constant inclusion. I was considered a brother to my friends Jack and Dean, and to the rest of their family, and they were brothers to me too. And now that my good friend and former coworker, Billie, was married to Jay Cade, it was like my whole social circle was stuffed into one family.

Maybe I needed to get out more.

I'd grown up at Cade Ranch, spent my summers working the ranch, and it was a blessing since my mama had to work two jobs, sometimes three after my dad died, to keep us fed and sheltered. It was a wonder Jack ever convinced his dad to actually pay me. The guy was a real jerk, but I guess he'd known I'd work hard, and he couldn't say no to the help. He was a hard-ass, but I was still grateful, and it allowed me to help with the bills at home even though I was only fifteen. My other job, office work and errand boy for the local Sheriff's Department, was what had inspired my current occupation.

Sheriff Benny was the glue that held all of Teton County together back in the day, and I'd looked up to him. I supposed he replaced my father in a lot of ways, teaching me how to be fair but persistent and to always trust my gut. I applied his advice every day in my work.

"Kev and Luuk are still in the Netherlands. They'll be back next week."

"Again? This is like their third trip abroad, ain't it?"

"Yeah. Apparently, my little bro's been hit with the travel bug. And Luuk reconnected with some old friends over there, so they went for a little reunion get-together. Oly's back to work at the animal clinic full-time, so Luuk's takin' advantage of havin' two docs to cover the cases. But I'm bettin' this'll be the last trip for a while. Doc P's takin' Luci on an extended trip to Mexico for their first-ever honeymoon in September, so Oly and Luuk will run the clinic while they're gone."

"What are you, the town recorder?"

Finn laughed. "S'pose so. Everybody tells me everything. I am a superb listener."

I snorted. "And you have plenty of humility."

"Eh, well, whatever." With his back to me while he stirred

something on the stove, he shrugged. "So what's up with Mr. Aberforth? That old coot causin' a ruckus again?"

"Wha—? How the hell'd you hear about that already?" I asked, throwing my hands up in the air. We needed to publish the phone numbers of the Wisper Gossip Tree. That way, in an actual emergency, the Gab Club might be useful.

"Please, you know Abey can't keep a secret. She told Yola and Manny at the bar, and Yola called to tell Oly, but since Oly was indisposed, Yola told me. Are you still surprised about just how small this small town really is? You've lived here, what, almost twenty years now?"

Sighing and shaking my head, I said, "No, guess I ain't really surprised. Ah, well, Carl had some stuff go missin' from his barn. Nothin' important, just an old tent, a canteen, and a pair of boots, maybe a few other things, but there was a little bit of blood on the floor. At least it looked like blood. Like maybe somebody cut themselves pretty good, but not enough to kill 'em."

"Blood? Whatcha think that's about?"

"Honestly, I have no idea," I said, taking my hat off and running my fingers through my hat hair. I hung it on a hook by the door and unbuttoned my shirt. My friends wouldn't care about me eating dinner in my undershirt. Damn sheriff's uniform was polyester, and it trapped the heat to my skin like it was made of shrink-wrap.

"I dunno who would've stolen an ancient tent. The thing would probably disintegrate into dust if the thief attempted to set it up. There weren't any tread marks around the barn, but the lock to Carl's tack room was busted, so maybe they cut themselves on the latch. My guess is it was some teenagers causin' trouble. I'll look into it, but I don't expect to find much."

The savory aroma of sausage reached my nose, and my

stomach growled. I hadn't eaten anything since breakfast besides my decapitated cookie, and my stomach was wringing itself into knots, I was so hungry. "What're you makin' tonight? Smells good."

"Just makin' sausage and biscuits. A little breakfast for dinner," Finn said, trying to push me away from the stove with his elbow when I reached around him, aiming my finger toward the saucepan. "This one's for Ace. I made it with vegetarian sausage. Plus, Dr. Harris is a vegetarian, too, so I've been bulkin' up my recipes. One of these days, she'll show up for dinner."

The Cades had started a new equine therapy business a few years ago, and things were going well, but it meant a whole bunch of new people were living and working at Cade Ranch, and Dr. Harris was one. She was an uppity woman around my age who stayed mostly in her trailer behind the barn. Finn invited her to dinner several times a week, but she never showed. She was good with their veteran clients, though, and I figured that was the point.

"Ugch. Vegetarian sausage?" I pulled my finger back in protest of the non-meat meat. "What does that even mean?"

"It's a sausage-*like* product made from plants. It's actually pretty good. I adapted my recipe for her. Ace loves my sausage and biscuits."

"Oh, I bet she does!" Dean joked, laughing when he came down the stairs.

Finn tsked. "How're my nieces feelin'? They need their Unky Finn to tell 'em a story?" If anybody ever claimed cowboys were mean and gruff, all you had to do was point them in Finn's direction, and he'd prove them wrong.

"Since when are you the funny guy?" I asked Dean.

He smiled when we shook. "How ya doin', brother?"

"I'm good," I assured him. "Same shit, different day."

"I seem to recall you tellin' us you had a date last weekend, Carey," Finn said. "How'd it go?"

"Oh God," I groaned. "Don't bring it up."

"Why not?" he asked. "It wasn't true love?"

"She wears socks with sandals," I said, like it was the most important fact about Tanya Wrigley.

Dean chuckled. "You're pickier than an old lady. That's the fifth woman you've had an unsuccessful date with in the last two months."

Finn chuckled. "How exactly would you define success in this scenario, Dean? If he got laid…"

I glared at him. "Okay, fine," I said. "Maybe that's an excuse, but you know how much dirt I have on just about every resident of Wisper? Sometimes I can't get that shit outta my head when I'm talkin' to someone."

"Like what?" Dean asked, grabbing a fresh biscuit off the tray on the counter. Finn punched Dean's arm, making him drop the biscuit, but they both went for it and caught it between them. They pushed and shoved each other, fighting for the roll, till Dean snatched it and ripped it in half. He handed half to Finn, and Finn shrugged, then ate the damn thing. *Brothers.* Finn saw me staring at the crumbling pastry, and probably the longing in my eyes, then tossed another at my head.

I caught it and ate it in one bite. With my mouth full, I said, "You know I can't tell you." Grabbing a beer from the fridge, I shrugged and washed the biscuit down with a swig.

Finn raised his eyebrows. He knew damn well there wasn't anything I wouldn't tell my brothers unless it was a state secret.

"But it might have somethin' to do with, um, her flair for Jesus."

"A little religion won't hurt ya," he said.

"No, but it might be hard if I have to compete with him in the bedroom." I cocked a brow. "She has pictures of the Savior everywhere. And I do mean everywhere. And on every*thing*. Even on things Jesus's face should never be on… You get what I'm sayin'?"

Finn twisted around, and they both stared at me with confused expressions.

"Her personal… pleasure… *device* was made in His image…"

There was a beat of silence, then Finn doubled over, laughing hysterically. He slid down to the floor, kicking his feet like a three-year-old. "Her dildo? Oh my God! Oh my God, I'm gonna pee my pants!"

Dean was trying hard not to, but he couldn't stop himself from smiling. "Carey, it ain't right you're goin' around tellin' people about that." He tried to stay serious, but he lost it, too, and bent over, holding himself up with his hand on top of Finn's head, but their guffaws turned into snickers when their oldest brother walked in the door.

With his two-year-old on his hip and his wife by his side, Jack said, "What's so funny?"

"Nothin'. Hey, man." I extended my hand and we shook, and Jack Jr. took advantage of his dad's distraction to steal the ball cap off his head. He plopped it on his own head, but it was too big, and it covered his eyes till Evvie tipped it up with her finger and kissed the kid's cheek.

"Hey, Carey."

"Hi, Evvie. Doin' good?"

"Yeah. We're so good," she said, but she looked at both Jacks when she said it, overwhelming happiness clear in her voice and in her smile, and my stomach squeezed at the sight of Jack Sr. smiling back at her. I'd never admit that I was a little jealous that they were so happy, but yeah… I was. I wanted to find it for myself. And damn if I wasn't tired of going home alone.

"Carey was just spillin' some town secrets," Finn said. He laughed again and popped up off the floor, reaching for little Jack. "Gimme my nephew."

"Fine," Jack said, offering the kid up, "but stop teachin' him to flip us the bird. He does it all day long now."

I tried to hide my laugh under my breath, but Jack heard it and shot me a look.

With no hint of a joke on his face, Finn said, "That is an essential life skill, brother. If you ain't gonna set your kid up for success, I'll gladly do it."

"Gimme my kid back." Jack snatched his son out of Finn's arms, then smacked the back of his head, and Jack Jr. followed suit. His dad smiled at him, pride written all over his face. "Finish cookin' dinner, asshole."

"Yah hole," the kid cooed, and he smiled at Finn.

"Aw, his vocabulary's growin' so fast. I'm a proud uncle." Finn clutched at his heart, pretending to get emotional and wiping an imaginary tear away from his eye, then turned to stir his vegetarian slop. "Yeah, yeah. It's almost ready. Last batch of biscuits'll be done in two minutes. Hold your horses."

"Hold horsies," Jack Jr. said, and he made the cutest attempt at a whinny I'd ever heard, but it was really more like a wet snort.

Dean and Evvie set the table, and Oly finally came downstairs after getting their twin daughters to sleep. Finn's girlfriend finally joined us, and we all sat around the table, ribbing each other and talking about our days. More than one person asked about my failed date, but I successfully steered the conversation in a different direction both times while Finn grinned at me and winked.

But, as I looked around, I realized I was home. Yeah, I'd hoped to be settled down by now, but these people would always be my family. Maybe I was fine on my own. I didn't need a woman to complicate my life, especially not one who fucked Jesus. That was a lot to live up to, and I didn't think I had enough of the Holy Spirit inside me to get the job done.

CHAPTER FOUR

FRANNIE

"MAMA, who was here? Was it my daddy?" Grace asked hopefully, walking into the kitchen after Phil had left.

"No, carrot. It was Phil. She came to pick up her pie."

"Oh, well, so who's next? What are we makin' tonight?"

I chuckled, thinking about the mess we'd made the night before. She'd been covered in flour. Somehow, it had even gotten in her ear. "How 'bout we skip bakin' tonight? It's so hot in here, I can hardly take it."

"Okay," she said. "What should we do instead?"

Pulling the two crisp twenty-dollar bills from my pocket, I said, "Fancy a walk to José's Diner?" I wiggled my eyebrows.

"It's rainin', Mama, and we already ate."

"Oh, never mind that. It's barely drizzlin' now. Besides, maybe it'll cool us down. The sunset is so pretty tonight, and I bet José will have somethin' tasty on the menu today. Your sugars have been good all day, and we deserve a treat."

A smile grew on her lips. "Okay! I'll go get my flip-flops."

So maybe the rain was a little heavier than a light drizzle, but Grace didn't seem to care as we talked and walked through our neighborhood toward downtown.

Wisper was a rural town and didn't have sidewalks, so we walked on the side of the road, gravel crunching beneath our feet, holding hands and kicking rocks here and there. We waved to Mrs. Dixon when we saw her sticking little American flags all over her front yard, jabbing the little metal posts in her grass, and she'd hung red, white, and blue flowers in baskets on her porch to celebrate the upcoming Fourth of July.

The smell of pine was strong after the rain we'd had, and the red maples lining the streets dropped their seeds everywhere. Grace called them twirly helicopters, and she picked one up every few steps and tossed it in the air to watch it twirl and twist its way back to the ground.

I'd always loved the trees here, the cottonwoods so big and wide, providing shade in the summer and vibrant orange leaves in the fall, and the chokecherry trees, with their little red berries. Being so close to Yellowstone and all the diverse wildlife and plant life was a definite plus on Wisper's pro/con list.

We walked past one pretty, two-story log home after the next, and the shame I felt about our tiny, run-down cottage grew with each step. I wanted so badly to be able to provide a home like that for Grace, one with a manicured backyard and big trees she could climb and carve her name into.

That was another dream I feared would never come true. Since I'd lost my job at Brava, the only fine dining restaurant in town, when it closed down, I hadn't been able to find another I could work at while Grace was in school, so I needed the money my father doled out to us like we were his employees. But there had to be more to life than this. There had to be more than a shitty restaurant job that barely earned enough to buy groceries for the week. Who eats at a fine dining restaurant in a mountain town at noon on a Wednesday? No one, which is why it went out of business.

I suspected Doug was working somewhere since he hadn't been around causing problems lately, but I wasn't sure. If he was, it was probably ranch or farm work, so it wouldn't pay much, and it wasn't like he'd help with my power bill anyway. He didn't help with anything, not even his own child's medication.

But I was used to it, and even though it tore at my pride to have to rely on my father for money, I did it for Grace. I did it for the medical insurance she needed and for her insulin. There weren't a ton of full-time, decent-paying jobs in Wisper anyway, even though I looked every day for new job postings, hoping that today would be the day something amazing showed up, only to be disappointed again and again.

One house was set back from the road with a pretty, white front door. The door's glass window was etched with a filigree pattern, and it caught my eye. I cringed inside at the memories that house brought back and tried to ignore them.

"Mama, isn't that your old house?"

"Yep."

"Who lives there now?"

"The Danburys."

"How come we don't live there?"

"I lived there when I was a kid, but my parents owned the house. When your grandfather moved to Cheyenne for his job, he sold it."

To change the subject, I pointed to the house next door. "See that house there?"

"The one with the green door?"

"That's where my best friend lived."

"Sheriff Carey?"

"Yep."

"How come you're not best friends anymore?"

"Oh," I said, surprised by her question. "Well. I… I guess we just grew up. And I moved with your dad to Texas before you were born, so I didn't get to see Sheriff Carey much after that."

"But you still like him, don't you?"

"I do. Of course I do. He's a really good person. A good man. In fact, that was the house I'd go to when I was sad or mad or scared."

"Why?"

"You're just fulla questions tonight, aren't you?" I sighed before I answered. Thinking about that time in my life was bittersweet. "Because it was a safe place. Anywhere he was was safe and happy."

"Does he still live there, or did his daddy sell their house too?"

"He does still live there. His daddy passed away when we were a few years older than you, but he lived there with his mama. And when she moved away, she gave the house to Carey."

Grace stopped walking and looked behind us, thinking for a minute, then she looked back at Carey's house.

"Whatcha lookin' at?" I asked, noticing the big juniper pine in the front yard. We'd made a secret hideout underneath it the first summer Carey lived there and spent our days pretending we were treasure hunters or explorers.

"Nothin'. Just wanted to see how far it was from our house. It's not very far."

"No. Only four blocks. Why?"

"Maybe we could go there sometimes. It might make you happy again."

Oh, Grace. But she was right. It would make me happy. I

knew it, but it was just another dream that couldn't come true. I was still married technically, and I'd pushed Carey away before I left Wisper anyway. He wouldn't want me to come to his house.

I'd known Carey was in love with me when we were teenagers. It wasn't like he hid his feelings, always trying to hold my hand, and I'd loved him, too, but I was angry then. I wanted to escape Wisper and my father, and nothing could've stopped me.

But Carey had been my safe place, and I was too afraid to lose that. With all the crap my father put my family through, I'd needed Carey. I needed my best friend, not a boyfriend, but I pushed him away anyway so I wouldn't break his heart.

The distance I'd purposely put between us began with me sneaking away after school so Carey couldn't offer me a ride home. That led to me being busy when he called, and then I began going out with new friends, avoiding him, and living up to the disappointing reputation my father expected of me.

By the time I left when we were seventeen, I'd earned that reputation, and running away with Doug Morris was just the next logical step.

I didn't love him. I never had. He was simply an opportunity for me to get out.

Fat lot of good it did me.

Texas was an even more miserable and trapped existence than Wisper had been, and I'd quickly realized that leaving home was a mistake. A big one. When we finally moved back to Wisper, I felt like I could breathe again, but I was still stuck in the life I never wanted, being treated the way I swore I'd never let anyone treat me, by Doug and my father.

No matter how hard I'd fought against it, I was just like my mama.

The person I never wanted to be was exactly who I'd

become, and I didn't want Carey to know how weak I was, so I avoided him the best I could.

It was hard in such a small town, but he was the sheriff and busy, so I tried to stay out of his way. Still, I loved him, and now that he was a man and not a naïve teenager, I noticed things about him I'd never noticed before. Like the way he used his big, strong body to shield someone if they were upset or scared. The way his sheriff's uniform fit his body like a glove, and the thigh holster he wore was some kind of weird turn-on. I wasn't sure what that was about, but hot damn. Every time I saw him, it was always where my eyes went. The muscles strained against it, full of strength and power when he stood tall.

But all of that was meaningless. He wouldn't want me. Not the way I was now. If I was the same Frannie I used to be, sure, I could understand it, but not now. And not after I'd left and blown him off for years.

I hadn't wanted to, but I'd known how big the mistakes I'd made were, and I knew, if I asked, he'd forgive me, but I also knew I didn't deserve it.

"Mama?"

Looking down at my beautiful daughter, I tried to remember how to be happy. Even if life hadn't turned out the way I'd meant for it to, I had Grace, and she was the only reason I needed to smile.

"I am happy, carrot. If you're with me, there's nothin' that could make me happier."

She rolled her eyes and snorted. "Mama, you're kinda silly."

"Oh yeah?" I laughed and said, "Well, the apple don't fall far from the tree, now does it?"

CHAPTER FIVE

CAREY

WHEN I GOT HOME, ready to sleep and not be disturbed for at least twelve hours 'cause I had the next day off as long as Teton County stayed quiet, my house phone was ringing.

I answered, "Sheriff Michaels."

"Hi, baby."

"Hey, Mama. How you doin'? How's Arizona treatin' you?"

"Everything's good. I missed your call this mornin'." Her accent was thick in my ear, and it reminded me of all the times she'd taken me to the rodeo to watch my dad. She was a buckle bunny back in her day, which was how they'd met. That my dad had died falling off the back of a bull was fitting, and she always said he went out the way he wanted to and the way God had intended, but I saw the pain in her eyes every time and felt the lie behind the words.

"Yeah, sorry 'bout that. I was lost in a sea of paperwork. Guess I forgot."

"Well, so how was your date last weekend? You never said."

"Aw, Mama, not you too."

"Uh oh. This one didn't go well?"

"The guys bugged me about it all night." Sighing, I removed my gun and holster, placing them on top of the curio hutch I'd inherited from my Grandma Michaels, and I dropped my keys on the sofa table, then wandered around to the couch and fell onto it. I had a gun safe, but I lived alone, and sometimes I needed quick access.

"How's everybody doin' up there? I sent Evvie some outfits for little Jack. She texts me pictures of that sweet boy every time he wears 'em."

When she retired from her job as a nurse and moved south, I bought the house I'd grown up in, but without her here, it felt empty and lacking. It had been just the two of us for so long, and we'd had a lot of good times in this house and laughed a lot. Card games and movie marathons had been our thing. She loved gin rummy, and I made her sit through *Star Wars* more times than she'd probably like to admit. She tried to teach me to dance and cook, and I smiled, remembering the time I almost burned the place down. There was never any shortage of take-out containers in my house nowadays.

We talked for a while, and then she said she had to go 'cause she was late for her golfing lesson, and when I clicked off my phone and turned on the TV, there was a knock on my door.

Wait a minute, golfing lesson? It was ten at night, and Tempe was only an hour behind Wisper. I wondered what my mama was up to—why she'd lie about what she was doing— but I was interrupted when whoever was at my door pounded on it.

"What now?"

I knew I shouldn't complain. I asked for the responsibility of being the Sheriff, and I was proud of the title and proud of how I conducted myself on the job, but sometimes, attending to the needs of everyone around me became overwhelming. Was it so bad that just once I wished for a little peace and quiet? Was it so bad to wish for one thing I could keep for myself?

When I opened the door, I saw no one. There wasn't anybody on the other side… till I heard a squeak and looked down to see Grace Morris standing there, looking as scared as a faun.

"Grace? What're you doin' here? Where's your mama?"

With Fran living only a few blocks away, we should've been used to seeing each other, but it didn't happen very often, and Frannie kept to herself. When her mama died five years ago, her sister and Dad moved to Cheyenne, so I figured Frannie had come home to Wisper with her daughter and no-good husband 'cause Doug's mama still lived here, and since the loser didn't have a job, he probably depended on the ol' lady to pay for his rent and food. He didn't stay with Frannie anymore. Just like his best buddy, Vern, Doug Morris lived with his mommy like the mature, self-sufficient, and upstanding citizen he was.

Right.

Frannie was somewhat of a recluse. Sure, she was separated from her moron of a husband, but she hadn't divorced him, and I knew straight from the horse's mouth that he didn't take kindly to other men talking to the woman he considered to be his property. He was a lousy excuse for a man, but he was Frannie's choice and, unless he did something to warrant me throwing his ass in jail, none of my business.

Except now, I thought he might've done just that. Fran didn't let ten-year-old Grace wander around town, even though most kids her age were wild, running through town all summer 'cause Wisper was still a place people felt safe enough to let them do it, but I'd never seen Grace playing with them; she was always glued to her mama's side. So why was she at my front door at ten o'clock on a Friday night, fear written all over her face, looking like she was ready to cry or scream?

"Grace? What happened?"

Her voice shook when she spoke. "Mama said you're safe. Please," she whispered. "Help her."

My heart stopped beating for five seconds. "Where's your mama, Grace?"

"Home," she said a little louder, and I grabbed my gun and keys, picked that kid up so fast, and all but threw her in my cruiser.

"Can you tell me what happened?" I asked, shoving my truck into gear and punching the gas pedal.

She didn't say one word, but when I looked her over, tears were streaming down her face.

Flipping on my lights, I raced to her run-down house, radioing my deputy on my way. "Frank, you copy?"

"Yeah, boss."

"Meet me over at Francesca Morris's place on Elm Street. Code 3. Don't let anybody hear you comin'."

"On my way."

When we got there, I had a second of panic. It would take Frank a few minutes to get to us, and I couldn't take the kid with me or leave her alone. But Fran's neighbor, Mrs. Quinn, peeked her nosy nose out her front door, and I took advantage.

While she stood with Grace on her front porch, arms wrapped around her to keep Grace from following me, I approached Frannie's busted-in front door with my gun out, finger next to the trigger and my heartbeat hammering in my chest.

The pit of dread in my stomach was enough to eat an ulcer clean through it. I had a feeling Fran was unhappy in her marriage, though, on the rare occasion we did talk, she wouldn't say. She'd barely talk to me. I'd never gotten a report that the asshole was abusive, but now it was occurring to me that maybe that was what had happened.

I was furious at myself for not knowing it before, 'cause as I inched through her front door into the darkness there and saw the state of her house, I was sure of it.

CHAPTER SIX

FRANNIE

IT WAS ALWAYS the same dream. If you could call it a dream. Technically, it was probably more like a hallucination or a trauma-induced manifestation since it only surfaced when I was unconscious after a "talkin' to" from my estranged husband, though his fists sure didn't feel estranged from my face or my stomach.

But the dream was always the same.

It was the memory of when I'd realized I would have to fight tooth and nail for my future, the day my dad had come home and told my mama, my sister, and me that if we didn't shape up, he would replace us with a family who would. Because he was running for county office, he needed his family to behave properly, so if we couldn't live up to his impossible standards, he'd find a better one. I hadn't been the poster-child daughter of a politician with my mediocre grades and my tendency to be a dreamer, and after I'd discovered he was having an affair, I acted out. Benny, the sheriff when I was a teenager, had hauled me down to the station for bad behavior more than once.

The affairs continued, but I'd never confronted my father

—no one did. It wasn't a thing anyone did to Bradley McKinnon—so when he threatened to leave us, I was afraid he'd really do it, and I couldn't let that happen to my mama and sister.

The dream was a memory of the day Jilly had decided to become a lawyer, just like my dad. It was the day my mama had gone on the "diet" that later killed her, and it was the day I knew I wanted out of Wisper. I wanted to get away from my father, and nothing could've stopped me.

Not even love.

That was the part of the dream that always got hazy. I looked for anything I could find to help me, something to prove my worth to my father, but there was nothing, and I ran out of the house, never to return. Every time, I thought I would find the thing that would make it all better before I woke, but I never did.

All I could see was a copper-colored glow. I felt the smile in the cloud billowing in front of me and the feeling of welcome it offered to me, but I could never see it properly. It never spoke or made a noise, but somehow I knew it was safe, and if I could only reach it, everything would be okay.

I'd spent my entire adult life wishing for that feeling.

But just like every other time I'd had the dream, when I stretched my arms out to reach for whatever this thing in front of me was, this thing that called to me like love, I woke up with a jolt.

And this time, it only took two seconds for me to realize where I was and what had happened.

"Grace! Grace, where are you? Baby, it's okay. Mama's okay. Please come out. He's gone. It's over."

Jumping up on unsteady legs, I tried to shake the dream from my head, and the darkness of my reality pulsed around me, making me dizzy. I felt like I might vomit when I remembered Doug throwing the living-room lamp against the wall. I knew the bulb had shattered all over the floor, so I was careful when I stood 'cause my feet were bare, but honestly, what was another cut? My body was full of them. By now, I'd shed so much blood because of that man, it was a wonder I had any left to live. But it wasn't important.

"Grace? Please, my girl. Where are you?" Had he taken her with him when he left? I was passed out. I had no idea where my daughter was, and I was terrified. Things hadn't been this bad since Texas, and I was scared now that this would be our normal again.

My front door creaked open, and my heart fell even further into the pit in my stomach. I wasn't sure if I could survive round two with Doug, and I knew for a fact that Grace couldn't live with any more fear or disappointment.

I backed into the corner, hoping I really was in darkness and it wasn't blood in my eyes making it impossible for me to see. I felt the sticky warmth trickling down my face, so I knew it was a possibility. *Grace, please, stay where you are, baby. Don't let him see you.*

A flashlight flicked on. It was excessively bright, and the glare hurt my eyes and made my head pound, but I was glad to be able to see. The harsh light wasn't aimed at me yet, though, and it blocked the dark figure behind it so I couldn't tell who held the flashlight. Feeling around me, I tried to find something I could use as a weapon. There was nothing till my fingers bumped into a broomstick leaning against the wall. I gripped it, flipping it upside down, ready to poke my husband with the end, not that I expected it to do much damage, but it was something at least.

The flashlight slowly moved through my living room, then a deep voice whispered, "Frannie? Where are you?"

Relief flooded my body. "Carey?" I'd know that voice

anywhere. It was the sound of home, even though I'd abandoned my home years ago. I'd abandoned him.

"Yeah," he said, and he shined the light on me. "He still here?"

He didn't need me to tell him what had happened. He'd figured it out. I couldn't hide it from him anymore. "I-I don't think so. Is his truck in the driveway?"

"No."

"Then he's gone. I kinda remember him leavin', but I'm not sure, and I-I can't find Grace." The panic was starting to take over, and I stumbled through the words. I wasn't sure if he could even understand me. "I think he t-took—"

"She's next door with Mrs. Quinn. She's safe. She ran all the way to my house to get help."

"Oh, thank God." The overwhelming relief was immediate and so thick, I could barely breathe. Letting the broomstick fall beside me, I slid down the wall, my legs unable to hold me up any longer. I knew Doug couldn't be bothered with his own daughter, and he certainly wouldn't be bothered to care for her medical needs, but I was always afraid I'd wake up after one of these "conversations" to find my daughter taken from me. Again.

And I would find no help then. Not from Doug, and not from my family. I almost laughed at the image in my head of my father running to my rescue, till I realized how sad it was that he wouldn't.

Carey followed me to the floor, squatting in front of me, and he spoke into the radio on his shoulder when we heard another car pull into my driveway. He shined his torch away from me, and I was finally able to see his face a little. The more I concentrated on his rugged features, the more relief I felt. He looked different from the last time I'd seen him. His cheeks and chin were covered in stubble, but his kind eyes were the same. His frame was tall and solid, and I wanted to throw myself into his arms. Just the sound of his voice slowed my racing heart a little. "I'm inside, Frank. Keep an eye on the kid and Mrs. Quinn."

Frank Sims's baritone voice came through Carey's radio. "Everything okay in there? Need me to call for a bus?"

Carey's eyes assessed me carefully, looked over the cut at my hairline, at the blood beading there. He cocked his head to the side, then reached forward with his fingers to gently touch my face, and I almost allowed myself to lean into them. "I'm gonna have Frank call for an ambulance, and I'll give your dad a call."

My head snapped back. "No!" Jesus. That was the last thing I needed. "Please, Carey. I'm fine. I don't need an ambulance, and please don't call my father. I-I don't wanna bother him."

"Frannie—"

"You don't understand. Please. I can't involve him in this. Please, will you just let it go?"

"Let it go? You're bleedin'. You blacked out. No, I'm callin' for an ambulance at least. If you don't want your dad to know, that's your business."

The problem was, if I went to the hospital, it would become my father's business. Someone would call him when they found out I was the State's Attorney's daughter.

I begged, leaning up on my knees and gripping his shoulders. I looked in his eyes, the light from his flashlight a wash between us, willing him to see it my way. "Please, Carey? Please? If I ever meant anything to you, please let this go. I'll go to Doc Whitley's clinic. I promise."

It was cruel, I knew. I'd made a lot of promises to him when we were young, and I'd kept none of them. And I knew he'd cared for me—more than I'd wanted to admit back then

—so it was a low blow for me to use it to leverage him now, but I couldn't take the chance that my family would hear about this.

It was enough that I'd embarrassed my father by trying to divorce my husband, but I did it anyway. It hadn't come through yet, though, which was why I kept finding myself in these messes, why my daughter lived in fear, and why my face looked like a well-used punching bag. But my father and sister lived several hours away in Cheyenne, and they rarely made the trip out to see us. *Out of sight, out of mind.* But I needed it that way, and I needed his money and his medical insurance. If he disapproved of how I was living my life, he'd stop giving me that money, and it would mean Grace's health would be in danger.

More than it already was, and I couldn't have that.

Carey was resolute. "Say the word, and I'll make it stop."

He was pleading with me; I saw it in his eyes. He still cared for me even though I didn't deserve it. I hadn't deserved it in a long time.

And there was nothing he could do.

If I didn't report the abuse, there was nothing anyone could do. Even if I did report it, I had learned the lesson time and time again that nothing would be done, so I pulled my hands away, leaning back on the balls of my feet, and lied right to his face, "Thank you, Sheriff. This was my fault. I… I tripped on the rug, knocked over the lamp, and fell. That's all that happened. Please, just go. I'll head over to the clinic, but I'm fine."

"Dammit, Frannie—"

"Stop callin' me that. We ain't kids anymore."

I stood and walked past him still on my floor. Taking the deepest breath I could, I felt a bruised rib, at the very least, protesting the inhale, but when I got to the door, I ignored the sharp, stabbing pain and yelled out into the night, "Grace! Grace, honey, I'm okay."

My daughter ripped her way out of Mrs. Quinn's arms, jumped down the porch stairs, and ran to me. Relief flooded my body when she crashed into me. The pain in my side would've liked to take my breath away, but it was nothing compared to the pain I could've been feeling if she'd been hurt or if Doug had taken her.

"Mama?"

When I heard her scared voice, my breath rushed out, and I was whole again. Nothing and no one would hurt my girl. Not ever. And I would do whatever I needed to keep her safe and healthy.

I held her as close to me as I could without suffocating her, and there was so much belief in her deep gray eyes, exactly the color of mine. Belief in me while she held me as tightly as she could, arms wrapped as far around me as she could reach, and my heart shattered again for my sweet girl. It broke for her every time her father laid his hands on me. It broke for the loss of innocence she didn't deserve, for the fear she was made to feel because she was born unlucky, and for the shame I knew she'd feel when she realized someday that it was all my fault.

───────

"FRAN, I think I need to call the authorities."

"It was an accident," I lied to the doctor. "I told you, I fell."

Doctor Whitley didn't believe me. He might've been old, but he was still sharp as a tack, and it wasn't like he couldn't guess what kind of man my husband was. Children didn't stop talking for no reason all of a sudden, and bruises didn't appear on perfectly healthy women for no reason either.

Doug hadn't hit me in a long time. When we were in Texas, it was a regular thing, but since we'd moved back to Wisper, he'd controlled himself. Or tried to. I thought he must've been afraid of what might happen if people around here knew the truth—Carey specifically—and he didn't want anything to mess up his life. Not that he hadn't messed it up himself, but he knew he was more likely to end up in jail here than he had been in Texas.

"Anyway, I already spoke to the sheriff. Everything's fine, Doc. I promise."

He looked in my eyes, doubting me and dabbing blood away from the glue he'd just used to close the cut on my forehead. "Fran, I don't feel comfort—"

"Doc, please..." I begged him with the look in my eyes not to say anything more in front of Grace. I'd bribed her with my busted phone, and she was playing a game, but I knew she was listening to every single thing I did or didn't say. It was past midnight, and she had to be so tired.

He took my hint and, instead, grabbed a red sucker from the glass jar on his desk. "Grace Mae, would you like a sugar-free lollipop? And then I'd like to check your A1C. Last time it was a little low, and you ladies have had a long night."

She looked up but shook her head when she spotted the candy between his fingers.

"Do you have a green one, Doc? Grace's favorite color is green." I smiled at Grace, but she didn't smile back. She probably wouldn't for at least a week. Each time we went through this, it took longer and longer for the light to return to her eyes.

"Of course," Doc said. He dropped the red sucker back into the jar and lifted a green one, then handed it to Grace and she put it in her pocket. "How are you set for Grace's insulin, Fran? I know you said you have it covered, but I always have some here if you need it. You just let me know."

"We're okay, aren't we?" I winked at Grace, but she dipped her head, looking down at my phone again. She didn't like to talk about her diabetes. She wouldn't say so, but I was sure she knew it was part of the reason we were stuck with her father. It was the thing my own father held over our heads so I wouldn't embarrass him by living my life the way I wanted to. Without my father's money, and with no job of my own, I couldn't afford the medication. The cost of insulin in the United States was a joke, but if I took handouts from Doc Whitley, my father would hear about it. He'd find a way to punish me for it. I knew he would, and Grace knew it too.

Every day, she shrank a little more inside herself, trying as hard as she could to not be a burden, and no matter how many times I told her how untrue that was, she didn't believe me, but we'd gone too long without her insulin too many times for us to risk losing access to it, so it was the reason I wouldn't chance making my father angry. With Doug Morris for a dad and my father for a granddad, Grace was doubly unlucky, but I tried hard every day to make up for them both.

Dr. Whitley turned away from Grace, and speaking in a low voice, he said to me, "I don't see evidence of a concussion, Fran, but that doesn't mean you don't have one. If you and Grace stay the night in my guest room, I won't call Carey… this time."

The word "no" was forming on my lips, but he raised a brow and cut me off. "Before you answer, let me remind you that Mrs. Whitley will have something to say about it, so there isn't much point in you leaving. That woman, God bless her, will be on your front porch in under an hour in her curlers and housecoat and everyone will hear about it. And if you don't stay, she'll have my head, so it benefits us both. That way, I can keep an eye on you. If you're still feeling okay in the morning, you can go. Do we have a deal?"

"I-I…" Looking at Grace, I took a deep breath. I really didn't want to take her back to our house when the living room was still in shambles. And maybe she'd get more rest here. She'd probably feel safer if we stayed, so I released my breath and surrendered. "Fine. Deal… Thank you."

"IT'S SATURDAY. Wanna go to the river? We could take a picnic," I coaxed, trying to perk Grace up. My head felt like it was in a vice, throbbing to the beat of my heart, but ibuprofen would work wonders. I hoped.

Doc Whitley had let us go after he'd reexamined me, shined a light in my eyes, took my temperature, and grilled me about how I was feeling, and we walked six blocks home. Grace had felt safer there, and she slept like a log.

"We need to return your library books and get more, and then we can hang out by the river and read. How's that sound, carrot?"

Grace shrugged and took a small bite of her oatmeal. She hated that crap, but it was cheap and unprocessed. I added bits of cooked apples and sprinkled a little cinnamon on top to help the bland flavor, but she still despised it.

Someone had cleaned up the broken glass and tried to repair my front door, and I had my suspicions that it was Carey, or maybe Doc had asked someone to clean up. I wasn't sure how I felt about that—someone being in our house without me knowing—but they'd been trying to do a nice thing. I couldn't find my broom, so they must have taken it with them when they left, probably because it was filled with shards of glass. I'd have to buy another one at the dollar store. Whoever it was had tried their best, but a strip of light still broke through where the doorjamb had been kicked away from the frame, and Grace glanced at it, hoping I wouldn't see her looking, but I did.

"C'mon, kiddo. Go get dressed and we'll get goin'. I'll pack us some snacks."

Pushing her bowl away, she stood from the table and walked to her bedroom, but still, she wouldn't smile, and I fought the urge to cry. But I couldn't.

Not in front of her, at least.

CHAPTER SEVEN

CAREY

FINALLY, I had a day off. Abey and Frank were handling the calls in the Wisper office, and Jody and Ed in the Jackson main station. Teton was a large county, but we had outposts in more than a few places. It was a lot of driving to and from the different towns and townships, but it wasn't a hardship. In fact, I preferred it to being stuck in one place. At least driving, I could see the sky, the mountains all around me, and the air was fresh. A little dusty this time of year, usually, but still clean and refreshing.

Wisper was my favorite place to be though. It was home, and it didn't matter if I was on the clock or off. It was where I belonged.

Today was no exception. The sun was high in the big, blue Wyoming sky, wisps of clouds streaked here and there, and I was tucked away in my favorite fishing hole along Fish Creek. Most of the holiday vacationers would be further north, or they'd join the rest of the Wyoming tourists on Snake River, but this was my secret spot. It was a freshwater tributary that forked off from the main creek, full of cutthroat and brook trout, and it was the most peaceful place on the planet, in my humble opinion. It was where I came when I needed a breather, if I could take the time off.

Last night, seeing Frannie like that, beat to hell and still trying to protect that waste of skin she called a husband—

It was enough to make me want to commit murder.

But she wasn't mine, I reminded myself again. She'd never been mine, and she never would be. But damn, didn't she know there was a whole different kind of life she could be living? And how could she condemn her kid to her bad choices? I wasn't uncaring of her situation; I'd observed many women in her exact position, but she had to know I'd help her. All she had to do was admit that the abuse was happening and ask.

Maybe that wasn't so easy though. I knew that too.

Once again, Frannie McKinnon was breaking my heart.

Or, well, Fran Morris.

I tried to push it out of my head, tried not to see the blood on her face and the bruises that would soon appear, tried not to see the fear in Grace's eyes.

It was impossible. I dropped my gear on the ground, kicked off my boots, tore off my shirt and jeans, and stomped into the river in my boxers, just to feel the pull and push of the water on my legs and the hot sun on my shoulders. Just to feel something other than anger. When I looked south, I saw a mama elk and her calf, the tiny spotted thing following behind her, lapping at the water every now and then but still looking around, scared of the world. Scared of predators. Scared of the unknown.

It wasn't till the elk took off that I realized someone was standing behind me.

Two someones.

Normally, anybody coming to engage in watersports or boating would be rowdy and make too much noise, so it was surprising to me that whoever was standing behind me on the riverbank was whisper quiet, like only prey could be.

"I'm sorry. We'll go. We didn't know anybody would be here," Frannie said when I turned to look at her and her daughter. She must've remembered this fishing hole from our many summer days spent here, playing pirates or plotting Frannie's culinary-world takeover.

Fran's eyes were glued to my bare chest, and then they dipped lower toward my shorts, and I rushed forward to grab my T-shirt. Pulling it over my head, I yanked it down, trying to cover myself while Grace looked back and forth between Fran and me, shielding her eyes from the bright summer sun, holding a book in her other hand, but when her mama went to pull her back down the trail, Grace stomped her foot.

"No!"

"Grace?" Frannie froze, looking as surprised as I was that the kid was throwing a fit. Up until last night, I wasn't sure Grace Morris could talk at all, but she was talking now. In fact, I wasn't sure she'd stop.

"You said we could read by the river. Here's the river and here's my book." She held it up in the air and shook it. "I wanna read! You keep promisin' me things, and then you take 'em away." She glared her mama down, and the look on Frannie's face was pure heartbreak.

It was plain to see she didn't want to take the afternoon away from Grace, but as she looked back and forth between the kid and me, she was afraid to stay. I didn't think she was afraid of me, more like she was afraid of what her husband would do if he found out she was anywhere near another man, especially since he knew we'd been friends in another life. The fact that I always carried a gun probably made no difference to the idiot, and I was sure it didn't give Fran any comfort either.

"I'll go. You ladies stay and enjoy the river." I said the words, but I wanted to punch a tree. Seriously? I was losing my day off and my fishing hole too? But I wouldn't show my frustration to the kid. Poor thing had enough to worry about, that was for sure.

I couldn't hide my scowl from Frannie, however. She cringed when she saw it as I grabbed my jeans, boots, and fly box and stalked past her. The beach sand and pebbles rubbed between my toes, and it was stupid, but the burn it caused and all the anger and hurt I'd felt when she left in high school was bubbling up inside me. Every time I saw her, the urge to scream at her grew.

She had always been so special, the life of the party, and she was fierce and brave. Everyone loved her. She was supposed to make something of her life. She was supposed to be magnificent. But she wasn't. Far from it.

And her decision to pull away from me, to distance herself from our friendship 'cause she thought I wouldn't ever go anywhere, it pissed me off. I may not have left Wisper, but I had made something of myself, and what had she done?

Where was the light that used to shine in her eyes, in her hair, in every breath she took?

I didn't mean to, but when I walked past her, I spoke low so only she could hear. "Have it. Have my river, Frannie. Just take it all. Maybe you can hide it away with my heart, wherever it is you keep that."

A breath rushed from her mouth, and she clapped her hand over it. I heard her fingers slap the skin.

Shit.

"I want him to stay, Mama."

Huh? Stopping in my tracks, I turned toward Grace. It was the last thing I'd expected to hear.

Frannie turned to her daughter, too, dropping down to her knees in the rocks along the bank so she was eye to eye with Grace. She was wearing cutoffs and a black tank top, and as hard as I tried, I couldn't keep my eyes off her ass. A hint of its curve showed at the tops of her thighs, and the urge to press her up against my body so I could feel it was trying to steer my brain in unwanted directions. Seriously unwanted.

We were so far past teenagehood and stolen glances now, but I realized how attracted I was to her still. It was inappropriate, though, so I pushed the thoughts away.

"Grace? Are you okay? Maybe your sugar's gettin' low."

"It's not. I'm just mad at you."

Fran sighed, but she looked a little worried. "Baby, Sheriff Michaels can't stay. I'm sure he's got lots of things to do. He's a busy man."

"He doesn't look busy to me. He looks like he was plannin' to go fishin', but we messed it up. So why can't he fish while we read?" Grace stood her ground. "You don't have to talk to him if you don't want to, but I like when he's around. I'm not scared when he's around."

That stopped her mama cold. Frannie seemed to be choking on air, and I couldn't have been more uncomfortable. I didn't want to deny the kid, but I also didn't want to make things worse for Frannie. It was unlikely that Doug Morris would happen upon my secret spot in the woods, but it wasn't impossible for someone else to wander through and then tell some loudmouth in town who they'd seen.

"I, um, well…" Frannie turned on her knees, and she begged me with the look in her eyes and the pained smile on her lips. "Sheriff?"

She would do anything for that kid, I was sure, even if it was uncomfortable.

Looking around, I assessed the little bend in the creek, the opposite bank, and I checked behind me. There wasn't anyone else around, and most likely, I'd hear it if someone were to approach. And when I looked back at little Grace Morris, my decision was made for me 'cause she was smiling up at me. Big.

"You sure?" I said to Frannie, trying not to let Grace hear the lingering annoyance in my tone.

Fran looked back at Grace, at the open smile on her face —even I could tell the kid looked more relaxed than she had in a long time—then turned back to me. She nodded. "Please, Carey?"

"Well, I s'pose I could stay for a while, but don't you go scarin' my fish away with your girl talk and giggles." Stuffing my anger deep down inside, I smiled and winked at Grace. If it were possible, her smile grew bigger, and she gave me two thumbs up a little awkwardly with her book still in one hand.

"Okay, that's settled," Fran said, and she stood to fetch her cooler bag from where she'd dropped it. "Grace, are you hungry?"

"No, Mama." She rolled her eyes. "I just ate breakfast."

"Oh, right. Well, go ahead. Find a spot and crack that book. Hagrid awaits."

"What are you gonna do?"

"Uh, well, I'm gonna talk to Sheriff Michaels for a minute."

"'Kay then." Grace shrugged and nestled herself into the crook of a tree trunk twenty feet or so away.

Frannie watched her daughter's every move till she was settled and reading. When she turned back to me, she couldn't stop herself from glancing over her shoulder every thirty seconds to check on the kid.

"Frannie, I can see her plain as day. Relax. If there's any danger, I'll spot it comin'."

She nodded, but she didn't look anywhere near relaxed. The knot on her forehead that Doc Whitley had fixed up was red and angry looking, and a bruise had formed on the apple of her cheek. It hid her freckles, and it pissed me off.

My eyes zeroed in on the bruise like a laser. "You gonna tell me what really happened last night?"

Looking up at me, she squinted against the sun. It lit up her gray eyes, and I could've sworn the tiny green specks around her irises sparkled. Her hair had fallen out of her ponytail a little, and pieces of it framed her face. It was so red in the sunshine, and I felt the urge to tuck it behind her ear, but I didn't 'cause I still wanted to yell at her. And I couldn't 'cause we didn't have that kind of friendship anymore.

"Are you askin' as the sheriff or as a friend?"

"We ain't friends. You made that clear last night."

"I told you, I fell." She shrugged, like it was no big deal. Like her husband using her beautiful face as a target for the frustration he felt over all the misery he'd created in his own life was her fault. Like last night was your run-of-the-mill Friday and there was nothing more to be said. *Fell, my ass.*

"Okay then." That was all I said before I turned and set myself up on a fallen log a few feet closer to the water. If Fran was bound and determined to protect someone who didn't deserve it, there wasn't much I could do. Legally, my hands were tied, but that didn't mean I couldn't keep my eye on him unofficially.

Opening my fly box, I found my favorite fly and attached it to my line. I pretended I couldn't hear the river rocks knocking together when she walked up behind me, and instead, I focused on the sound of the water ebbing and flowing over rocks lazily, catching on logs, and trickling downstream.

"Carey?"

"Hm?"

"I'm sorry."

"What for?"

"You helped us last night, and I'm…"

"You're what?" I said, testing my line, and I rolled it back.

"I'm not bein' very thankful."

"No need for that. Just doin' my job."

"Okay."

We both stood there, silent. I didn't look at her, but I didn't want to walk away. I liked being near her. The same attraction and pull I'd felt back in high school was tugging at me now. Her feelings had never been the same, but still, I stayed rooted to the rocks 'cause it felt like, just for a moment, that maybe I could at least have my best friend back.

When I didn't respond further, she said in a small voice, "I better go check on Grace."

Peeking over my shoulder, I saw Grace still reclined against the tree, but she wasn't reading her book. She was watching her mama and me again, but when Frannie approached, she stuck her nose back in the book, pretending she'd been engrossed in the story the whole time.

The kid saw everything, and I wondered if Frannie knew.

Wading into the water, I tried to lose myself in the feel of the river, the sway of the barely-there breeze, the hot, late-June sun shining down through the fir trees and soaking into my skin, and I concentrated on my roll casts—the feel of the line flying away from me, the *whip* of it catching in the air and the *thunk* when it landed and sunk under the water.

Twenty minutes later, after my heart had slowed to a normal pace again and my shoulders had relaxed, I heard a tinkling voice behind me. "I've never seen anybody fish like that."

"Wha—?"

Grace was three feet behind me, up to her knobby knees in the water. The kid was stick thin. "Sorry," she said, looking up at me nervously, fiddling with the hem of her shorts. "Did I scare the fish?" Her mama had fallen asleep against the tree, and I wondered how long it had been since she'd had a good night's rest.

Chuckling, I said, "Yeah, I think you did. Ah, well, lucky day for the fish, eh?"

"You're not mad at me?"

"No. You didn't mean any harm, did you?"

She shook her head, and her curly, golden-red hair bounced around her shoulders. It was a little wild, and I thought back to her mama when she was around Grace's age, when I'd first moved next door to her. Frannie hadn't liked to brush her hair either. She was a bit of a tomboy back in the day, usually turning up at home for dinner covered in more dirt than me.

"Do you eat 'em?"

"The fish? No. It's called 'catch and release'."

"Hm." She stepped beside me, looked up and down the river, then down at her bare feet under the dark, glassy water, her tennis shoes and socks forgotten on the shore. She bit her bottom lip and peeked up at me. "I think that's mean."

"Mean?"

"Yeah," she said quietly, but then a little louder, "If you're gonna put a hook through his mouth, then you should just put him out of his misery and eat him. Imagine how the fish feels when he gets caught. I bet he's scared.

So if you don't eat him, he went through all that for nothin'."

"Oh. Huh, guess I never thought about it like that."

"People shouldn't make other people feel scared for no reason."

"No, you're right. They shouldn't. But fish aren't people."

"No, but they're alive." She shrugged one shoulder and walked a few feet away, bending down to pick rocks from the riverbed. The current was steady, but the river was only a few feet deep where we were, so I kept my eye on her, but she was just a jump away. "Just sayin'."

It felt weird to me to be concerned about Fran's kid. I mean, protecting people was a part of me and it was my job, but this felt different somehow.

Grace threw the rocks across the river and took a deep breath, then bent forward and submerged her face under the water. When she came up, the water dripped off her chin, soaking her pink T-shirt. "I didn't see any fish down there."

"No, they're probably over closer to the other side. See the foam on top of the water by the bank?"

"Yeah, it looks gross and moldy."

Laughing a little, I said, "Ever heard the expression 'foam is home'?"

She shook her head, scrunching her nose up like she smelled something bad.

"It's just air bubbles, but it's a good place to cast your line 'cause the fish hang out there, lookin' for bugs to eat."

"Yuck."

I laughed again, and she dropped down so the water covered her shoulders, then leaned back and let it rush over her head. I worried her mama might get mad about her swimming in her clothes, but the air was so hot, she'd dry off quick enough.

Right then, Frannie woke up and she was frantic. "Grace? Grace! Where are you?"

I raised my voice so she could hear me. "She's right here. Don't worry."

"Where?" Frannie pushed off the tree and ran to the riverbank. Her hair had fallen completely out of the ponytail now, and it fell over her shoulders in kinked waves. It seemed odd to me that her hair looked so soft and relaxed but the rest of her body was as tense as a stretched rubber band.

I pointed to the big air bubbles popping over Grace's head under the water. "Right there."

"She can't swim!"

"Frannie, the river's only a few feet deep here." But I stepped closer to where Grace had disappeared. "She's one dive away from me."

Grace popped up, wiping the water away from her eyes, and Frannie gasped. "Grace Mae Morris! What's gotten into you today? I thought you were scared of the water. You don't like to swim."

"I'm not swimmin'. I'm standin' in a river. There's a difference. It's like takin' a deep bath, 'cept colder. Duh, Mama."

Frannie looked back and forth between Grace and me, at the smile on Grace's pink lips, and finally, she seemed to relax. So much, in fact, that we spent the rest of the afternoon fishing together. I always had an extra rod or two with me in case one snapped, but Frannie said she hadn't fished since I taught her how when we were kids, so I showed them both how to cast. Gracie liked my false casts the best, to clear my line of water or to reposition it, but she got mad and stomped up a fit when I actually hooked a fish. The fish got loose and made his fast getaway, and Grace giggled with way too much glee.

She didn't use a hook, but she seemed to like the action of casting her line, and when she eventually got bored of it, she had a ball digging through my lures and laying them out on the riverbank in order of their "prettiness."

Frannie was quiet most of the day, and at first, it annoyed me. I missed her loud mouth and endless opinions like when we were teenagers, but after a while, her presence became a comfort. She spoke to Grace occasionally, usually to warn her not to get in my way, like she was used to worrying about the kid bothering other people, even though Grace was no trouble.

She talked a little about her sister, Jilly, telling me how successful Jill had become as a young lawyer and then as her father's "right-hand woman." It was the only time she mentioned her father, and when I brought up her mama, she went from relaxed to stiff again in a second.

"I'm sorry about your mama, Frannie," I said once Grace went back to reading her book and Fran and I fished in silence for a while.

"Thank you."

"Were you able to spend much time with her before she passed?"

"No," was all she said.

"They were in Cheyenne by then, so I hadn't seen her in years, but my mama was really sad to hear about her passing. You know how close they used to be."

"Yeah." When I looked at her, it was easy to see she was holding back tears. The choked sound of her voice was a dead giveaway too.

"Sorry. I shouldn't have brought it up again."

"It's okay. It's just… I hadn't seen or spoken to her for a long time before she died, and I… I regret that. Deeply."

"She knew you loved her."

Fran scoffed under her breath. "Did she? I'm not so sure."

"I am. She was a good woman, and she loved you and Grace. My mama told me all the stories she heard from yours about Grace when you were down in El Paso."

"It was all secondhand information from Jilly. She was the only person I kept in contact with when we were in Texas." Fran pulled her line from the water and looked at me. "My mama never even met Grace."

"Why not?"

"It's… Never mind. It's not important."

"That seems important, Frannie."

Taking a deep breath, she hung her head and said quietly, "I said some awful things to her after I left town with Doug, and then I basically cut her out of my life. I don't know how she could've forgiven me. I've never forgiven myself."

"Fran, she was your m—"

"Please, Carey, can we stop talkin' about this?"

"Yeah," I said. "'Course." But the regret was written all over Frannie, and it made me sad. She closed her eyes and held her breath, and I was sure she was still trying not to cry.

I didn't want to make it more difficult, so I changed the subject. "So, Grace likes to read?"

Fran laughed through her sadness. "If she could do it all day long, she would. Sometimes I have to force her to play outside. That's weird, right? She's ten. Remember when we were her age? You couldn't force us *inside*, and if anyone had told us to read a book over summer vacation, we woulda run away screamin'."

Agreeing, I laughed, and the mood was lightened.

Normally, when anyone interrupted me while I was fishing, it ruined my day. All I ever wanted was a little peace and quiet. I didn't ask for much, but this was the thing I did to release all the sorrow and heartbreak I saw on a daily basis. It was the thing I did so I wouldn't go around pissed off and hating the cruel world around me. But today, watching Grace play and laugh, seeing her curls bounce in the sun, and watching Frannie smile when she saw it, I felt peace.

I knew I shouldn't, but I did, and I let it wash over me while the sun began to set. I felt that warmth in my bones, and I wondered if it was too much to hope that I could feel it again.

CHAPTER EIGHT

FRANNIE

"HI, JILLY. HOW ARE YOU?" I could hear my sister typing on her laptop. It wasn't unusual for her to put me on speakerphone so she could do eight other things while she talked to me. I knew she'd want to know about what happened the other night, but it was awkward when she asked. I tried to keep it from her, but she always seemed to find out.

"I'm fine, and don't call me Jilly. Jesus, Fran, I'm not a little kid anymore."

"Yeah, well, you're still little Jilly to me, and you always will be."

"Whatever. Anyway, that's not why I called."

I wanted her to be calling to find out if we were okay, not to gauge the mess she might have to clean up for our father, but whether she cared or not, and no matter what she was doing, it was always her motive.

"Then why did you?"

"Daddy knows there was a dustup between you and Doug again."

I breathed a laugh. "A dustup? Really? That's the term you're usin'?"

"Fran." She sighed, like she was annoyed that I'd had the nerve to get punched by my husband. "Are you okay? Is Grace okay?" She asked the question, but it felt like it was a formality, and once she'd asked, she could move on.

"We're fine."

Looking up at the usually blue sky in the overgrown backyard behind our rental house, I sighed up at the storm front moving through western Wyoming, turning the sky gray. While I wished for rain, hoping it would come soon to knock out the relentless humidity and cool the air some, I watched Grace picking dandelions, dancing around the yard like a Disney princess. I smiled, but it was fleeting. We needed a lawn mower, but I couldn't afford it, and I was not about to ask my sister to ask our father for more money.

Occasionally, Mrs. Quinn had the teenager who mowed her lawn do mine, but only the front yard and only because my foot-high grass embarrassed her. "Do you really wanna know, Jill? Every time you ask, I feel like…"

"What?"

"Nothin'. Just… like you have more important things to do."

"You can't be mad at me for being busy. I'm sorry, okay? But Fran, you know the position I'm in. It's all I can do to keep Daddy in line. If it got out that you…"

"That I what? That I exist?" The failed, loser daughter of the almighty and so important Bradley McKinnon who had the audacity to let her husband hit her? I scoffed and turned away from Grace so she couldn't hear me. "Careful, Jilly. Can't let him know you might actually have a heart. He can't run for president if his *good* daughter isn't a cold, unfeelin', successful bitch."

"That's not fair, Fran, and you know it."

"No. Maybe not."

"I love you and Grace. You know I do. Don't you think this is hard on me, being the go-between? I hate how he treats you, how he keeps you captive with the money. If I could, I'd give it to you. You believe me, don't you?"

When I didn't say anything, she sighed. "Mama told me to look out for you. That's what I've been trying to do, but you don't make it easy. Doug hasn't done this to you since Texas. What did you do? I mean, do you have to antagonize him so m—"

"Antagonize him? Are you kiddin'? He came here drunk and high. He didn't care that Grace was here. He never cares. I'm a punchin' bag for that man no matter what I do. He's a monster, and I'm trapped, Jill. Grace and I are trapped." I stopped. I didn't want to make her mad. I hadn't asked her about my divorce petition in weeks, but every time I did, I felt like that was a bother to her too. But she was my family, and she was a lawyer. Who else could I ask? "Have you heard anything about my divorce? Last time I asked, you said there was somethin' wrong with my paperwork, but Jill, I kept copies and I checked it. Everything's correct."

"No, I haven't heard anything. It takes time."

"It's takin' forever. What am I doin' wrong? I need to be divorced, Jill. Grace needs it too."

"You just have to be patient. I'll have my assistant check again, but even if it's gone through, you know you can't say anything until after the election. It's only a few more months. I know you don't like it, but appearances matter. You know Daddy has very conservative friends, and they won't like to hear about your marital problems. It makes a difference, Fran."

I hoped she couldn't hear the judgement in my laugh, but I wasn't sure my little sister could hear anything besides her own ambition anymore. Since our mama had passed, it seemed like all Jilly's heart had flown right out the window, and sometimes I wondered if her morals and conscience followed right after. I felt guilty about that. I wasn't here when Mama died, and Jill had to deal with it all alone. It was another regret I'd have to live with for the rest of my life, and even if I could push it out of my mind, Jill never let me forget.

"That's what you said before the last election, which was why I didn't file back then." But I could dish it to my sister just as good as she gave, even if it made me feel guilty to do it. "Do you have any idea what a jerk that makes you sound like? Some champion of women you turned out to be. Mama would be so proud."

"That's not fair either, Fran." She sighed again. "Listen, I called 'cause Daddy wanted me to tell you that we're coming to Wisper next week, okay? So get ready. You still have the makeup I sent you to cover the—"

Rolling my eyes, I said, "I gotta go, Jilly. My kid needs me, and unlike some families, I'm here for her, no matter what. No matter how it makes me look. But don't you worry, when Daddy shows up, I'll be there with bells on. My makeup will be flawless, I'll plaster on a fake smile, and no one will ever know he's a shit father and grandfather, and that all my baby sister cares about is votes."

"Fran—"

I hung up. I didn't care if she was mad. I couldn't listen to her anymore. I loved my sister, even if I couldn't remember why at the moment, but I couldn't take it anymore, couldn't handle the reminder of just what a disaster my life had become and what a disappointment I was to them both.

I was well aware.

"Okay, Mama?" Grace asked when she stopped spinning in the little pocket of sunshine peeking through the dark clouds, and she stumbled to the side a couple steps. Her feet were bare and dirty, the high grass poking up between her toes, and I flashed back to when she was born and those toes were the size of mini jellybeans.

"Yeah, baby. I'm good. Just gonna look in the paper again for a job. Maybe today's our lucky day, huh? Careful you don't fall on your head."

Grace zigzagged her way over to me perched on the back patio step. "That's not possible," she said, giggling, and I couldn't stop staring at the spark in her eyes. It was new, and it was my favorite sight in the world. "I was thinkin'. Maybe I could stay with Sheriff Carey when you get a job. I had fun fishin' with him. That way, you won't make your new boss mad if I have to go with you or you have to leave early."

"Sweetie, I'm real glad you like the sheriff. He's a good man, but he's busy and he has a hard job. Sometimes it can even be dangerous. It's no place for a little girl."

"Oh. Well, maybe I could get a job in his office. Then I could help pay for my medicine, and I'd be safe so you wouldn't worry, and I wouldn't be in his way. I promise. Maybe I could be the radio person, like the one he used the other night. I could be the person on the other end who says 'ten four, boss.' That'd be a fun job."

God, this kid. Could she be any more perfect? It broke my heart. "I bet you'd be really good at that job, but, unfortunately, you're too young to work. You've got a few more years left to grow before you can apply for a job. I, on the other hand, am way past the right age," I said, opening the crinkled *Jackson Hole Daily* Mrs. Quinn had left on my front porch after she'd finished reading it. All the coupons would be missing by now, and the pages would be out of order, but it wasn't a big deal. The paper was bigger than the *Wisper Gazette* used to be before Mr. Anderson retired and closed up shop, but still pretty small so it wouldn't take long to read from start to stop anyway. And there most likely wouldn't be any good jobs, but I had to look. There had to be something I could do that wasn't more than a couple miles from our house. Distance was yet another obstacle since I wasn't sure my car was reliable enough to make it back and forth to Jackson every day, and I really couldn't afford the gas.

"How come we don't open our own restaurant, Mama? That's your dream, right?" Grace asked before she twirled off again. "Let's just go find a restaurant, and we'll tell 'em how good you cook. They'll let you be the boss if you make the sugar-free pineapple cake you always make for my birthday. That'll definitely impress 'em, and we'll be rich."

Great plan, kiddo. If only it were that easy.

CAREY'S TRUCK was parked downtown outside the little Wisper sheriff's station on Main Street, and the sun glinted off its hood when we passed it in our old, run-down Kia. My radiator was just about kaput, and I was pretty sure I needed a new alternator, but I kept crossing my fingers that it would last another month, another week, sometimes one more hour. It was a hunk of junk, but that little car had gotten Grace and me through more rough nights than I could count, and for that, I loved it.

Something inside me was making me want to stop though. To talk to Carey. To explain. To make him understand why I'd left all those years ago. To tell him I loved him still, and that I wanted to be his friend again, but that I'd left because I wasn't good for him. My father had drilled it into my head for so long, and there was only so much of that you could hear before you believed it.

I did. I believed it down to my soul back then. And since, all those years alone, stuck in a trailer in the middle of the desert—wishing Grace's dad would come home so we could eat, and then wishing he'd leave as soon as he did before he'd had a chance to get drunk and take his frustrations out on me —those years hadn't done much to change my mind.

Some kind of awareness was coming to life inside me, though, like my eyes had been open all this time, but they'd been covered by thick goggles and I hadn't really been able to see.

And now, I saw everything every day in Grace. She made mistakes like I had when I was young. She wasn't perfect, didn't get straight As in school, but she loved and laughed, and she was a whole, worthwhile, and utterly loveable person, no matter her choices. I couldn't imagine not loving her because she got an F on a test or broke a vase.

So why hadn't I been enough for my father the way Grace was enough for me?

Maybe I had been. Maybe it was his problem and not mine.

Why did I deserve to be treated like I wasn't worthy of his love? How had my father or Doug or anyone known that I was weak like my mama and, if they took my power away, I wouldn't fight back?

What right did they have to take it? Or had I given it to them? Why would I do that?

I'd seen this documentary on TV about a woman who was raised in a cult. Her parents were idiots, and they'd been sucked into this dangerous religious ideology, and the girl had grown up believing that if she wore the color yellow, she'd be damned to Hell. She'd been beaten for wearing a yellow wildflower in her hair. Years later, the police had raided the compound and saved all the kids who'd been living there, and now they were all trying to figure out who to be and how to live in the regular world.

The girl was realizing that all the things she'd been taught were now falling away from her way of thinking, like the shedding of hair. One by one, the negative beliefs and ideas about who she was or who she was supposed to be dropped and fell away.

I was ashamed that it had taken so long for me to wake up, that it had taken the fading light in my daughter's eyes to rip the goggles off my head, but maybe I was like the cult girl.

Maybe all my misguided beliefs were falling away now too.

And maybe I wanted to tell Carey that.

I didn't, though. Instead, I kept driving.

TERRE FINKLE PAID me fifty bucks every Sunday when Grace and I helped her make meals for the elderly members of her church and I helped her with the pastries her husband sold at their coffee shop downtown, Coffee Shot. They'd offered me a job, but it was an evenings and weekends gig. There wasn't anywhere for Grace to be while I worked, and I wouldn't leave her with a babysitter, no matter how well-meaning they were. Doug had a knack for overpowering little old ladies. He'd done it before, and he'd do it again if I gave him the opportunity. His charismatic personality shone through every damn time, even though he was the opposite of a kind and caring man in reality. Leagues from it.

He took any chance he could to punish me, and I was done making it easy for him. It wasn't right for Grace to be in the middle. She didn't understand why her dad was so cruel, and as much as I hated him, I'd never let her know what I really thought of him. She deserved to have good thoughts and memories of him—which, if I was honest, was laughable.

Actually, what she deserved was a *good* dad, but since she wasn't going to get that, I promised myself I'd never talk ill of him when she was around. Lately, though, it was becoming harder and harder to do.

We'd had a break from the constant "dustups" since moving home, but the fear and anxiety that the old Doug would reappear was always there. In Texas, he never bothered to hide the abuse, so she'd seen far too much already, and there wasn't a lot I could do about that, but I wouldn't add to it. I'd just keep trying to replace the awful memories with good ones, like the river yesterday.

I was desperate for my divorce to come through. Maybe it was wishful thinking, but I thought, if it did, that would be a permanence that would put the final distance between my husband and me, and maybe then, he'd stop hurting us.

When I pulled into Terre and Walt's driveway on Mountain Lake Lane, I couldn't get Carey out of my mind. It had been so long since I'd felt safe enough to relax. Whether it was Doug and his stupid antics or Grace's illness, I was always on high alert.

But the other day in the sunshine, with Carey's calming voice and the clean smell of his skin mixed with the water and fresh air, somehow the same way he'd smelled when we were teenagers, I'd relaxed enough to fall asleep against a tree. I couldn't remember the last time that had happened, and I wondered if it was a normal thing for most people. Did everyone else feel safe enough to forget their worries for a few hours every day and get real rest?

I couldn't imagine.

And the way Grace relaxed around him, the way he

smiled at her and made her feel safe? It was the sexiest thing I'd ever seen.

There were a lot of things I was noticing about Carey, things I'd never noticed before, like the way his lips would part when I was talking and he was really listening, or the way his eyes lingered a second too long on my lips when I stopped. His biceps and shoulder muscles flexed in the smallest ways when he pulled his fishing line, adjusting it to a better spot on the water, and he spread his legs and planted his feet, never losing his stance against the current. He was always solid. He was always good and strong.

"Well, hey there, girls," Walt Finkle called out, waving to Grace and me, and he wiped the sweat off his neck with an old-fashioned cotton handkerchief, then stuck it in his back pocket and pushed his lawnmower back and forth along the side of his house. His yard was twice the size of ours. Walt and Terre lived toward the edge of town where the properties weren't quite rural, but they weren't the small 1920s cottages like ours, or the newer log homes people seemed to like to build in town with barely enough room in their yards to plant a tree.

Walt's little push mower seemed like it was made of emeralds, afternoon sunshine glinting off the green metal, and I wondered if it'd be rude to ask to borrow it, but then again, I never asked anyone for anything, 'cause if I did, in this small town my father would hear about it. He'd throw a fit, and I'd never hear the end of it. God forbid I ever made him look weak. Jilly never let me forget when I did, and they'd taken their support away more than once for less, so I was trained not to test him.

"Hi, Mr. Finkle. How're you today?"

"Fran, how many times I gotta tell you, call me Walt. And I'm just fine. Tryin' to get the grass mowed before this heat gets too unbearable. How 'bout you, Grace? Would you like to help me?"

Looking down at Grace, I wished I didn't have to say no. Not that she loved mowing lawns, but I longed to let her be a normal kid, to be the kind of kid who could run around in the summer sun, getting sunburnt and dirty. But I wouldn't and she knew it, so she never asked.

Softly, she said, "No, thank you, Mr. Finkle," and she looked at her scuffed-up tennis shoes.

Walt and Terre knew Grace was shy, and they knew not to push her or she'd disappear further inside herself. "Alright then," he said. "Get outta this heat. Terre's inside, waitin' on you two. I hope you're gonna make me some more of those dinner rolls you made last week. I gave myself a bellyache, I ate so many."

Grace giggled. She loved Walt. He was more of a grandpa to her than my father had ever been, and it broke my heart that I couldn't let her help him. I knew she wanted to.

It wasn't that I didn't trust Walt, but it wouldn't have surprised me to see Doug drive by at least twice while we were there. He knew they paid me cash, and sometimes, when he needed money, he'd come and take it, like he did the other night. And I wouldn't ever be so stupid again to let Grace play outside without me when he was around. He'd use it against me, say that I was a neglectful mother. He'd done it before. Or he'd just take her and dump her at his mother's house for the day. Just to make me worry. Just to be a dick 'cause he could. 'Cause he wanted to prove that he was a man, and I was a woman, and that meant there wasn't a damn thing I could do about it. The courts were always on his side, no matter how awful he was to us or how unfair.

Women still didn't have much of a say in the eyes of the law, at least not where we'd lived in Texas.

And Grace had been so little then. Her opinion hadn't mattered, even though she'd begged and cried with the judge when he made her see her dad for visitation. The misogynistic asshole had basically said that Doug couldn't be that bad if I'd stayed married to him all this time, and that Grace should want to spend time with her father, and if she didn't, that was my fault, and I shouldn't try to poison my daughter against her daddy. I should respect him, no matter what he'd done.

Judge Hayes had said all that to me while he looked at the black and blue around my eye and the split in my lip. I'd been trying to divorce Doug for years, but there was always an issue with the paperwork, and once my first petition had finally gone through, the hearing kept being delayed or postponed. And when we'd made it to the final judgement, the judge had just flat out said, "No."

Doug showed up once to take Grace for lunch, but when she got home, she told me he made her wait in the hot truck while he went inside one of his buddies' houses. She sat there alone for three hours, and when he brought her back, I smelled beer on his breath. That was the last "visitation" he'd ever put her through, thankfully. He wanted to be a father like he wanted a hole in his head.

I kept trying to get rid of him. Now that we were back in Wisper, I was hoping we'd get a judge that I knew or who knew my father. Maybe that would make the difference, or maybe Jill's influence could help. I wasn't trying to shame my family. I just wanted my daughter to be safe and happy. Was that such a bad thing?

"C'mon, Grace. Let's go bake," I said, nudging her toward the house. "You can help Terre measure. You like doin' that, right?"

She tried to smile, but it looked almost painful, and I plastered a fake smile on my own face, then took her hand to lead her into the Finkles' garage.

When we walked in the kitchen, blessed air conditioning blasted us, and it was almost a shock, coming from the high-nineties temperature and skyrocketing humidity outside.

Terre Finkle was a welcome sight and voice. She came with good memories, mouth-watering scents, and she always had a smile on her face. "Grace Mae! How are you, sweetheart? Magnolia's been waitin' for you," she said as her ancient cocker spaniel raced up to Grace in the middle of the kitchen. The dog hopped up and down on her hind legs with her front paws on Grace's stomach, and it looked like she was smiling. Grace patted Magnolia's head and scratched under her chin, and Magnolia kicked her foot like a jackrabbit when Grace hit just the right spot.

"So, how was your week?" Terre asked me. She was asking to be polite, but I could hear the worry in her voice when she noticed the makeup on my face I'd used to try to cover the evidence. It was clear she suspected Doug was abusive, at least verbally. This was the first time I'd shown up with a bruise on my face, but she'd noticed me flinching at a loud noise, or how I apologized up and down if I did something wrong, but I'd never admitted it to her, or anyone in Wisper for that matter. I'd learned my lesson in Texas after reaching out to people over the years. No one helped. Sure, maybe they cared and they were sorry it was happening, but no one wanted to be involved in another family's drama.

Terre was a good woman, and she was supportive and kind, but there was a stigma to being a battered wife. In the back of everyone's mind, I knew they couldn't help thinking I had deserved it or it had somehow been my fault.

Sometimes, *I* had a hard time convincing myself it wasn't my fault. I was the idiot who eloped with Doug. I was the one who dropped out of high school and who had a child with a man who was cruel and useless.

I was the one who gave up on my dreams.

"Good."

"Fran, you're under no obligation to tell me"—she leaned across her kitchen island, lowering her voice—"but I see the bruise on your face. Your makeup isn't thick enough to hide all that. Darlin', what happened?"

Peeking back at Grace while she rolled on the floor with the dog, giggling and peppering Magnolia's muzzle with kisses, I said in a small voice, "It's nothin'. Don't worry about me."

She looked at Grace, too, then nodded and pulled a baking sheet loaded with a huge pile of dough from her refrigerator. "Okay. I understand, but I'm here when you're ready." She took a deep breath, mustering up a smile and wiping her hands on her pink apron, then raising her voice, she said, "Alright. While you're makin' dessert, Fran, who's gonna help me make lemon chicken, sauteed green beans, and dinner rolls?"

"Me!" Grace jumped up. "Can I make the rolls?"

Terre chuckled. "You most certainly can, sweet girl. The ones you made last time turned out perfectly. When I delivered the meals after church services, I told Mrs. Hodges you made those rolls, and she ate three right then and there."

Grace gave a beaming smile. "Really?"

"You bet. I think you've inherited the talent from your mama. You two oughta start a bakery down on Main Street."

"Oh, I know," Grace said, finding a little confidence. She trusted Terre like a grandma. "I already told Mama that, but she said no."

I laughed, glad for the change of subject. "No, what I said was maybe someday, but it's just not feasible right now."

"What's 'feasible'?"

"It means your mama thinks it wouldn't be a good idea right now," Terre said, "but personally, Fran, I think you're wrong."

"Me too. You're the best baker in the whole world, Mama. You could do it."

"Grace's right, Fran, and Wisper doesn't have a bakery. The treats we sell at the coffee shop don't count. You love making all those French pastries. You have a way of makin' 'em down-to-earth and not so hoity-toity. I'm tellin' you, it'd be a hit."

"Maybe," I said, trying not to sound too defeatist in front of Grace, but I didn't finish culinary school, and starting a business would take a lot of money. "But I'm not really prepared for that."

"Maybe you could look into bringing on an investor, like the Cades did with their new equine therapy program out at Cade Ranch."

Huh. I hadn't thought of that. "An investor?" I asked, pulling wax paper and piping supplies out of the island drawer. I was making chocolate éclairs, which were one of my favorites to make and to eat, and they were a great dessert to bake in such high humidity because, as long as you got the moisture content right, the evaporation of the steam during the baking process was what made the pâte à choux pastry so light and airy.

"Yeah. The man who invested with the Cades lives in town now. Apparently, we impressed him so much, he and his sister moved to Wisper."

"Oh. But, I mean, I couldn't just walk up to a stranger and ask him to give me his money."

"Well, 'course not, dear. You'd need to write up a business plan. And I expect for a food-related business proposal, you'd need to bake for him. Show him what you can do."

"A business plan?" I had no clue how to make one of those. The school I attended for all of two months before Grace was born offered business classes, but I hadn't gotten that far before Doug blew through the rest of my tuition money, betting on horses at the rodeo. As hard as I tried, I'd never been able to save that much again, and I hadn't trusted him enough to leave Grace with him every day to work a full-time job. So culinary school or my own bakery was just another faraway dream, and most likely one that would never come true.

"Well," Terre said, patting my hand on the countertop, "somethin' to think about, huh?"

"Sure. Yeah," I lied. I knew I wouldn't do it. No one I knew would think it would be a good idea to hand thousands of dollars over to me. Besides, my father would never let me have that, nor would Doug.

Since I was seventeen years old, I'd made one bad decision after another. All any investor had to do was look at my GED, my failed attempt at college, and my failed marriage to a man I never should've been involved with.

That was all proof enough that I wasn't worth the risk.

CHAPTER NINE

CAREY

"WE GOT another call from Carl while you were out, boss," Abey said from behind her desk when I walked in the station with our lunch from José's Diner. Chicken clubs all around, and José packed them up in a little box with an ice pack at the bottom to keep the food cool. Our little station in Wisper was my home base, though I spent plenty of time at the Jackson station during the week, where too many people and too many problems to solve waited for me every day. Here, it was quiet. We only had a handful of employees, and that was how I preferred it.

The temperature was climbing higher every day, and everybody in town seemed to be inside with their air conditioning on full blast to avoid the heat and humidity. The sky was dark, but it still hadn't really rained, and there was an eerie sort of calm and quiet outside on Main Street for a Sunday. Normally, the town would be a buzz of kids playing at the park, customers strolling down Main Street, shopping at the local shops, people sitting outside Coffee Shot, drinking their lattes, filling each other in on town gossip. Even the farmers market was quiet today.

I'd seen Fran drive by earlier. Her right taillight was out, and I probably should've pulled her over to tell her, but it had been awkward between us at the river when she and Grace left. She seemed like she wanted to talk more to me, but she wouldn't.

Maybe she didn't want to say anything in front of Grace, or maybe she realized, after all these years, she didn't actually have much to say to me anymore. I had no idea. There was a whole lot I wanted to say to her, but I definitely couldn't get all that off my chest with Grace around. And technically, it wasn't really my place to inform Fran of all the ways she'd gone wrong in her life.

But dammit, I was tired of seeing her look so defeated.

When would that end? When would she grab hold of life like she used to, by the balls, and whip that shit into shape? She'd never had a problem doing it before, and it was a sad sight now to watch her just getting by. It hurt me to see it, actually caused a real, physical pain in my chest.

"Hear what I said?"

"Oh yeah. Sorry, Abey. Got a lot on my mind. I'll call Carl back. He's probably lookin' for an update, but I haven't found—"

"Nope, he called this time 'cause somebody knocked his west fence down and his whole herd crossed the highway. He wrangled some of 'em, but he couldn't find a few. I called over and asked ol' man Milson to send a couple of his cowboys. Max Gordon and Buckey went over to help Carl, but they haven't called back, so I don't know if they found the cows or not."

"Did you send Frank?"

"Yeah, he's there now."

"Nobody was hurt?"

"No, and Carl didn't see it happen. He only noticed when

he realized his cows were gone, and no one reported an accident."

"Okay, well, that's a little concernin'," I said. Most people would probably wave it off, but coincidences didn't happen often around Wisper. A broken lock, blood, and now a busted fence? It didn't sit right with me.

"Radio Frank and let him know I'm on my way. There's somethin' buggin' me about this. And call Emergency Services just to make sure they haven't heard anything, in case the driver didn't report it till they were out of Teton County. Maybe there's just a glitch in the system."

"Will do."

"And Abey, will you check the air, please? Feels like a damn sauna, it's so hot in here."

"I already did. I called Shelly, too, to ask if there was some trick to coolin' it down, but she said no. But I think she might be lyin' so we're miserable without her here while she's on maternity leave. I think she wants us to know just how needed she is." Abey snickered and I smiled, shaking my head. It sounded like Shelly. Abey slumped back in her chair, fanning herself with one of her *Mud & Trucks* magazines. "I lowered it, but it's just too hot. The AC can't keep up."

"That thing is old as sin. Just add that to the list of shit we need but the state won't pay for."

"Right?" She laughed. "We could modify our uniforms. Tank tops and bootie shorts?"

I laughed too. "Yeah, that'd look real good in sheriff brown, but maybe it'd make us a little more popular with the townsfolk. Although, I'm not sure the state of Wyoming would approve the request."

"True dat," she said. "Oh, that reminds me, Kay called again."

"Oh yeah?" I said, looking at my lunch with longing since

I knew I wouldn't have time to eat it till dinner, and by then it'd be soggy.

"Yep." Abey popped her lips together. "Says she wants you to call her back. I'm thinkin' she wants to go out with you again."

"Mm hm."

"Oh, jeez. What's wrong with this one? She's nice."

"She is. Yeah," I said. "Nothin' wrong with her."

"But you won't take her out again, will you?"

I finally looked at her. "Probably not."

"And your date with Tanya was a bust." Abey shook her head. "Boss, you know you can talk to me, right? If there's somethin'…"

"I'm okay, Abey, but thanks."

"Alright, well, I hate to tell you this, but the perfect woman ain't gonna wander into Wisper and snatch you up. So, say yes. Go out and have some fun. You deserve it. You work hard."

"I'm just not feelin' it," I said.

Abey rolled her eyes. "You haven't *felt* the last five women, and that is not a pun. There was a swarm of hotties at the county employee picnic, waitin' for you to take 'em out. What gives?"

"Nothin' gives, and mind your business." I tossed the lunch container toward her, and she caught it. "Put that in the fridge 'fore it goes bad."

"You're gonna go bad if you don't—"

"Good grief, Abey. Get your own life, would ya?"

"Oh, I got one," she said, "and my life thinks yours is a sad state of affairs."

"Oh yeah? Well, my life thinks your life—ughh, why do you do this to me? You're like the annoyin' little sister I don't remember askin' for. I gotta go."

"You know you love me," she sang as I pushed back through the door on my way back out into the heat and misery.

Before it slammed shut, I said, "I can't remember why right now, but sure."

———

"DAMN IT ALL TO HELL, CAREY!" Carl yelled at me when I stepped out of my cruiser. I'd parked on the side of the road where his fence was busted into several jagged pieces of wood, and as I shut my door, I got a good eyeful of the mess. "You said you'd look into this, and now, all hell's done and broke loose."

"I am lookin' into it, Carl. I haven't found anything yet, but maybe now we'll have more to go on. Did you see anything? It was the middle of the day."

"No, young man, I did not see anything."

"I'm not a 'young man,' Carl. I'm the sheriff, and you know it. I know you're pissed, but I still need a little bit of respect from you."

"Well, that's just fine. Meanwhile, my farm's gettin' ripped up and broken into, and you're just standin' there."

I was usually a little more tactful, but it was so damn hot out, and it made me more tired than I could remember being in a long time. I couldn't help it. I sighed loudly. "Now, just 'cause you can't see me workin', don't mean I ain't. Frank, what'd you find?"

"Not much. Just a bunch of torn-up wood," Frank said, rivers of sweat dripping from under his hat down the side of his face and neck while he crouched, looking for any clue as to who could've done this. His uniform was soaked. The guy was a mountain of a man, forty years old and built like a

Sherman tank, but quiet as a mouse. "There's some tracks in the dirt there," he said, pointing to the tire tracks next to the fence, "but seems to me they look like ordinary truck tires. We'll get somebody out here for a tire cast, but…"

Frank knew, just like I did, that it would be a wild goose chase down a lonely road, trying to identify the driver of the vehicle based on tire tracks, especially if it really did turn out to be an old truck. Who didn't drive a truck in Wyoming?

With my hands on my hips, I squinted out at Carl's property. His farm was set off Route 20, about three miles from town, and it was surrounded every which way by wild, western beauty. I wasn't sure if the ol' guy knew how lucky he was that he'd inherited the land from his dad. It was bound to be worth more money than I'd ever make in my life.

Which got me to thinking. "How's business, Carl? How's the farm doin'? You havin' any troubles I don't know about?"

"I'm doin' fine, *Sheriff*, and I don't appreciate what you're insinuatin'." He huffed over-stuffed pride from his chest and planted his hands on his hips, mirroring me. Carl was sweating, too, beads of it dripping down his forehead into his eye, and it had to burn, but he wouldn't blink or look away.

"I ain't insinuatin' anything. I'm askin'. I need to know. You havin' any trouble with customers, with the bank, with anybody?"

"No. And I'll tell you same as I told those fancy land developers, my farm is still viable. I ain't sellin', I don't need help, and y'all can take a long walk off a short pier."

"Land developers, Carl? That didn't seem like somethin' I should know? Who? Who are they?"

"They's just some jerks from I don't know where, wanna buy my land, and not even for a good price. They said they wanna use it to"—he lifted both hands to imitate quotations with his fingers—"strengthen the cattle industry in Wyoming and give jobs to the community, but I don't buy it for one second. Soon as they got their grubby hands on my property, they'd flatten it and build condos to sell to millionaires. You shoulda seen the way they were dressed. Like they'd walked right outta some magazine." He raised his eyebrows, shaking his head. "Ain't never gonna happen. Not on my watch."

"You got any paperwork on that? An offer? A business card? Anything?"

Frank stepped next to me, catching the general drift of my thoughts. In a hushed voice, he asked, "Where you goin' with this?"

I flashed him a look to be patient, waiting for Carl to speak.

"No. I threw it away."

"You don't remember the name of the company? Or the name of the guy who brought the offer?"

"It was a woman who was in charge, but no, I can't recall her name. Why? You think she had somethin' to do with my busted fence?"

"Well, now, I'm not sure, but I plan on findin' out. When was she here?"

"I dunno. Maybe two weeks ago. It was before my tack room got broken into. You think it's connected?"

"Frank, get on the phone to the Jackson station. Get someone out here to cast those tire tracks. I got a few phone calls to make. And Carl, I need to be your first call if you hear back from these people, hear me?"

"Yeah, yeah, I hear you."

"You got somebody to help you with this fence?"

He waved me away. "Milson's sendin' Max back. He'll fix it up, I reckon. He's a good kid. He and that Buckey found all my lost cows." Carl fixed his hat on his head, pulling it low over his eyes as he walked away without another word. He wouldn't show it, but he was probably pretty scared. He knew he didn't possess the resources to win any kind of legal fight.

If someone wanted Carl's land, it wouldn't be hard to get to. He was an old man living and working alone. His operation was small, and he didn't produce much. Mostly he sold to the same loyal customers he'd had for years, but he wouldn't hire anyone, and he wouldn't accept help from local ranchers. I was surprised he'd let Max help with the fence. He was a son of a gun, but he was an honest man and a long-time part of the Wisper community, and I planned to figure out who was doing this to him.

Nobody was gonna bully my town and get away with it.

Which reminded me. "Frank, let's head out. I got another matter I want you to look into."

CHAPTER TEN

FRANNIE

WHEN MY FATHER and sister pulled up in front of the Wisper courthouse in their black town car, Grace and I were posted there like I'd promised we'd be. My sister thought the close-knit family show would convince the public what a good and decent politician our father was, but if the residents of Wisper knew the truth, they'd realize he was a selfish, dishonest man who cared only about himself.

Gone was the time when seeing my father still made me sad, when I wished for him to hug me or ask me how I was, when I wished for him to care. He didn't, and instead of allowing good memories to swamp me in those instances and try to punch holes in my heart, I thought about other things from my childhood. Carey was a frequent visitor to my memories because he had been the best part of it.

My father stepped out of the car in his deep navy blue suit and red tie, and his eyes locked onto me, looking me up and down. His hair was completely silver now, no hint of the black it used to be, like it was the last time I'd seen him. I'd always thought he'd come to hate my red hair because it was the same color my mama's had been. He once told me it was what he'd first fallen in love with when they met, but as she got older and sicker and he became more obsessed with his career, I watched him fall out of love since she couldn't win him any votes.

He smiled when he saw me so that anybody passing by would be convinced of his fatherly love, but I saw the disappointment in his eyes. When they met mine, he had a hard time holding his smile, and I was sure he was seeing the fading but still visible bruises on my cheek. I'd tried to cover them up with the makeup Jilly wanted me to use, but it couldn't hide the yellow-green undertone to my skin. The makeup just made me look like a clown, and I hated it. The only time I wore it was when one of them was around. I liked how I looked without it—it was him who couldn't stand the sight of me. Jilly reminded me of that fact often, too, always sending stupid dresses and shoes for Grace and me to wear for photos or appearances, though those had become few and far between, 'cause God forbid a photographer got a picture of SA McKinnon's daughter wearing jeans. And what if they could see what his family really looked like underneath the makeup?

He was a popular man in Teton County. Some people still remembered him from when we'd lived in Wisper when Jilly and I were kids, but everyone knew about the money he'd brought to the area with the many deals he'd made with backpacking gear and outdoor adventure companies. Big ones. My father had made a show of it, showering the money he'd made all over Jackson and the surrounding towns, building new parks and shiny new schools, attracting more people to buy homes in Wyoming, more people to spend money here, and making him look like some kind of hometown savior, and that was eventually what had won him the State's Attorney title.

What the grateful community never knew was how much money and how many kickbacks my father had probably received from those deals, and how much favor he'd likely earned with incredibly rich men, men who had sway in Washington, which was exactly what he'd been after. It was all he used to talk about at the dinner table.

He didn't do any of it because he loved where he lived and wanted to make it better, but because he had plans for his future that included a run for governor and then the Senate. He was obsessed about that, too, when I was younger. He couldn't have cared less about Wyoming.

It made me sick to my stomach, but I smiled back and focused on Jilly when she stepped out the other door. Grace lit up when she saw her. She loved her Auntie Jilly, and she still remembered when Jill used to visit us in Texas and bring her fancy butter cookies and teddy bears.

But the last time that had happened was before we moved back to Wisper because Doug was convinced he could revive his rodeo "career" if we came home. I'd been so relieved to move home though. The middle of nowhere Texas had been a scary and lonely place for a woman who was basically a single mother and her young daughter, broke, broken, and alone.

Since we'd been home, though, my father couldn't be bothered to come see us. He sent Jill, and she stayed ten minutes before she had to dash off for a meeting. The stuffed animals she'd given Grace were probably yellowed and unstuffed by stray animals on the run-down property where the trailer we'd lived in still sat, if it hadn't been condemned and torn down by now.

At least here in Wisper, we lived near other people. In Texas, it had been over two miles to the nearest neighbor. Two miles to run to get help when we'd needed it. Two miles to walk to get formula or milk for Grace when she was a baby and her dad couldn't be bothered to bring it home for her or let me drive his crappy truck to go get it. Two fucking miles with a baby on my hip in the scorching sun and dry desert heat while my loser husband sat in air conditioning at the bar, drinking our grocery money—

"Francesca," my father said, still with a false smile fixed on his face, his accent gone and replaced by some posh-sounding tone. "She looks like a ragamuffin. Did you even brush her hair?"

"*She* has a name," I gritted out, my eyes boring into his empty ones, displaying the anger I could never voice. I hoped to God Grace couldn't hear us.

"Grace," he turned to her while she hugged Jilly by the car. "Come, dear, give your grandfather a hug." He reached one arm toward her, expecting her to run to his side, but she was reluctant. Of course she was. He was practically a stranger to her. "Now," he said, and I nodded when Grace looked at me, asking permission to go to him.

Grace walked to him slowly and stood by his side while he patted her hair, then he dropped his hand, and it twitched, like it hurt to touch his only granddaughter. He looked her over, inspecting her like she was a suit that didn't fit, the same way he always looked at me.

And that was it. That was all we got from my loving father after not seeing him in almost a year.

Thank God Mayor Covey appeared, forcing his hand into my father's, and he started in with questions and concerns from the residents of Wisper, hoping to get some answers from a government official about the help they needed with so many different issues around town. I hoped the mayor wouldn't hold his breath. Unless what Covey wanted lined up with my father's plans, he'd turn blue in the face before my father would help.

Jilly followed behind when they walked toward the court-house, and she motioned for Grace and me to follow with a wave of her French-manicured fingers. Grace hurried to hold my hand, and she walked beside me, her little legs trying to keep up with Jilly's pace.

"Fran, I asked you to wear the pink skirt suit I sent. What even is this outfit? You look like some gothy teenager." She huffed a sigh, nodding toward my black T-shirt dress and dollar-store flip flops while she flicked notifications away on her phone like they offended her. She wasn't even looking at my clothes, and what did it matter? There wasn't anyone around. No one but my sister and my father cared. I was dying in the hot sun, but wearing the opposite of what my father wanted and expected was a small dig, one of the only ones I could get in without too much punishment. It was childish, but it felt good. "And Daddy's right." She lowered her voice and leaned closer to me. "Grace needs a haircut. I'll make an appointment for her. Maybe they can chemically straighten that bird's nest."

"What?" I stopped walking, pulling Grace to my side. "You're not touching her hair."

"Calm down, Fran. It was just a suggestion."

"Suggestion my butt, Jill. Why does it matter what we wear or how we do our hair? How in the world can that matter to our father?"

She rolled her eyes. "I wish you wouldn't call him that. Can't you just call him daddy, like I do? It shows a stronger familial bond. C'mon." She tugged on my arm and pulled me to walk again.

"Whatever. How long do we have to keep up the charade this time? Are you staying all day?"

"We'll be here until tomorrow. Daddy has a few meetings scheduled in Jackson this afternoon and tomorrow morning, and we're hoping to catch the governor tonight at the restaurant here in town. What's that diner called everybody loves? I can't remember. Anyway, that's where the governor will be tonight. I think we can get her endorsement for the next election, but it's going to take a little schmoozing. She and Daddy don't exactly enjoy each other's company." Jilly shrugged and took a deep breath, looking away from her phone finally. Her eyes did a slow perusal of my outfit. "Really, Frannie. Could you try just a little harder? And Grace, how are you? How's school going?"

"It's summer," Grace said, her eyebrows rising slowly, like she was only just figuring out how out of touch Jilly really was. I'd known for years.

"Oh, right, of course. So are you having fun then, doing all kinds of fun summer things? Do you guys have a pool in that rental?" she asked me.

I laughed. "Do we have a pool? Are you kiddin' me right now?"

"What?"

"We barely have electricity and food, Jilly. No, we do not have a pool."

"Don't be overdramatic. What about the community pool?" my ridiculous sister asked, then to Grace, "Have you ever made a lemonade stand, Grace? That would be fun, huh?" Her eyes flicked up to mine, and she cocked her head to the side. "And it would be a great opportunity for campaign photos."

"I don't let her drink lemonade, you know that." I stopped walking. "What's really goin' on here, Jillian? *Daddy* never visits, and when he has to come here, he spends all of ten minutes in Wisper before you whisk him off. Last time he was here, he couldn't be bothered to see his family, so why would he stay here for a whole twenty-four hours?"

"There's nothing going on, Fran. Daddy has business here, and he really did want to see you and Grace. It just happens to line up with the governor thing, that's all. Oh, I'd like him to visit Grace's school too. She goes to the one he had rebuilt a few years ago, right?"

"Again, Jill, it's summer. There is no school right now, and there's only one elementary school in Wisper. You know this. You went to it."

"Right. You're right," she said distractedly, pulling her phone up again when it buzzed in her hand, swiping and clicking away. "Oh no, the people we're supposed to be meeting later are already at the hotel. Daddy! They're early!" she called, jogging in her black heels to catch up to him. I thought my sister was supposed to be a high-powered attorney, not the Wyoming SA's grunt.

My father looked back at me and Grace, and some kind of look flashed across his face, like maybe he wanted to say something to me, but he didn't. It wasn't anything new, and it was probably just a lecture about how I had let him down, but he wouldn't want the mayor to hear.

Leaving Mayor Covey talking to himself, Jill ushered our father back toward their car. "You can go, Fran," she said, waving Grace and me off. "I'll text later and let you know what time to show up to the diner. Just wear something a little nicer, okay?"

"Mama, do we have to go?" Grace whispered while Jill helped him into the car, like he was ninety years old and helpless. He swatted at her, like he didn't like her doting on him, but he didn't stop her. He'd looked relieved when his conversation with Mayor Covey was interrupted, though. Probably because the mayor was what my father would call a bleeding heart. It didn't matter that Mayor Covey loved Wisper and genuinely wanted only good things for the people who lived here. If he disagreed in any way with my father, then my father wouldn't respect him. It was his way or the highway.

I smiled down at my beautiful, wild-haired daughter. "Yes, carrot, we have to. But as long as we get some good veggies in you, you can have a few bites of those pancakes you love with bananas and blackberries. Remember? José added extra fruit so they're sweeter, and you didn't even miss the syrup."

"Okay, Mama." She nodded. "I'll go for you. I know it's important to you."

"Thank you, baby." I smiled again, leaning down to kiss her forehead. It wasn't important to me at all, but it was important for Grace's health, so we would go, even though it would be absolutely unbearable.

***

"DAMMIT! THIS STUPID CAR."

"Mama, don't curse. It hurts my ears," Grace called out the backseat window while I kicked my stupid tire, cursing my car, which wouldn't start. It was completely dead in front of our house, and we were going to be late to the diner. The mood that would put my father and sister in had me panicking.

"Sorry, bub," I said, then to no one, I moaned. "What are we gonna do now?"

"Don't worry," Grace said. "The sheriff will be here any minute. He can drive us."

"What? The sh—?"

I was interrupted when a police siren *whooped* at me, and I spun around to see Carey's cruiser pull up behind my car.

He jumped out. "Frannie? What's wrong? I got your text."

"My text? Huh?"

"Borrowed your phone," Grace said, holding my phone out the rolled-down window with a mischievous glint in her eye. "You can have it back now, but this would be so much easier if I had my own."

"Grace Mae Morris, you are in so much trouble."

Looking out the far window, she shrugged, trying to hide her smile.

I turned toward Carey, completely embarrassed. My face had to be the color of raspberries. "I am *so* sorry."

He laughed under his breath, but then turned and bent down to speak to Grace through the window. "Gracie, this isn't technically an emergency. You can text my personal phone any time you want to, but you can't text the official Sheriff's number and say there's an emergency when there really isn't. That's actually illegal."

Grace's eyes became the size of saucers, and she looked terrified till Carey smiled and tipped his hat back. "You get one free pass. This is it, but don't do it again, okay?"

"O-okay, sorry, but Mama doesn't have your phone number in her phone."

"I'll be sure to give it to her. Deal?" Grace nodded, and Carey patted the door lightly, straightening and smiling at me too. "What seems to be the problem?" He looked so sheriffy right then, and without my permission, my eyes did a slow perusal from the top of his brown cowboy hat, down, down, down all of his very non-little-boy muscles that oddly looked amazing in sheriff brown polyester, down to his steel-toe boots.

I gulped before I said, "It's the alternator. I need a new one. Well, actually, I need a new car, but until we win the lottery, I think I just need a new alternator."

"Lemme have a look. Pop your hood."

I groaned in my head. Did he really have to be so nice and say things like that? The images swimming around in my mind were so not appropriate for this situation.

"Carey, you don't have to do this. I'm sure you're busy."

"I'm actually not for once. I've gotta be at José's Diner in about thirty minutes, but it won't take a minute for me to have a peek."

"The diner? Why?"

"Uh…" He looked uncomfortable, his eyebrows lowering and his lips pressed together. He took his hat off and ran his fingers through his copper hair.

"Oh! I'm sorry. Do you have a date or somethin'?"

"No, I don't have a date. I'm s'posed to be there for your dad," he said, walking to the front of my car. "He requested me as his personal security. I'm just surprised you didn't know. Your sister didn't mention it? She's the one who called me."

"Oh, um, no, I-I'm not really privy to their—well, anyway, no. I didn't know you'd be there too. That's where we're tryin' to go. We could walk, but I can't be late, and it's so hot. We'll be sweatin' like pigs by the time we get there."

"Pigs don't actually sweat, Mama," Grace added helpfully, "which is why they like to lay in the mud. 'Cause it's cool."

I shook my head and laughed at my little know-it-all, and I was relieved to see the calmness and laughter in Carey's eyes. He should've been angry about getting a crank 911 text from a ten-year-old, but he wasn't.

"Alright," he said, stepping back around the front end of my car. "Then why don't I drive us to the diner, and after, I'll have a look at your car. Sound good? Mike Williams over at the auto shop owes me a favor. If the alternator's all you need, you just have to buy the part, and he'll install it for you."

"Thank you. That's really nice of you," I said, hoping he couldn't detect the panic I was feeling. I didn't want him to know how destitute we were, but how much did an alternator cost? I wasn't sure I could afford it.

"Ready?" he asked, nodding to his cruiser, and the panic disappeared 'cause all I could think about was how thankful I was that Teton county had swapped out its fleet of SUVs for pickup trucks. Carey was definitely sexier in a truck. Just him standing next to the truck was hot with his hat and his thigh holster... *Dang it, Frannie. Cut it out!*

I cleared my throat. "Okay. C'mon, Grace."

"Told you he'd drive us," she said under her breath when she climbed into his back seat.

"Put your seatbelt on, little miss nosy Parker."

"Who?"

"Never you mind," I said, then lowered my voice. "I can't believe you texted the sheriff."

She whispered back, shrugging again when she clicked the seatbelt into place over her lap, "We needed help. He's a helper. What's the problem?"

CHAPTER ELEVEN

FRANNIE

MY FATHER and sister weren't at the diner when we arrived, thankfully. Whenever my presence was demanded, I tried to get there early. If I got there before they did, my father could at least think I was prepared or organized or respectful, whichever of those things was important to him on that particular day. I wouldn't know since he barely spoke to Grace and me.

Plus, it gave me time to get comfortable and calmed down. When I was forced to play the part of his happy, perfectly-put-together daughter, I got flustered. I didn't belong in that life, and I always worried people would see right through me, and it would be another thing my father could hate me for.

Memories from my childhood tried to surface again—memories of my daddy holding my hand while we waited in line for a movie, memories of him reading fairytales to Jilly and me at bedtime, or just him laughing. He never laughed now. I was pretty sure he'd forgotten how. Not that I ever had the chance to witness his lack of laughter, but it was apparent in his general demeanor.

Grace had a way of centering me, though. If she was with me, when we were together, it was me and her against the world. Big carrot and little carrot. That was what she called us, or carrots squared.

And this time was no different. Except this time, Carey was with us, and that made us carrots times three. It was silly, but I spent the entire time waiting for my father to show up trying to think of a better name for three redheaded friends.

The governor's black SUV pulled up in front of the diner, and two photographers were there, waiting on the sidewalk to capture pictures of her saying hello to a few Wisperites, shaking their hands and patting their children's heads. I didn't know much about Governor Buchanan, but she was a woman, so that made me hopeful that she was a good public servant, as opposed to the man she would soon be meeting: my father. It was kind of a sexist point of view, but the men in my life had proven to be untrustworthy. I supposed the complete opposite could've been true about the governor, but I was optimistic.

Except for Carey. He was always someone I could trust.

"Be right back, gotta shake some hands," he said when Grace and I were settled at the long diner counter with menus in our hands. He turned to head toward the door, but he stopped, looking back at me. "You okay though? You look nervous."

My stomach tightened at the feeling Carey's concern caused in me. Even now, he still cared. And he still looked at me as if the stars shone in my eyes, like I was important to him. Like I meant something to him and we were still the best of friends.

Like we loved each other still.

"I'm okay. Just wanna get this over with. My father, he—

they like me to be at these things, to show my support, but I'd rather be anywhere else."

"You're a good daughter," he said, and he smiled and walked outside to greet the governor.

I didn't correct him before he walked away, and I watched through the big front windows as he shook Governor Buchanan's hand. She was probably twenty years older than Carey, with dyed platinum-blond hair and a boring black pantsuit, but she looked him up and down in his uniform like she was considering whether to order him for dinner.

Not that I could blame her. When we were young, he was cute, but now, Carey was an insanely good-looking man. Solid, handsome, and superbly fit, with a defined and stubbled jaw and eyes that could melt you on the spot. And she probably didn't know what it felt like, but I still remembered the fire he'd put inside me when he'd kissed me. Who was I kidding? I still dreamt about it. If she knew how Carey's kisses felt, the governor would jump him and grind herself against him, never mind the photographers.

I wondered if Carey remembered our kiss. It happened before I left, before I pushed him away. Before we went from being glued at the hip every day to barely speaking when we passed each other in the hallway at school.

That kiss was a part of the reason I left.

One winter night between my house and his, everything changed. It was the spot where all our important moments seemed to happen back then...

"Frannie, I wanna kiss you," he said. "Will you let me?" His eyes were hidden by evening shadows, but he tilted his head a little, and then I could see them better, and they were clear. We were sixteen, and most kids our age would fumble through that kind of declaration, but he knew what he wanted.

"You're my best friend, and I don't wanna mess it up, but... you're all I think about."

"I am?" Those eyes fell to my lips, and my stomach dropped into my winter boots when I realized he wasn't what I thought about day in and day out. I had thought about him in that way, the boyfriend way, and I loved him, but I'd become obsessed with changing the trajectory of my life. That was the thing to occupy most of my thoughts. I could not end up like my mama. I just couldn't, but that was the way things looked to be headed.

"Yeah," he said, stepping closer to me, looking in my eyes, and I wasn't sure it was a good idea, but I wanted badly to know how it would feel if he kissed me.

"Okay." And maybe if he kissed me, I wouldn't feel anything, and then it would be easy to walk away from him when I left Wisper. I'd miss my best friend, but I wouldn't be losing the other half of my soul.

That was when I realized I'd already made my decision. I would leave. I needed to. Doug Morris had already invited me to go to Texas with him. He had plans to make it to the pro-rodeo circuit. It was a dumb dream in my opinion, but it didn't really matter. I just needed a way to escape. Once I made it out and I was free of my father, I could make my own way in the world.

Carey reached forward, holding my face between his hands, his thumbs tracing soft lines along my jaw, and he moved in, closing the distance between us, and I began to panic inside.

What if I did feel something for him? Something more than best friends? It had been building between us for a while with every look and touch he gave me, but I'd been trying to ignore it. Could I leave him? But I had to. If I didn't, I'd end up in a life I didn't want, always trying to make my father proud of me. Always trying to please someone who couldn't be pleased, at least not by me.

Come hell or high water, that wasn't going to happen.

But when Carey's lips touched mine and I closed my eyes, it was like fireworks went off inside me. Places in my body that had never been ignited before were exploding with happiness, expectation, and desire. It was overwhelming. It was everything, and I kissed him back.

Suddenly, it was me snaking my tongue into his mouth, my fingers digging into his hips to pull him closer.

Carey gasped, and he tilted his head, swallowing my kiss and making it his own. He tangled his fingers in my hair and pressed our bodies together, and in that moment, everything became clear to me: If I stayed, I'd love him. I'd love him hard, and I'd have to stand by while he built a career and pursued his dreams. I'd become my mama. I'd give up everything because I loved him enough to be that person.

If I stayed, I'd be unhappy, and I'd ruin both our lives, and he deserved better…

My father's car pulled up alongside the governor's, stealing my attention away from the past, and he and Jilly stepped out, and the governor visibly stiffened. Carey noticed it, and he looked back and forth between my father and the governor several times, but he didn't say anything. I'd long ago stopped wondering what my father could be up to, but it wouldn't have surprised me to hear that he was trying to blackmail the governor or she'd caught him getting involved in something he shouldn't be.

Out of the corner of my eye, I noticed my asshole husband lurking on the sidewalk across the street, behind a lamppost. I didn't think he'd seen me, but he could guess Grace and I would be here since my family was. He knew

how my father liked me to be present at his ridiculous political showings.

Since the unfortunate day I married him, my father and
Doug had had maybe a handful of interactions, but Doug was
usually hiding nearby on the off chance he could get something from my father. Money was his typical motivation,
though what my father provided for Grace and me from my
mama's inheritance came from Jilly, which I supposed was
the same thing since she went everywhere my father did and
doted on him like he was her child instead of the other way
around.

My father kept control of the money, doling it out when
he saw fit, and Jill would transfer it to a bank card for Grace
and me. She'd never give me more than a hundred bucks at a
time because she said Doug would get his hands on it, and
then it would be gone and I'd be sorry. The payments for
Grace's insurance came directly from her account to the
insurance company because she thought that was way too
much money for me to handle on my own, like I was an irre-
sponsible child.

She still thought I was a starry-eyed idiot, with dreams for
brains, and it hurt to know she thought that about me. I hadn't
given her much of a reason to think otherwise, though, so she
was probably right. Or she had been. And she was right that
Doug would blow through any money she gave me.

But Jill had no idea what I'd had to do for Grace. I'd give
Doug the money if he threatened me for it, but only because it
would pacify him and we could avoid another "dustup" in
front of Grace.

She was the reason for everything I did, every decision I
made.

The usual feeling of fear and dread stomped around in my
stomach when I saw Doug standing there, but I knew Grace

and I would be safe from him with everyone around, especially Carey, so I tried to relax. It certainly wasn't unusual that Doug would be nosy about my family, and he showed up wherever I was regularly, if just to knock me down a peg. To put the fear he knew he could make me feel inside my gut. His cruelty really knew no bounds, and I had plenty of scars to prove it.

Once my father, Jill, the governor, and all their various staff were inside the diner and seated, eating and discussing things I couldn't follow or understand, and didn't want to, the evening passed slowly. I looked frequently for Doug, but I'd only glimpsed him that one time.

José was there, though, and he made Grace's wheat pancakes and brought us low-sugar cookies for dessert, which of course were delicious. He and I'd had many conversations about them because he had quite a bit of healthy-cooking knowledge, and he had encouraged me to start a bakery too. More than once. He said there were a lot of people in town who requested baked goods, and he thought I had good ideas about pastries I could provide for customers seeking healthier dessert options. He didn't have the time or the space himself to get into doing that. He was plenty busy cooking for the diner and catering luncheon events.

José's food was really good but inexpensive, so whenever I had a little extra money, I'd take Grace for lunch on the weekends or breakfast before school in the winters. His homemade chili was a staple around here, but most of the time, José refused my money. He was the best chef I'd ever met, even though he'd never call himself one, and he was an even better human being.

Grace and I weren't included in the conversation between the governor and my father, except when he pointed us out to her, saying something about his "other" daughter and his granddaughter, and the governor noticed me then. She kept looking over at me, where Grace and I were perched at the diner counter still, silently eating and praying this thing would end soon. When no one was looking, we played rock, paper, scissors, and Grace drew rainbow-colored cats on a paper menu with Crayons José provided.

Carey stood diligently behind the booth where my father and the governor sat. There wasn't any danger, and the governor had her own security, so I had no clue why my father wanted him there. Maybe it was protocol, but more likely, it was probably the same reason he wanted me there— for appearances, to make him seem bigger than he was, more important than he was, a different kind of man than he really was.

When he could look away without my father noticing, Carey would smile at Grace and me discretely, wink, and be goofy, and Grace loved it. He had a way of making anyone he gave his attention to feel included and happy, like he had your back, like he was a true friend, and like you were, well… loved.

Neither Grace nor I had any idea how that felt anymore, to be given attention from a man who cared whether we were happy or not, and Grace soaked it up. I had a feeling it was the reason she'd texted Carey earlier. For his help, yes, but also because she *liked* him. He was easy to like. I wondered if he had any idea what a big deal it was that Grace was already so comfortable with him. She wasn't like that with anyone else but me, but when Carey was around, she was a normal ten-year-old girl.

When dinner was over and the governor had left, and after Jilly had scolded me for not helping more, though I had no idea what I could've done to help or even what she needed help with, we were all set to leave. José waved us off with a

Tupperware container of Grace's cookies, and Carey had come back inside after escorting the governor out to her car when a man stormed into the diner. The door hit the wall, and the jingle bell on the door handle fell to the floor with a loud *clang*.

Doug appeared across the street again. He'd been hiding in the alley, which also wasn't an unusual thing for him to do, but he stepped forward under the streetlamp, like some creepy marauder in an old movie. He wasn't watching me or Grace though. He was watching the commotion between my father and this man when the man stepped right up to my father, his face red and angry. I remembered the guy from my childhood but couldn't recall his name.

"What are you doin' about the violence and destruction around here?" the familiar man demanded of my father. "Some attorney you are. You're supposed to protect your voters. I voted for you. I thought somebody from Wisper would give a shit, so how are you gonna protect me? My farm's at risk!"

"Carl," Carey warned, stepping between the man and my father. When Carey said his name, I remembered who he was. He was Harold Aberforth's dad, a kid Carey and I'd gone to school with, and not a particularly nice guy—father or son— but they'd lived in Wisper their whole lives and were a part of the tight-knit community. "Calm down, now. It isn't SA McKinnon's job to investigate crimes. It's mine, and I'm doin' it. You're gonna have to be patient, but this ain't the right avenue for your complaints. Take a step back please."

Carl's face seemed to grow redder, and he was holding his breath in anger, but Carey kept looking at him, and from where I stood, it seemed like Carey was trying to communicate something to Carl without actually saying anything.

The way Carey cocked his head and the tone of his voice

brought back so many memories from when we were kids. One memory specifically was really clear. We were fourteen, so neither of us had a driver's license yet, and we'd snuck out and hitched a ride to the movies in Jackson one summer night. When we got home and got caught, Carey tried to help me talk my way out of trouble when my father interrogated me. But he'd tried to accomplish this silently, like he was a mime. He expected me to know what he'd meant from the terrified expressions on his face.

Needless to say, my father grounded me for a month, and later, when Carey climbed back through my bedroom window after my parents had gone to bed, he laughed at me, saying, "I told you what to say!" Except back then, all I could see when he looked at me was his smile, his gorgeous butter-brown eyes and freckles, and the love he had for me. Reading his secret thoughts or ulterior motives was a lost cause.

But now, I saw that there was something more behind what he was saying out loud to this man, Carl, and I wanted to know what it meant, and why wouldn't he just say it? Why would he try to hide something from my father?

My father couldn't be bothered. "If you have this under control, Sheriff, I'll be going. Thank you for your services."

"Yessir," Carey said, turning to shake my father's hand while Carl backed away silently, fidgeting and waiting impatiently until Carey would explain what had just happened.

My sister, on the other hand, was all too keen on Carey's weird movements, and she was studying him, like she was surprised by what was happening. She glanced out the window, her eyes landing on the place across the street where Doug had just been posted, like she'd seen him or had known he was there, but there was no way she could have. She had even less to do with my husband than my father did, and Doug was gone now.

When she noticed me watching, her patented "every-thing's okay now, let's just pretend this never happened" smile spread over her lips, and she reached her arms in Grace's direction. "Come here, sweetie. Give Auntie Jilly a hug before I go."

Grace did, and my father patted her head like a puppy while Jill hugged her, then he walked from the diner to his car, staring off into the night and tapping his foot while he waited impatiently for his driver to open the back door.

Carey promised to call Carl later and, with not a little persuasion, Carl went home, and then so quickly, everyone was gone, and Carey and I stood on the sidewalk staring at each other silently, while Grace clicked away at her favorite game on my phone.

Doug was nowhere to be seen, though I was worried he was still watching, and I was worried about what kind of chaos that would cause later.

"GRACE, YOU MIND GOIN' for a ride with me and your mama?" Carey asked while he drove us slowly down Main Street. He'd been nothing but professional helping Grace and me into his car to give us a ride home. At least from an outsider's perspective, it was just the sheriff giving a ride to a mom and her kid, nothing more. And that was all it was, but it felt like so much more.

Doug knew Carey and I had been best friends when we were younger, and he had always been jealous of that fact, so I knew I was potentially poking a hornet's nest, but it felt good to be around Carey, to be protected, even if only for a short time, and to feel happy and safe. Those weren't feel-ings Grace or I experienced very often, and I knew how much she liked Carey, so I hated to take them away from her.

Or from me.

Wisper was dead quiet, and it was still so hot, even though the sun had set more than an hour ago, but Carey didn't turn on his air conditioning. Instead, he rolled down the windows, and it was like the fresh air was laced with sedatives. My anxiety over the whole evening seemed to recede into the background, and I held my arm out my open window, wiggling my fingers in the air, feeling the wind push and pull. I could smell dry sage and dusty earth, and it was the most peaceful scent.

It, too, brought back memories of so many summers growing up in Wisper, covered in that dirt and dust, my cheeks sticky after eating popsicles from the ice cream truck, running home to make sure I'd get back by my sunset curfew with my shoes dangling from my fingers because the feeling of Wyoming dirt between my toes made me feel free. Carey and I used to hold hands while we raced to make it back to our houses before the neighborhood streetlights turned on for the night, and we'd meet again between our houses first thing the next morning for whatever adventure awaited us that day.

"Sure," Grace said, and she yawned. She'd eaten her plain-but-balanced meal with a few bites of her favorite pancakes as a small treat, I'd already given her an insulin injection, and now she was full and tired.

She began humming along to the song on the radio, and Carey peeked at her through his rearview mirror, then turned it up. It was that boy-band guy who went out on his own. I couldn't remember his name, but every ten-year-old girl on the planet was in love with him.

When Carey sang the words at the top of his lungs, Grace and I both jumped, and Grace laughed. "Watermelon Sugar!"

They sang together then, till the song was over, and I tried not to laugh. It was the sweetest thing, but Carey's voice was awful. It didn't seem to bother him or Grace though.

"So," I said when the song was over and Grace had gone back to playing her game on my phone, "where we goin'?"

"Oh, I just thought a drive might be nice," Carey said. "That okay? You up for that?"

I nodded, smiling like a fool, happy that being around him after all these years still felt comfortable.

"I've been workin' on this case, and sometimes, drivin' helps me think and process, you know?" He looked at me and then back between the seats at Grace, laughing under his breath. "Did she fall asleep that fast?"

I peeked at her and laughed too. "Yep." Reaching behind my seat, I picked up my phone from the floor where it had fallen when Grace dozed off. "I'm not surprised. It's been a long day. She always gets sleepy after she eats."

"Is that hard to manage? The diabetes, I mean?"

"No," I said. As long as we had the medication she needed. I didn't mention that part wasn't easy.

"Why doesn't she use a pump. I noticed you givin' her an injection earlier."

"Grace doesn't like the pump." She'd said as much, and that she was scared and embarrassed to use an insulin pump —she was shy enough without a box permanently stuck to her body—but I knew she could get over that. The real reason was that it was too expensive. Injections were the cheapest way to treat her diabetes.

Carey faced forward. "Can I ask you somethin', Frannie?"

"Yeah, I guess," I said, still holding my arm out the window, watching it in the passenger-side mirror like it belonged to someone else.

"What's goin' on with you and your dad? Did you two have a fight? He barely said two words to you tonight."

"No, we didn't have a fight." And I left it at that.

"When we were kids, he was the whole world to you. You looked up to your ol' man like he was a god."

"I suppose he was to me back then, but we're all adults now."

"Yeah, we are, but has he done somethin' that, I dunno, made you mad or sad?" He reached for my hand between us and held it, and I closed my eyes and concentrated with my whole being on the feeling of my hand in his. I still remembered the last time he'd held my hand, and it had been almost thirteen years. It felt different now though. It felt like more. His hand was big, and it enveloped mine, the rough texture of his skin sending shivers down my arms. I hadn't felt like that in more than thirteen years either. I had a husband, sure, but no one had ever made me feel the way Carey had. "I could feel somethin' goin' on between you two tonight, and with Jill. Everything feels different. Y'all used to be so close."

It was awkward, but I tried to change the subject. "How's your mama?" I asked, hoping he wouldn't press me further. Knowing Carey's kind nature, he wouldn't, but also knowing him, he'd see right through me.

He nodded once. I saw it out of the corner of my eye, and he squeezed my hand, then let go and gripped the steering wheel at ten and two. He knew I was avoiding his question. "Uh, she's okay. She lives in Arizona now. Tempe. She's takin' golfin' lessons, if you can believe that."

I didn't mean to, but I blurted, "So, what's this about? I mean, this drive?" Not that I wanted it to end, but it wasn't like we were close anymore. Why all of a sudden were we acting like we were? All the feelings and memories I was suddenly drowning in were scaring me, and the kiss from all those years ago wouldn't leave my head, no matter how hard I tried to force it out.

"I told you—"

"Yeah, drivin' helps you think, but we don't spend time together, Carey, so why are we now?"

"That ain't my fault, Frannie. That's all on you."

He wasn't wrong. But the reasons for my distance from him hadn't changed since we were teenagers; they'd only intensified. Either way, I didn't plan on involving Carey in the mess my life had become.

No matter how much sitting next to him in a quiet truck felt right.

Even if it felt like home.

"You're right. It is my fault."

"Will you tell me why?" When I didn't answer, he lowered his voice almost to a whisper. "If this is about Doug—"

I peeked back to make sure Grace was still asleep. "It's about everything. You don't wanna be my friend. I wouldn't be good for you. You have a great life. A great job. Good friends. I don't wanna mess that up. And besides, I'm still technically married. How would it look?"

"I don't care how it looks, Fran. I have plenty of married women friends. Nobody seems to have an issue with it. What's this really about?"

"Yeah, well, none of those women are married to Doug Morris. I am."

"And why's that? I've waited half our lives for you to tell me why. Why you left with him, why you didn't come home when things got bad, why you…"

"What?"

He pulled to the side of the road and got out, then walked around and opened my door. Peeking back at Grace once more, I was satisfied she was asleep and would be okay for a couple minutes while I shut this conversation down. It wasn't safe to let it continue, but when I stepped out and closed my door behind me, I faced Carey, and he wrapped his arms around me, pulling me against his body, hugging me. I felt his breath in my hair and on my neck, and my knees buckled at the relief and overwhelming feeling of belonging I felt.

He caught me and held me against him, saying nothing. We just breathed, and it felt like it used to. Like that day he kissed me.

"I'm sorry," I whispered.

"Why, Frannie? I loved you. I woulda loved you forever. Why'd you go?"

CHAPTER TWELVE

CAREY

HOLDING HER, it was like time had stopped the day she'd left Wisper. Like she hadn't left, hadn't married Doug, and hadn't become this shell of a person. Like she was still my Frannie, my best friend, and the only woman I'd ever really loved. She even smelled the same, like warm summer nights and wild roses.

"I've missed you," I said, hugging her like both our lives depended on it. All the dreams I'd had as a young man of me and her together came slamming back into my head, and they made me breathless. "I missed my best friend."

"I missed you too." She tried to hide it, but I heard the catch in her voice, like she was trying not to cry.

It was all I could do to not feel her against me, her chest heaving with breath, because when we were in each other's arms, it felt just like it used to when we were teenagers and every touch lit a fire inside. I'd only kissed her the one time, but I never forgot how it felt.

With my lips dangerously close to her neck, I said, "Talk to me then. Tell me what's goin' on with you. Please? I can still see the bruise on your beautiful face, and I saw the destruction that husband of yours caused the other night. I'd do anything for you to tell me why you let him do that to you, Frannie. Why're you lyin' for him?" I pulled my head back a little, swiping her hair away from her face with the tip of my finger, and my eyes landed on the bruise. I couldn't help it.

My mention of the asshole seemed to snap her out of the mood she was in while we held each other. She pulled out of my arms, and I missed her warmth immediately, even though it was probably a hundred degrees outside.

Her expression was hard and closed off when she said, "We can't do this here. We're in the middle of town. There's lights everywhere. If he happens to drive by, you have no idea the problems he'll cause."

"I think I have some idea," I said, remembering the other night and many others when I'd been called to break up a fight between her husband and some unsuspecting bar patron or some Joe Schmo walking down the street. Doug blamed the world for his failures in life, and he took it out on just about anybody who looked at him funny, but as I was coming to understand, maybe he took most of it out on Fran. I was furious that it had taken me this long to see. Some investigator I was. "But you're right. I don't wanna make it worse for you and Grace. C'mon, I'll take you home. We can put her to bed and talk there."

"DO you know why your dad was meetin' the governor tonight?" I asked Frannie while I carried a sleeping Grace to her front door.

"I'll take her, Carey. But thank you." Frannie scooped Grace out of my arms when we reached her doorway.

"Fran—"

"Thank you for drivin' us, but please, just go. Things will only get worse for us if you stay. Don't worry about my car. I'll call the auto shop tomorrow."

"I just wanted to talk to you, Frannie. Nothin' more."

"I know, but it's…" Her eyes dropped, and she stared at Grace's face, like she wanted to make sure the kid was still asleep, but she was avoiding me. I was sure of it. "It's just really not a good idea, okay?"

I hadn't realized how much I wanted to talk to her, just to be in the same room with her a little while longer. All the old attractions were back, though they felt different now—stronger—but I really had missed my best friend. It broke my heart to leave her like this, but resigned and disappointed, I nodded. "Yeah, okay."

"B-but thank you," she said, and she looked up quickly and smiled. It wasn't radiant, though, like her smile used to be. It was barely there.

"Any time, you know? You can call me any time. You have my number now."

Dipping her chin, she nodded once and closed the door.

Dammit.

I LEFT, but I didn't go home.

I just kept driving.

What the hell was going on with Fran's dad? There was something there tonight, under the surface, between him and the governor. Jillian was weird, too, but I thought that might just be her normal state, and Frannie seemed oblivious to it all, whatever it was.

Fran's dad and the governor spoke in hushed voices most

of the evening. There were regular folks enjoying dinner at the diner, talking and laughing, so even though I wasn't more than five feet away, all I could hear were a few stray words here and there. They talked about the upcoming election, and I did hear it when Mr. McKinnon asked straight out if Governor Buchanan would endorse him to be the next governor when she ran for the Senate in the next election. She didn't seem to want to answer him, continuously dodging the question.

Other than that awkward exchange, I didn't get much else.

And when the governor left, after I cleared out all the hangers-on hoping to meet her, Carl stormed in. That damn idiot. I knew he was upset, but what had he really expected to accomplish by pulling that stunt? Thankfully, the photographers had already left by then.

McKinnon had seemed properly surprised by Carl, and I didn't think he or his daughter noticed Fran's husband perched like a vulture across the street for most of the night.

I couldn't imagine how either of them could possibly know anything about the small crimes connected to Carl's farm or the land offer he'd gotten, but it gave me an avenue to investigate, and when I pulled up in front of Carl's old, run-down farmhouse, he met me on the porch.

"You here to arrest me for exercisin' my civil rights? I had every right to demand answers from that asshole."

"No, Carl, I'm not here to arrest you, but next time, could you give me a heads-up?"

"Why would I do that? If I want answers, why would I involve the man who works for the dishonest backhanders over there at the capital? Ain't gonna do me one bit of good."

"Carl, I work for the people of Teton County. I work for

you, and you know you can trust me. You've known me most of my life."

He scoffed, but he knew he wouldn't win the argument. "What's this about, Carey? It's near ten at night."

"Yeah, I'm sorry for the late hour, but I got a question for you." I pulled my phone from my pocket and searched for a picture of Jillian McKinnon, right hand and daughter to Wyoming's State Attorney and Frannie's baby sister. When I showed it to Carl, I asked, "Is this the woman who was here offerin' to buy your land?"

"No. That ain't her. She's got light hair, and I know who that is. That's the SA's daughter. They used to live in town when the girls were kids. The woman who was here had dark hair, almost black. She was a white lady, kinda tall—well, she had on those ridiculous stick-heeled shoes, you know the ones—and her face was kinda pinched. Know what I mean? Like she's unhappy, or maybe she just hates her job."

"Okay, but other than tonight, you haven't spoken to the SA or his daughter lately? Haven't had any contact with 'em?"

"No. What reason would I have to talk to them? Is that all you wanted? I gotta be up with the sun in the mornin'. I ain't really got time to answer all these stupid questions."

Rolling my eyes at Carl's attitude, I sighed. "Yeah, that's it for tonight, but don't forget to call me if you remember anything else or you hear from the woman again."

"Yeah, yeah," he said, and he yanked his screen door open and disappeared into his house.

Well, that was a dead end. Not that I expected Fran's family to be directly involved in something so obviously nefarious, but there was definitely something there tonight. Something weird in the air.

When we were younger, I was around Jill because Frannie and I were always together. She followed us to the creek or the playground nearly every day, but that was years ago, and now, I didn't know a whole lot about her. Beside the two facts that she lived in Cheyenne and was a lawyer, I knew even less, except for what Fran had told me, which wasn't much.

Looking at her and her dad tonight, though, Bradley and Jillian McKinnon seemed more like people from a big city rather than people who'd grown up in Wisper, and that somehow gave me a little pause. Not that there was anything wrong with big cities, but you could always tell when someone was from a small town like Wisper. There was just an open friendliness about a person, a relaxed way they related to people. Fran's dad and sister no longer had that quality, and their presence here felt forced and like they disdained Wisper and her residents.

There had been something in both of their eyes tonight, and I was bound and determined to figure out what that was. I had a feeling it wasn't something good, and I had an even bigger suspicion that it did have something to do with Carl's busted fence.

I just had no idea what it could possibly be.

DRIVING AIMLESSLY WASN'T GETTING me anywhere, so I did the only thing I could think of: I called my friend Billie. I reached in my glove box and fished around till my fingers bumped into the hard plastic that was my unregistered, commercially bought cell phone.

"For fuck's sake, Carey. What now?" Billie groaned into her cell phone and yawned. "Why do you always call when I'm sleeping? You know how important my sleep is to me."

"And you know how important my job is to me."

She tsked her tongue. "Fine. I want to, but I can't argue with that. What's up? What do you need me to do this time?"

"I need you to do a little diggin'," I said.

"Yeah, that's usually why you call. In fact, I think maybe you should get the words 'I need you to do a little diggin'' tattooed somewhere, but about who this time?" She yawned again, and her voice softened when she cooed at her husband. "Go back to bed, Jay. It's just Carey."

"You act like the only time I call is when I need somethin', but I just talked to you two days ago 'cause you were freakin' out about Jay askin' you about havin' kids."

Whispering, her voice was muffled when she said, "Hey, that's confidential. I still don't know how I feel about it, so zip your lips, dude."

"Please, you know you want kids. I've seen the way you look at your nieces and nephew. You're smitten. And it ain't like you to waffle back and forth on a subject. Dive in head-first, that's what you usually do."

"You think you're so smart," she said with attitude, but I could hear the smile in her voice. "The truth is, I don't know. Maybe we'll adopt, or maybe I'm just destined to be the greatest auntie who ever lived. Whatever. I'm not gonna decide in the middle of the night on the phone with you, so what do you need me to do? What am I looking into this time?"

"This has to be discreet. No one can know what you're up to. There can't be any trail."

"Ah, is that why you're calling on your super-secret burner phone? You know, when you call me on this phone, your name comes on my contact list as 'Dork'?"

"Yes, that's why I'm callin' on this phone, and yep, I actually did know about your nickname. Thanks for that, by the way, but you're not the sleuth you imagine yourself to be."

"Alright, fine. Lemme have it," she said, and I spilled all my suspicions and questions. If anybody could find dirt on SA McKinnon, his daughter, or Governor Buchanan, Billie would be the one to do it.

CHAPTER THIRTEEN

FRANNIE

MORE THAN ANYTHING I'd felt in a long time, I wanted Carey to come inside when he carried Grace from his truck, just to feel his friendship a little longer, to feel safe and surrounded by a man who was strong and who loved instead of hated. I couldn't deny that I wouldn't have minded Carey's eyes on me in more than a platonic way too. Until recently, I'd almost forgotten how it felt, and I found myself wanting it so much, I ached for it.

It was a bad idea. I knew that, but I still argued with myself for hours, indecision making me pick up my phone eight thousand times, wanting him to come back, but then I'd click it off and back on more times than I could count. Finally, I turned it completely off, and at three in the morning, I fell asleep, but I woke soon after when I heard Grace calling out for me.

Jumping out of bed and running to her room, I flipped on her bedroom light and tried to comfort her while I looked around, making sure there wasn't really any danger and it was just a bad dream. I'd never tell her, but I was scared of the dark too. Scared of being alone in the world without another adult to have my back. I hadn't always been this way, and it made me feel weak that I did now. But it was how I felt.

Peeking out her window, I made sure there were no monsters lurking there. "Grace, it's okay. You're okay." Her dinosaur night-light was out, and she'd probably woken and was scared by the darkness.

"I heard a noise outside," she said, crying softly. She reached for me, breathing rapidly and crushing me against her when I sat on the edge of the bed. Her little heart was beating a mile a minute, her springy, red ringlets wet with sweat and tears and stuck to the side of her face, and her cheeks were pink from the heat. God, what we both wouldn't have given for working air conditioning.

"Everything's all right. I'm here. It was probably just a deer or a bunny or somethin'."

I shushed and rocked her in her bed for a few minutes, and she was quiet, and then she pulled back a little, looked up at me, and asked, "Why doesn't my daddy like to be with me?"

I froze. "What?" I'd really hoped I would have more time to come up with an answer to this question. One where I wouldn't have to lie but where I wouldn't have to tell her the bald truth either: that her father didn't care about her. That he was her father in DNA and name only, and it was all he'd ever be.

"I saw a girl at the diner with her daddy tonight. They were eatin' hamburgers and laughin' together. Why doesn't my daddy do that with me? He only comes here when he's mad at you."

"Oh, Grace, I-I... Well, the truth is that I... don't know. I don't know why your daddy gets so mad or why he doesn't come to see you. I just don't know. I'm sorry."

"It's okay, Mama. I know he says it's your fault, but I

know that's not true. And I don't think I'd like it if he did come to see me anyway, but I was just wonderin'." She looked away, pushing her hair away from her face and avoiding eye contact, like she was afraid to ask her next question. But she did. "Do *you* like it when he comes here?"

Gently, I guided her face toward mine again, and looking in her eyes, I said plainly, "No, Grace, I don't." Honesty was the best policy, even if the truth wasn't what she might want to hear.

She nodded, sniffling again. "So maybe we could just tell him not to come anymore. I think that would be better. I don't like when he hurts you, Mama."

"I know. Oh God, I know." I pulled her back to me and hugged her so hard I thought I might break her little body. "I'm so sorry."

"I love you," she said in the sweetest voice, "and I want you to be happy. Don't you want that too?"

"More than anything in the world, I want *you* to be happy. If you're happy, then I will be too."

"Okay," she said, patting my hands with her own small ones when I lay next to her on her bed, snuggling in close.

"It's too hot for us to huddle up together under the covers, tellin' our stories, but I sure do like cuddlin' my little carrot." I buried my nose in her hair, drawing in the scent of everything perfect and pure in the world, and Grace rolled to face me, and she kissed my cheek.

"Me too. Let's just pretend it's not hot. We can pretend we're at the North Pole, and there's penguins and polar bears all around, except the polar bears are nice. They won't eat you, and they wanna sit in our igloo and listen to our stories. And we can only tell stories about wintertime."

"What a great idea. I'm feelin' cooler already. You sure

are smart, my girl, and I love you bigger than the whole world."

"I know. Love you too." Moonlight was trickling in through the cheap metal blinds over her window, and Grace used it to study my hands, trailing her fingers over the lines on my knuckles. She was working up a breath to ask me something else, and finally, she said, "Mama?"

"Yeah?"

"You know, Sheriff Carey is a carrot too."

"He is. He has red hair like us."

"Hm."

"What?"

"Oh, nothin'." She smiled at me and twisted a lock of my hair between her fingers. "Are you gonna give him those letters you wrote?"

"What? How do you know about that? You read them?" I thought I'd been so stealthy all this time, waiting till she was asleep to write my letters. I never planned on giving them to him, but writing them made me feel like Carey and I were still connected. Like we were still a part of each other's lives. I'd started writing them years ago, after Grace was born, to tell him about her, and I never stopped. My fifty-cent notebook had traveled with us to every trailer we'd lived in, and as soon as we'd get settled in a new place, I'd find the safest place to hide it, but since Doug didn't live here anymore, I'd left it on my nightstand a few times, and I was now realizing that had been a mistake.

"Not all of 'em, but Mama, this is a small house, and sometimes I have to get up at night to pee."

"Grace Mae, you are incorrigible. And no, I'm not giving them to him. They're private. Like a diary."

"What's 'incorrgable'?"

"It means you're a little stinker."

"That's fair," she said.

SUNDAY MORNING ROLLED AROUND AGAIN, and Grace and I took a walk through downtown Wisper before we were due at Terre's house. It was too early for the stores to be open, but we were only window-shopping anyway. Aubrey, the owner of Your Local Bookie was setting up a display in front of her store, and she said hello and handed Grace a free paperback copy of *Anne of Green Gables* when we passed, and Avery from the flower shop tucked a purple flower behind Grace's ear when we said hello. Everyone was preparing for the hot day by setting up early.

The sun was shining, but it had yet to blanket us in its scorching heat, so the air was still cool but humid. Constant humidity was unusual for this part of Wyoming, and it made Grace's hair even more wild. Her frizzy curls bounced when she skipped ahead of me to stick her nose against the ice cream parlor's big front window.

Jabbing her finger at the window, she pointed inside. "Mama, look! They have bubble gum ice cream with actual pieces of gum in there! See that poster on the wall? I want that."

"Bubble gum ice cream for breakfast?" I said, looking in the window too.

"No, silly, after breakfast."

"Hm, well, I suppose we could get you a little taste, but you know you can't have a whole ice cream cone. Sorry, bub."

"It's not fair. All the other kids get to eat whatever they want, and I have to eat stupid vegetables and gross oatmeal. I hate diabetes."

"I know it stinks. I wish you could eat whatever you want, but you can't. That's our reality, and we've just gotta make the best of it."

"I know," she conceded, backing away from the window with a frown on her face. "It just really *sucks*."

"Gracie Mae," I said, gasping and acting shocked, "don't cuss. It hurts my ears."

I smiled and she rolled her eyes. "Whatever, Mama."

We walked another block, and the smile came back to her face when she held my hand, and we swung our arms in time with our steps.

"You know, Sheriff Carey calls me Gracie too?"

"He does?"

"Yep. I like it."

"I'm glad," I said, thinking I liked the way she was loosening up toward people. It hurt my heart for her to be so closed off. She had me remembering that Carey called me Frannie instead of Fran or Francesca, too, and I remembered what his voice had sounded like when we were young when he said it.

"Why you smilin' like that?" Grace asked, and I tried to wipe the ridiculous grin off my face.

"No reason."

We walked a little more, and I said, "It's nice out today. I bet Terre will make you a glass of her special peach water later when we go over to help her cook. We can sit out on the back porch and watch Magnolia chase squirrels when we're done."

She groaned. "I hope she never catches one. That would make me sad."

"Well, it's a good thing they're fast and that Magnolia is an old dog. I don't think her eyesight is what it used to be."

"Oh! Let's make her those peanut butter oatmeal treats

she likes. We always have oatmeal, and you're nuts for peanut butter." She smiled up at me, hoping I caught her joke.

I laughed. "I am not nuts for peanut butter."

"Yeah, y'are. You put it on everything. I'm surprised you don't plop a big spoonful of it in your coffee every mornin'."

I tickled her neck with my fingers. "You are *so* funny."

"Ooo, Mama, look!" She dropped my hand and ran to a big flyer in Coffee Shot's window when we passed it. It was the only store open and was already full of early-morning caffeine seekers, and Walt was busy, slinging coffee behind the counter, but it looked like his two employees had things covered and Walt was in the way. Terre was always going on about how Walt found every innocent excuse not to go to church with her, and I laughed when I remembered, waving to him just as Grace pointed to a poster for the EveryBody Rides Barn program at Cade Ranch with pictures of kids of all ages, grooming and riding horses with handlers helping. Everyone was smiling in the photos, and the mountains in the background looked grand and majestic.

"Could I do that?" she asked with wonder and awe in her voice. This kid and animals—she'd always had a connection to them that I couldn't understand.

"Oh, I don't think so, baby. I think it's a program for kids who have disabilities."

"Well, I have diabetes. Doesn't that count?"

"No, technically—"

Someone passed us on the sidewalk, carrying two cardboard trays full of iced coffees, and then a happy female voice interrupted me. When I looked up, it was Evvie Cade, of all people. I'd seen her picture in the paper and knew of her, but we'd never met.

She was grinning from ear to ear. "Would you like to learn how to ride?" she asked Grace as she set her coffees down on a nearby outdoor table, and Grace looked up at her and nodded. "Well, then today is your lucky day. I might know the owner, and I think he's got a spot open for you."

"Oh, no, no," I stopped her. "Thank you, but we couldn't —I mean, I'm sure the program is out of our price range. But it's really nice of you to offer." I winced a little, feeling stupid and like a complete failure because I couldn't give my daughter everything she wanted even though she deserved the world.

Evvie smiled and patted my arm. "The EveryBody Rides Barn is a not-for-profit. We do have some clients that are referred by their doctors, and we bill their insurance, but not all of them. And we have a scholarship program that pays for the kids whose parents might not be accustomed to the insane cost of caring for a horse, which is just about everybody." She bent down a little toward Grace. "And I bet if you promise to groom the horse after you ride him and feed him some hay and apples, then that's all the payment we'll need."

Grace's eyes lit up, and she looked up at me with so much hope on her face, clasping her hands together. I couldn't decide if she was begging or praying that I'd say yes. Probably both.

"Grace, I—"

"Oh my gosh. Please forgive me," Evvie said, turning a little and speaking quietly so Grace wouldn't hear her. "I should've asked first. It's just that the ranch and horses changed my life, and when I see a little kid get excited about joining the program, I have a hard time controlling my enthusiasm." She chuckled and shook her head. "Sorry again. I'm not doing a very good job of convincing you. You're probably thinking I'm some weird lady on the street. Hi," she said, offering her hand for me to shake. "I'm Evvie Cade. I'm married to Jack Cade, one of the owners of Cade Ranch.

You're Fran, right? I've seen you around town. I think you went to school with Jack and his brothers."

"I did, yeah. And Dean, Carey, and I used to hang out together. I was friends with Oly Masterson back in the day, too, but we don't really know each other much anymore. I've seen her at the animal hospital a few times. We used to have dogs, but…" I didn't finish my sentence, not wanting to upset Grace by reminding her of the puppy her dad had given her and then took away when Axle peed on the floor 'cause Doug was too drunk to take the poor thing outside.

"Oh, that's great. So you've probably been out to the ranch before. Really, Fran, I'd love it if you and Grace would come out and give it a try. We started the program a few years ago, and it's been going really well. We have a lot of kids learning to ride on our horses." She looked at Grace. "All kinds of kids. Kids with disabilities, kids without disabilities. Big kids, little kids, and sometimes adults too. Horses are really good at making you feel happy, and riding is just about the coolest thing ever."

Evvie's open happiness was infectious, and Grace was nodding with enthusiasm. There was zero chance I could say no and not pay for it without massive pouting sessions and possibly the biggest meltdown a kid had ever had, and that wasn't usually Grace's style unless her blood sugar was low. But I could see the utter heartbreak peeking through her bright eyes, ready to explode out of my child if I passed on the unexpected opportunity.

Evvie looked back and forth between Grace and me while I contemplated taking her up on her offer. I was only skeptical because I knew if Doug found out we were involved with the Cades, he'd have something to say about it. He wasn't their biggest fan. He'd had a run-in or two with Evvie's brother-in-law, Kevin Cade, and several years later, I still remembered how angry it had made him. And he generally didn't like it when Grace or I found something that made us smile, like culinary school or puppies.

Evvie must've thought I still wasn't convinced it was free because she said, "I promise, there are no hidden costs. There's nothing you need to do except show up and watch Grace ride. She'll love it, and we have amazing handlers and teachers. My husband is one of them."

"Really? It's free?"

"Yep. Completely. It's that simple. It's our donor's gift to the kids."

"Wow. That's really kind. I've heard about an investor. Is that the same man?"

"Yes," Evvie said, nodding across the street. "His name is Theodore Burroughs. He bought the old newspaper building there, and he's working on building a community center. He's an amazing man, more generous than anyone I've ever met. He and his sister moved here a few years ago. She's actually dating my brother-in-law, Finn. We don't see a lot of Theo these days, but he's around. Anyway, I know he'd love it if your daughter took advantage of his scholarship."

Turning away from Grace a little and feeling like the biggest loser, I admitted, "My car isn't the most reliable. Cade Ranch is fifteen or twenty miles from here, right?"

"Yes, but me or one of the guys is always running to and from town, so if you need a ride, call me. Here, give me your number." She pulled out her phone and waited for me to recite my cell number. When I did, she sent me a text. "There. Seriously, call or text any time. And I'm not just saying that, so don't go home and then never call 'cause you think I didn't really mean it. I do mean it. Okay?"

"O-okay. *Thank* you." I tried to convey how grateful I felt through my voice. It was such a nice thing for her to offer, something I could never afford on my own, and Grace would be gaga for the horses. I could barely wait for her to start, just to be able to see the perma-smile she was sure to be wearing for at least a month. I hoped we could keep it from Doug, but if not, it was worth it to see that smile.

"You're very welcome. I'll text you when I get home and can look at the schedule. Then we can set up Grace's first lesson." Evvie looked at Grace, raising her eyebrows in mock sternness. "There's a lot to learn. Are you sure you're ready?"

"Oh, yes, thank you, thank you, thank you!" Grace was practically vibrating with excitement, bouncing up and down on the tips of her toes, looking back and forth between Evvie and me.

"I thought so." Evvie winked at her. "All right. Talk to you later today. I've gotta get this coffee back to the ranch, or I'm gonna have some big ol' grumpy cowboys on my hands." She winked at me this time.

Waving kind of lamely as she walked away, I shook my head. Well, what a start to a day, and the smile on my daughter's face was epic.

"Thank you, Mama!" Grace threw herself at me, hugging me as hard as she could when Evvie drove off in a big, dusty, red truck. "Oh, thank you! I want a white horse. No, I want a splotchy one. Can it be a girl horse? Oh, or maybe a baby horse. Will I ride the same horse every time or a new one every time? Have you ever ridden a horse? What color was it? How big was it? Can I get a cowgirl hat and boots?"

"That was nice of Evvie, wasn't it?" I asked as I peeled her off of me and held her hand while we continued walking. "Are you happy, my Grace?"

"Yes. More happy than I've ever been in my whole entire life!"

"Me too," I said, laughing a little. How could I not be

when I looked down to see my daughter smiling bigger than she had in the longest time? So long, I wasn't sure I could pinpoint the last time. Seeing that smile was my goal every day, and I was once again grateful for the community we'd found back in Wisper.

CHAPTER FOURTEEN

CAREY

"WHATCHA GOT FOR ME?" I asked Billie when I saw her at Cade Ranch Sunday evening. Seriously, they fed me at least twice a week. The thought that I probably needed to get my own life kept flashing through my head, and also that maybe I should've been chipping in for groceries all this time.

"Not much," Billie said while she plopped a big piece of meatloaf on her plate, right on top of an even bigger pile of mashed potatoes. "Thanks, Finn. This smells so good, and I'm so hungry, I think my stomach is about to eat itself."

"You're weird," Finn told Billie, carrying some kind of humungous salad in a bowl to his girlfriend, Aislinn, the dreaded vegetarian, which was a rarity here in cowboy country where steak and hamburger reigned supreme, but Finn seemed to have no end of fun coming up with things to cook for her. "Here, Ace. This is your couscous salad with tofu and mushrooms."

Billie made a disgusted face as Finn set the bowl in front of Ace, who smiled and reached her arm out toward his hip, feeling around till she found a belt loop. She stuck her finger in it and tugged him closer. Ace was also visually impaired, which was ironically fitting since Finn was a recovering ladies' man. Pretty much every woman in town said it was a shame that Ace was blind since she couldn't see "what a looker her boyfriend was."

But they didn't need to see each other to love each other, and boy, did they. He leaned down to kiss her lips, and just watching them interact made me ache. If I was honest with myself, I'd have to admit that I was aching for Frannie.

She was off-limits, though, and it just made the ache worse. But she crossed my mind a thousand times a day, especially lately since we'd been running into each other more than usual.

I kept wondering what it would be like if she was my girl-friend or my wife and Grace was my daughter.

Yeah, it was a crazy thought, and it freaked me out a little that it kept popping into my mind, but there it was.

And if they were mine, they wouldn't be living in that run-down old house with no air conditioning and shit furni-ture. They'd have a car that actually ran, and dammit, they'd smile, like Grace had the other night when we were singing that ridiculous song.

Billie's snarky attitude drew me out of my thoughts. "Yo! Carey, are you listening to me?"

"What?"

"Are you for real right now? You asked me a question, and I'm answering it, but you haven't heard a word I've said."

"Sorry."

"What's up with you? You've been distracted lately."

The entire Cade family, little kids and all, were sitting around the table, and now every single one of them was staring at me. To throw them off the scent, I laughed. "Nothin's wrong. Jeez, Billie. Can't a guy be tired after a long day? It's hot as balls out there, and I've been outside most of the day."

Oly stomped her foot under the table. "Carey!"

"Oops. Sorry, Oly."

One of Oly and Dean's twin daughters, Fiona, asked, "Mama, what's 'hot as balls'?"

"Well, Fifi"—Billie lifted her finger in the air, preparing to explain the phrase to the three-year-old—"'hot as balls' means—"

"Billie," Oly warned, "don't you dare." She stared Billie down until Billie relented and dropped her hand back beneath the table, and even Jack looked scared of Mama Bear Oly. "Fiona, Uncle Carey just meant that it's really hot outside, but he said it in a rude way. *You* don't say it like that, okay?"

"Okay, Mama," Fiona said, smiling, like she knew exactly what it meant and was ready to repeat the words at precisely the right moment. Dean was sitting next to Fiona, trying really hard not to laugh, and Oly glared him down too.

"So, Carey, what's goin' on with Carl now?" Finn asked when he sat and loaded a huge slice of meatloaf onto his own plate. He chugged his beer. "You were just out at his place a couple weeks ago, but I heard someone mowed down his fence the other day. Somebody messin' with him?"

"I'm not sure. Somebody's doin' somethin'. It's eatin' at me, but I don't know what's goin' on."

"I heard the McCluskies had somethin' happen out at their place too," Dean said. "They found some of their herd sick in the pasture, and it looked like they'd been poisoned. Marvin thought maybe they got into some kinda plant they shouldn't have, or maybe the heat caused some bloat, and I woulda thought he was right, but when I was out at Bob's Feed the other day, Bob was tellin' me about some other small incidents around the county. They're startin' to add up."

"He did?" I asked, surprised, and Dean nodded. Fiona's sister, Mitch, was perched in his lap, and he was holding a fork loaded with green beans out in front of her. She was looking at it like it was a centipede, shaking her head furiously, an unspoken "no" on her lips. "Why wouldn't he call to tell me that? Damn gossips in this town. They report shit that ain't a crime, but when there is one, nobody makes a peep."

"Carey!" Oly screeched.

"Ah, shit, sorry."

Fiona kicked her booster chair under the table, singing, "Shit, shit, shit," and little Mitch giggled.

"Uncle Carey?" Oly practically growled. "You're grounded." She stared me down to the ground this time, and I winced. I felt terrible. I really did try to curb my language around my friends' kids, but Rome wasn't built in a day.

"I apologize, Oly," I said, using my most judicial smile, and to Fiona, I said, "Uncle Carey said a bad thing. Uh, more than one, but if you promise not to repeat the bad words, I'll bring you, Mitch, and Jack Jr. a real sheriff's star next time I come over, okay?"

"Okay!" She smiled, looking satisfied and content like only a little kid could be, and I went on, pleased with my negotiation skills and thinking out loud.

"Seriously, how did I go from people callin' me about everything to no one callin' me at all?" I shook my head. "I'll run over and drag the gossip outta Bob, but this could be serious. Carl had someone come to his farm and offer to buy it from him. Sounds like they were pretty pushy. He'll never sell, but it doesn't feel right that this is all happenin' at the same time. It feels like Wisper's ranches and farms are bein' targeted. Okay, fine, maybe that's conjecture at this point, but I got a feelin'…"

"Your feelings are always on point, Carey," Billie said. "Trust your gut, man. It's never led you astray before."

———

"UH OH. It wasn't me, Sheriff, I swear it!" Bob joked when Frank and I walked into his feed store the next morning. His hands were up in front of his big belly, and he backed away from his cash register like he was about to be cuffed and stuffed, but his usual smile and the twinkle in his eye was evident.

"Funny, Bob, but you are in a little bit of trouble."

He dropped his hands. "What for?"

"We heard there's been some curious things happenin' on the farms around here," Frank said, his deep voice echoing throughout the empty store. "Y'all talk and gossip to each other, but no one thought to inform us?"

"Oh, well, I apologize, guys, but it's just little things, like Don Headstrom had a fire in his barn. He got it out quick enough, and he thinks it was probably just faulty wirin'. You know, his barn is old as sin, and he shoulda updated all that stuff years ago. Then I heard from the McCluskies that they lost a few goats, but Marvin thought it was probably a bad batch of feed. That's how come I know about it, 'cause he asked me to look into it. But I called the feed company and wasn't nothin' wrong with it, so maybe the goats just ate somethin' bad. You know how goats are." Bob shrugged and yanked his baggy jeans up. "Little things like that. Maybe Wisper's just havin' a bout of bad luck."

"Ain't no such thing," Frank said. "A whole town can't be unlucky."

"You never know."

"You got a pen back there?" I asked, nodding behind the counter at a big pile of old magazines and dusty papers. "I'm gonna need you to make a list of names and anything out of the ordinary you've heard about lately. Anything at all. I don't care if a horse stubbed a toe. If the farmers or the hands thought to tell you about it, then it was important enough, and we need to know about it. And I wanna know who said what. Write it all down."

"Alright," Bob said. "This mean I'm your deputy now?"

"You wish," Frank said.

Rolling my eyes, I shook my head. "Just hop to it, Bob."

"Aye, aye, Cap'n."

WHEN I STOPPED BACK out at Cade Ranch a day later to check in with Billie 'cause she'd called to tell me she found something about SA McKinnon and his daughter, I was met by a gaggle of little kids holding out their dirty hands, waiting for me to drop shiny plastic sheriff's stars into them. I pulled them from my pocket, laughing under my breath 'cause they all looked so much like their parents. Jack Jr. was the spitting image of his dad, but that's where the similarity ended, 'cause that kid was happiness personified. He was always laughing, and you couldn't get him to stop talking once he'd learned how, but his dad was the star quarterback of Team Grump.

I placed one plastic sheriff's star in each grubby hand and patted three heads. The twins ran off to show their aunt, pulling Jack Jr. behind them. Evvie waved from the mouth of the barn, where she ooh'd and ahh'd over the kids' newest treasures, and I waved back and walked up to the house to find Billie sitting at the table inside the Cade's kitchen.

"S'up?" she said without looking away from one of her three laptops, which she'd set up on the dining table. She'd bought a computer chair for herself that looked more like a purple throne. The chair did things I hadn't known chairs could do, and it had three cupholders. Who the heck needed three cupholders at one time?

"Why're you workin' from here? You've got that swanky office all decked out at your house. Isn't this the kinda thing you're supposed to use it for?" The chair at her and Jay's house looked like a silver spaceship, and it had massage capabilities.

"I like to be near Jay, and he works here. Plus, it's so quiet there, you know?"

"You won't find quiet here, that's for sure," I said, and we both laughed when we heard the twins squealing outside. "Alright, so what'd you find?"

"Okay," she said, straightening from the hunch she'd been sitting in and taking a deep breath. I sat, too, and Billie dove in. "So I'm not finding anything devious on State's Attorney McKinnon. I mean, other than the fact that he seems like a pretentious idiot, but"—she paused for effect—"did you know that his oldest daughter, Francesca Morris, has filed for divorce from her loser douchebag husband, Doug Morris?"

"No. I didn't know that." Why wouldn't Frannie tell me that? I didn't clue Billie into the fact that I knew Francesca Morris more than she might've suspected. "I thought they were separated."

"Well, I guess, technically, they are, but yeah, she's actually filed twice. The first time was several years ago back in Texas, but that petition was eventually denied. Then she reapplied after they moved back here. I don't think I have to tell you that getting a divorce shouldn't take this long, especially since they don't have assets or complicated financial issues to wade through. I thought that was weird."

"Yeah, I mean, sure, that's a little odd, but what does that have to do with her dad or sister?"

"You are so impatient, Carey." She rolled her eyes dramatically. "So, Francesca's sister, Jillian McKinnon, works for their dad, and she's got her fingers in everything the SA does. She takes meetings for him, she signs all kinds of papers that he should be signing, and she basically runs the dude's life. Like, she signs his name, but she doesn't even try to mimic his signature. It was really easy to tell who signed what when I looked through a bunch of paperwork for some big case the SA's office just won."

I nodded slowly, then shook my head and threw my hands up, relaying my confusion and impatience, earning me a death glare from Billie.

She scoffed. "Bite me. Anyway, something made me dig into the divorce petition. Before Francesca filed the first time, there were four domestic violence incidents she was involved in. At least four that the cops were called out to address when Doug Morris beat the shit out of his wife, and two when there was something wrong with the kid. Once, an ambulance was needed. That happened in Texas, not here, and it was never Francesca—"

"Fran. Just call her Fran."

Billie eyed me for a few seconds. "Fine, Fran. Fran never called the police herself. It was always a concerned neighbor or, once, just some dude driving by, but what he saw on the side of the road was bad enough that he called 911 from his car."

I cursed under my breath, "Dammit, Frannie." What hell had she been going through? Why hadn't someone done something about it? It made my blood run cold, and I wanted to kill something.

Or someone.

"Carey," Billie said slowly, "what does this Fran mean to you? You look like your head's about to pop off your shoulders."

"That's not—she's not—she doesn't mean anything," I lied, though I wasn't sure why I didn't come clean. I felt protective of Fran, and I wanted to keep the love I'd felt for her close to my chest. Or maybe it was my heart, which was broken all over again. "We were friends a long time ago. That's all."

"And you're just a really good guy who doesn't like to hear about anyone being treated like that?"

"Right."

"Mm hm. Sure," she said, clearly unconvinced.

"Billie," I warned. "Leave it. Just tell me what else you found."

She tsked her tongue. "Oookay. Alright, well, I get that it's not easy for someone to extricate themselves from a situation like that, especially with a kid, but Fran tried, hence the two attempts to divorce that fucking asshole. She went through the proper channels. She even had a lawyer in Texas, but from what I can tell, that guy got bulldozed by someone. And that someone was from Wyoming."

"Who? Fran's dad, SA McKinnon?"

"I don't think so." Billie shook her head, eyebrows raised.

"Not her sister, Jillian?"

"Well, it wasn't Jillian, not directly, but someone from her and her father's office. Someone named Vera. Fran's lawyer in Texas was actually disbarred because of complaints Vera made, and soon after, the first divorce petition was denied, and Fran, her daughter, and that no-good piece of shit moved back to Wisper.

"Doug didn't have a job in Texas for longer than a few months at a time, at least not that I can find, so there was no record of him leaving a job. I couldn't figure out why they moved back." Billie flicked her hand in the air, likely annoyed at not finding something she'd searched hard for. "And I haven't been able to find anything about him since he moved here, besides what you probably already know, that he's sometimes a day worker for some of the farmers around here, he gets into fights like the rest of us breathe, and he's an intolerant asshole—remember he and his buddies gave Luuk and Kev a hard time a couple years ago?" she asked, and I nodded. I did remember that.

"Oh yeah," she added, "and he beats his wife."

"Okay," I said slowly, trying to breathe through the anger trying to strangle me from the inside out, "but I still don't understand what any of this has to do with the SA or Jillian McKinnon."

"Guess who bailed Doug out of a jail cell the last two times he got thrown in one after the big rodeo in Cody?"

"Who? Jillian McKinnon?" I said in disbelief. I should've known the answer; he'd spent more than one night in my jail cell.

"Well, she doesn't do it personally, but she sends Vera, or she get the charges dismissed or whatever."

"But Jill's just a glorified secretary, it's her dad who's—"

"I'm telling you, Carey, Jillian McKinnon runs the SA's office. She was a lawyer before she went to work for her dad, and she's the HBIC up in Cheyenne whether she holds the title or not."

"HBIC?"

"Head bitch in charge," Billie said. "Duh."

I was supposed to know that? I shook my head. "I don't understand. I mean, I get what you're sayin', but why? Why on earth would Jill wanna stop her sister from divorcin' the guy who hurts her and her daughter? It makes no sense."

Shrugging, she said, "Well, you're the detective, so go detect. All I can find are documents and files, but I think you're gonna have to talk to people 'cause I can't get you gossip from my pretty laptop." She stroked the top of one of her computer screens with one finger like it was a prized jewel. "Why don't you just go ask your Fran about it?"

"She ain't 'my Fran,' and I have asked her, but she won't say."

"Ask harder. Give her your good ol' down-home smile. I'm sure she'll melt properly and spill her guts."

"Wait. What about Gracie?"

"Oh, the kid?"

"Yeah, can you get into the hospital files from when she was transported in the ambulance? Did that man beat his daughter too?" It was hard, but I clenched my fists under the table so I wouldn't pound it and break it.

"Carey," Billie said carefully, holding her hands flat out above the table, "no, not that I can find anyway. Grace has diabetes, and the file states that she didn't have her insulin. She was in a coma for two days, but she was okay."

I stood, and my chair clattered behind me. "Because her father didn't work, right? He didn't bother to get a job, so Grace didn't get her medicine because they didn't have money or insurance. Is that right? Is that what you found?"

"Yeah. I think so."

"Fuck that man!"

"Yeah," she said again. "Do you know how expensive insulin is without prescription coverage? Or even with it? But no, I couldn't find a record of Fran having medical coverage when she gave birth to the kid, and it wasn't until Grace was almost three years old that she was diagnosed and Fran's father applied for a medical policy for the kid. Fran's sister pays for it using an inheritance their mother left them when she passed away five years ago."

"Goddammit. She coulda died!"

Billie stood slowly and approached me cautiously, like she thought I'd erupt. "Carey, are you okay? I've never seen you like this."

I hung my head, trying to hold onto some kind of composure. It wouldn't do anybody any good for me to lose my shit. I breathed deeply, in through my nose and out through my mouth slowly until I could control it. In a tightly measured breath, I said, "It sounds like you're tellin' me that Jillian McKinnon has worked to keep her sister and niece in this situation, like she purposely wanted them to stay in a toxic and dangerous environment. Why, Billie? Why the fuck would Jillian want that?"

"I don't know, and maybe I'm wrong and Jillian bailed Doug out of jail in order to try to control the narrative. Maybe she was worried about how that might look for her dad. But I can tell you where to go for answers."

Looking up at her, I took a final deep breath and let it out. "Where?"

Billie grabbed a paper from the table. "Here. This is a list of travel receipts from when Jillian McKinnon went to Texas while Fran lived there. Four times. And the dates coincide with four 911 calls."

CHAPTER FIFTEEN

FRANNIE

GRACE'S first riding lesson was Wednesday afternoon. We'd spent the morning walking around town, looking for Help Wanted signs in shop windows again. I made a game of it, distracting Grace with rocks and flowers we found along the way—extra points when they were shaped like hearts—and hopefully, she never saw the desperation on my face.

Doug hadn't been around since the night he knocked me out, so Grace and I were feeling good and hopeful again, but I always worried it wouldn't last long.

The little money I had left was running out, and child support was a concept my "husband" hadn't heard of. I had Terre's fifty dollars still, but it wouldn't go very far, and pie orders weren't rolling in on the regular. I had yet to get my alternator replaced, so we were walking everywhere. Luckily, Wisper was small enough that we could get to most places we needed to go on foot, but Cade Ranch was too far for Grace's little legs to walk.

I hated to do it, but I had to ask for a ride. My car wouldn't start, and I was stressing hard that this was the end of its life. What would we do when it died?

"Hello?" The speaker on my ten-year-old phone crackled in my ear when Evvie's voice broke through.

"Yes, um, Evvie?"

"Fran? I'm so glad you called. I was just thinking about you and Grace. How are you? Is she excited for her first lesson?"

"She's so excited, she can barely stand still. But… is the offer for a ride still—"

"Of course. Text me your address. I was in need of a big ol' iced coffee anyway. I'll run down to Coffee Shot and then stop by and pick you guys up. What's your drink?"

"My drink?"

"Yeah, what do you usually order? Walt will make any drink iced if you ask him. Or are you a tea drinker?"

"Oh, no, I like coffee, but that's okay." I laughed a little awkwardly. She was already giving us a ride. I didn't want her to spend her money on me. "Thanks, but the caffeine would just keep me up all night."

"Are you sure? What about Grace? They have those fruit slushes. Little Jack loves the strawberry one. Can I pick one up for her too?"

"Thanks, but no. Grace has to watch her sugar intake, so we don't usually—"

"Is she sick?"

"She has type 1 diabetes, so we have to be careful."

"Oh, Fran, I'm sorry. I had no idea. That sounds scary. I get stressed out when I have to give Jack Jr. children's cough syrup. I couldn't imagine having to give him shots of insulin."

"You get used to it. It's not her favorite thing, but Grace is really brave."

"I can tell. You can see it in her eyes." Evvie chuckled. "Okay, so we'll skip the sugary drinks and coffee. If I'm honest, it's not good for Jack either. Then, while Grace rides, you'll have to let me know what kind of snacks she can have. I like to keep something here for our students, but we don't have any others with diabetes, and I'm sorry to say I don't know much about it."

"Oh, um, sure. Thank you. That's really kind."

"It's nothin'," Evvie said, and I didn't argue, but it *was* something. Grace was always embarrassed and disappointed to have to turn treats and snacks down when the other kids were clearly enjoying popsicles or candy bars, shoving them in their mouths, so Evvie wanting to have something available that Grace could eat without her sugar going through the roof—or worse, dropping—would mean the world to Grace.

Evvie picked us up in her truck thirty minutes later, and she was all chatter on the way to Cade Ranch. I thought she might be the most positive person I'd ever met, chipper and so open and welcoming. I loved being around her, and Grace seemed to too. She opened up with Evvie quick enough, telling her about her friend Magnolia, and Evvie was even more excited then to show Grace the ranch because they had dogs, too, and a cat, and so many horses, she told Grace she'd dream about them every night.

When we pulled up next to the big white farmhouse at Cade Ranch, memories came flooding back to me of Carey, Dean, Oly, and me hanging out there. We were in our junior year of high school, and Dean and Oly had started dating. I'd seen the love in Carey's eyes when he looked at me the way Dean had looked at Oly, but I was already planning my escape from Wisper by then. I brushed him off, and Carey was too much of a gentleman, even then, to push the issue.

I wasn't sure if he'd ever known how much I loved him though.

The ranch itself hadn't changed much. The house and

barn looked recently painted, and the big arena building behind the barn seemed bigger than the last time I'd seen it, but the mountains in the distance were the same rugged beauties they'd always been, and the fields were like a painting come to life with deep green grass and tiny blue and purple flowers dotting them all the way to the horizon, swaying lazily in the afternoon breeze.

There were a few horses grazing in the pastures, and Grace stood, watching them, completely mesmerized for a minute, until two little girls ran up to her and took her by the hand to the fence by the barn. They were precious little things, one with blond hair and one with brown. I knew Dean and Oly had had twins, and they looked like the right age, but they seemed older than three or four years the way they ran around like little ranch bosses. And Evvie's son, Jack Jr., was already the star of the show. He appeared on his dad's shoulders in the big open barn door, and Jack Sr. waved to Evvie.

"There's my boys," she said.

I could hear the pride and love in her voice, and I wanted to be her so much in the moment that it hurt. Not that I wanted her husband or son, but I wanted to be like her. I wanted my daughter to be able to run and be free in this valley between mountains with not a care in the world. I wanted Grace to laugh and cause trouble because she had the freedom to. And I wanted to feel a man's eyes on me the way Jack's were on Evvie, like he loved every single inch of her and everything she did or said captivated him. He watched every move she made, and I would've bet money, if she were in danger, the danger better look out—he'd kill it, whatever it was.

I couldn't ever imagine having that, and I wanted it so much that my stomach hurt.

"C'mon," Evvie said, and she touched my elbow to get

my attention when I didn't respond. "Jack'll keep an eye on the kids, and I'll grab us some cold waters. I'm really big on recycling, so I don't have bottles, but I ordered these reusable tumblers with the Cade Ranch logo, and we give them out to—" She stopped when I still hadn't moved. "Fran?"

"I-I don't—I'm not comfortable leavin' Grace. I'm sorry. I don't mean to be rude, but…"

"You're not being rude. You're being a mom. Why don't you stay here. I'll get the drinks, and then we'll get started. Go ahead. Go on down there and ask Jack to show you to Gertie's stall. Grace is gonna love her."

"Thank you," I said, shame heating my face. I wasn't ashamed that I was protective of my daughter, but I was embarrassed that I'd put us in the position of having to be so careful and defensive in the first place.

And I was ashamed that I didn't know how to trust anymore.

Evvie wouldn't hurt us, and I remembered Jack from school. He and his brothers were good people, but that didn't matter where Doug was concerned. He'd proven as much already.

"Hey there," Jack said when I made my way down a tiny hill to the red barn. "You probably don't remember me, but—"

"No, I do. I remember you and your brothers. Is Dean here? I haven't talked to him in years."

"No, he went to meet Oly to help her on a farm call. Somethin' about twin calves needin' to be pulled over at the Lindel farm."

I smiled, but I didn't really know what else to say. I had nothing in common with him other than the fact that we grew up in the same small town.

"So this here's your daughter?" Jack asked when Grace approached with two little twin monkeys glued to her hips.

I couldn't help it; I smiled like an idiot. Grace looked so happy. She didn't even mind that the littlest girl was pulling on her curls. She looked like a big sister, and it looked like she loved it.

"Yes," I said, "this is my daughter, Grace. Grace, this is Jack Cade. This is his ranch."

"Nice to meet ya," he said to her. "I see you've already met Trouble One and Trouble Two." He was trying to sound stern, but he couldn't help his smile either.

Grace nodded, and the taller girl, Trouble One, said, "I not twubble."

Jack laughed. "No? You sure?" he asked her, and she stomped her foot.

She reminded me so much of her mom right then, and I laughed too. "These must be Oly's daughters."

Jack chuckled, nodding. "How could you tell? Trouble One is Fiona, and Trouble Two is Mitch. Her name is Sara, but we call her Mitch 'cause she was named after Sara Mitchum."

Mrs. Mitchum was my fifth-grade teacher, and I remembered her taking care of the Cade boys after their mom was gone. When Mrs. Mitchum died a few years ago, the whole town was sad.

Jack Jr. twisted and fidgeted until his dad lifted him off his shoulders and set him on the ground, and all four kids took off back toward the fence. "And that there's Hellion Cade."

"Seems like y'all have your hands full."

"You too," he said.

"Nah, Grace is pretty easy." Our lives were hard, but

Grace was a piece of cake as far as childhood antics were concerned.

Jack was studying me a little, and it made me even more uncomfortable. I didn't remember him being very talkative in school, so I was surprised when he said, "I don't wanna scare you off when you just got here, but I saw the way you were worried about your daughter a minute ago. You don't have to do that when she's here. Hear me?" he asked, looking in my eyes and holding my attention. "You and your daughter are *safe* here."

A breath rushed from my mouth when I heard him speak those words because I believed him, but I was even more embarrassed because he seemed to know what I might be scared of, and the thought that the whole town of Wisper probably knew made me ashamed.

He nodded once silently and turned, beckoning me to follow with a wave of his hand. "We ain't goin' far. I just wanted you to see the horse Grace'll be ridin'. She's right here in this first stall."

I turned, watching as Jack opened a stall door, and the horse inside whinnied as if on cue. "She's beautiful. This is Gertie?"

"Yep. Gertie the gabber."

"Well, then you chose the right kid to ride her. She's shy around people, but Grace'll talk Gertie's ear off."

One of Jack's brothers, a very blond and tall Finn Cade—much taller than I remembered him to be—stuck his head out of a stall down the aisle. "Hey, Fran. What's up?" He said it like it was an everyday occurrence that I was in his barn, like we were friends and chitchatted all the time.

"Not much," I said, and I laughed.

Grace rushed in the barn, squealing and laughing with Fiona and Mitch following her and two large and scruffy dogs following them, and then little Jack appeared with a goofy grin on his dirt-smudged face and no clothes on his rear end.

"Boy," Jack scolded, trying not to laugh. "Your mama's gonna have my hide. Where's your britches?"

"What's britches?" Fiona asked.

Jack groaned. "Aww, sweet Jesus."

Jack and Finn both looked to me, I assumed because I was the only mom in the barn. "Uh, britches are undies," I told Fiona.

"Okay," she replied so seriously, and then she removed her shorts and whipped her undies off too.

"Oh, shit. This is gettin' outta hand fast," Finn said, chuckling. He set down his shovel and walked over to whisk Jack Jr. and Fiona into his arms, and they disappeared up to the house for a change of clothes, the kids squealing and laughing all the way.

"Mama?" Grace tugged on the hem of my shirt, acting shy around Jack, but she was smiling. She whispered when I looked at her, "I *like* it here."

"Me too, baby." I smiled at her. "Me too."

GRACE WAS A NATURAL. Everyone said so, and I was proud of her for being so brave. Gertie was huge, but she was a comical horse, making all kinds of funny sounds and flashing her big horse teeth, and Grace was in love. Jack was her teacher technically, but the entire Cade family was weighing in by the end. Grace was the last client of the day, and after her lesson, it felt more like hanging out with friends than it did any kind of professional appointment.

Oly and Dean came to pick up their girls after they were done at their farm call, so the three of us sat and reminisced until the sun set behind the mountains in the west while Grace played school and duck-duck-goose with her new friends.

Finn declared it a "cookout kinda day," and he threw steaks on a grill up by the house. His girlfriend, Aislinn Burroughs, the sister of the Cades' investor, arrived a little later with the youngest Cade brother, Jay, and his wife, Billie, and it was like an instant party.

Kevin was the only brother missing, but he finally arrived in a blue truck with Dr. V from the animal clinic, and there was a police truck following them up the lane to the barn. The cop's lights were on, and my heart dropped into my stomach when I realized it was Carey.

He got out of his cruiser, swinging a set of handcuffs like he was about to arrest Kevin. I was confused. Had Kevin and Doc V been speeding or something? It hadn't seemed like it, but it all made sense when Kevin ran around the truck and hopped on Carey's back, pulling him down to the dirt. They wrestled but popped up, laughing, and Doc V spoke in a foreign language and swiped the dust off Kevin's lips with his thumb, then kissed him.

They were playing. Everyone was happy and goofing off, and they included us like Grace and I had always been there. When Carey noticed me standing next to Evvie by the fence, he smiled tentatively, but it disappeared quickly.

Evvie, Oly, and I talked all evening about healthy food choices for the kids. They'd both admitted that they'd taken the easy way out, feeding their kids processed food some-times and too much junk, and they both admired me for sticking to such a health-conscious diet for Grace, but the truth was that I would've given anything to hand her a bubble gum ice cream cone without checking her sugar first or worrying about it making her sick.

Carey was a little standoffish at first, but he relaxed the

longer the evening wore on. He was so carefree around his friends, joking with them and laughing. God, I loved his laugh. It was a very manly chuckle, and it hadn't changed since we were young, which was weird when we were twelve and most of the other boys' voices still sounded like a girl's.

We spoke a few times, though briefly, and every time, I wanted to throw my arms around his wide shoulders and hang on for dear life, but of course I didn't, and it wasn't until Jack lit a fire in a firepit alongside the big farmhouse and Evvie handed out glowsticks to the kids that Carey pulled me aside.

The pre-Fourth of July celebration was such an all-American scene, and I could've stayed there forever watching Grace play and run with Kevin and Finn, pretending to chase them. Grace laughed like she should've every day, and I was trying hard not to cry while I watched her, imagining what it would be like to be this happy all the time, but finally, Carey grabbed my hand and tried to lead me away from the crowd, and my ultra-Americana happiness bubble was popped like an overfilled balloon.

CHAPTER SIXTEEN

CAREY

"C'MON. COME WITH ME," I said, pulling Frannie behind me toward the barn. "I need to talk to you." I'd waited all night to *really* talk to her. It was hard to do, but every time I looked at her, all I could see was an image of her being carted off in an ambulance after being subjected to a beating by her husband, or I saw Grace 'cause she was sick from not having access to insulin. It made my blood boil, and I had to deal with that before I upset Fran with questions.

"I can't just leave Grace, Carey," she said. "We can talk here."

I turned back toward her when she stopped her feet, pulling on my hand. "Frannie, no one's gonna hurt Grace here. The Cades are my family, and there's no one I trust more."

"It's not them I'm worried about."

"What, you think your husband's gonna come tearin' up the lane and hit you? Without Jack or Dean noticin'? Without *me* noticin'? Ain't gonna happen. I'd shoot the motherfucker before I'd let him put another finger on you or Grace."

She closed her eyes, her head angled down toward the

dirt, like she was ashamed. *Ah, damn.* That reaction was exactly what I'd been trying to avoid.

"I'm sorry," I said, squeezing her hand a little, and she looked up. "We won't go far, just to the barn, but little pitchers have big ears." Nodding toward Grace roasting marshmallows with the other kids and Finn, I let go of her hand then and called over to Jack. He and Evvie approached us, with little Jack bouncing on Evvie's hip, tapping the side of her face with his blue glowing stick.

"Fran, please don't worry," Evvie said, correctly assessing the situation between Fran and me. It was probably pretty obvious to my friends that there was something between us. I couldn't help the way I looked at her, or the way I drifted toward her, no matter who I was talking to. I wanted to be near her, wanted to hear her voice. "We'll take care of Grace. I'll take the kids inside and put a movie on. I promise she'll be safe. I won't take my eyes off of her."

"I meant what I told you earlier," Jack said to Frannie. There was a vow in his words, and she took a deep breath and nodded.

"Thank you. Please call for me if she needs me."

"We will," Evvie said.

Taking her hand in mine once more, I tugged, and finally, Frannie followed me to the barn. I closed us in the tack room and locked the door so we were sure to not be overheard or walked in on.

She looked around at all the saddles and tack hanging on the walls, and finally, she said, "Livin' in Wyoming and Texas all my life, I feel like I should know what all of this is, but until Grace's lesson earlier, I admit, I didn't have a clue."

I turned to face her then. "What'd Jack say to you earlier?"

"Nothin'," she said, her eyes still wandering the room.

Her voice was quiet. "Just that Grace would be safe... you know, when she's ridin'."

That might've been what Jack said, but I knew it wasn't what he'd meant.

"I know we ain't friends like we used to be, but Fran, what the hell's goin' on with you?"

She looked at me finally, but she focused on my lips while I spoke, and I remembered the day she'd left town, when we said goodbye with our heads together, the breath between us the last part of her I'd had to hold onto. I'd remembered that breath every day when she was gone, and now even more because it was *my* Frannie's breath, not this scared lamb of a woman before me.

I wanted her to be my Frannie again. I wanted my best friend back, and I wanted more.

Nothing could've stopped me from closing the distance between us. It wasn't a choice. It was a physical necessity, and maybe the connection would remind her of who she used to be.

"What're you doin'?" she asked when I touched my lips to hers. They were warm, and I tasted the tiny beads of sweat from the hot June night above her lip. All those years. All the millions of times I'd wished I could kiss her again...

She was the heartbeat inside my chest, and finally, I was letting myself feel it.

I touched my forehead to hers. "Why didn't you tell me you'd filed for divorce?"

She gasped, looking up into my eyes. "How'd you—I-I... Because it doesn't matter. The universe won't let me divorce him. No matter what I do, I'm stuck with him."

"I don't understand why your dad won't help you. Does he know what Doug does to you?"

"He knows." It was the first time she'd ever admitted

what she'd been going through. I knew it, and she knew that I knew. She didn't say the words, but it was there between us now.

"Your dad and sister were weird at the diner the other night. It was like you weren't even part of their family. What's that about?"

"Nothin'," she said. "We've just grown apart, that's all."

"That's not all. I want you to tell me why your dad stands for it. I know you. Yeah, maybe it's been a while, but I *know* you, Frannie. I know there's somethin' more goin' on here. Is it Grace? Is she the reason why?" My eyes focused on the cut at her hairline, and this close, I swore I could still see a hint of the blue bruise, though it was long gone by now, replaced by a tiny pink line for a scar.

"I don't know what you're talkin' about."

I tried not to scoff. "Right." Shaking my head, I sighed, letting my frustration leak out, and tried to soften my voice. She'd been yelled at and scolded by enough men. I wouldn't add to that. "Why doesn't your dad do somethin'? Will you tell me that, at least? Why doesn't Jill? How can they let you live like this?" I touched the tips of my fingers below her cheekbone, and she looked up, focusing her eyes on mine.

"Carey," she whispered, her voice shaking a little in this moment between us, "there's nothin' for you to worry about. Everything's under control."

"Really? Is that why your daughter showed up at my house scared outta her mind? Why I found you beat up in your livin' room? If you've got it all under control, why are you so scared, Frannie? Why don't you ever smile?"

"I-I do smile," she stuttered, like she couldn't believe I'd noticed. "I smiled all day today."

"I know you did. You were beautiful today."

The look on her face then, the hesitant curve of her lips

and the tiny spark I saw in her eyes, it settled inside me, making me feel calm and warm, but my pulse was racing all the same, and her forehead was still against mine. "Your friends are great. Grace has been havin' a ball."

"Well, I'm glad about that," I said, "but I want you to have fun too. To be happy." My fingers found their way through her hair, the thick strands falling over my skin. I wanted to close it in my fist and pull her to my mouth again, but I knew she had to come to me on her own.

She closed her eyes. "Carey."

"I wanna kiss you, Frannie," I said, repeating the words I'd said to her so long ago. "Will you let me?"

She breathed, "Yes."

The apprehension in her eyes was so foreign to me—*my* Frannie wasn't scared of anything—but she'd said yes, and nothing could've stopped me from opening her mouth with my own. All the questions I had, all the worry and the anger I'd felt after hearing what she'd been going through, in the moment, it all disappeared. It dissipated like it had never been, and the building energy between us was all that existed in the world.

It felt electric, like it could zap me into a million pieces, but it could put me back together again and make me whole.

Maybe it was what we both needed.

My lips found hers again, and her breath rushed out, and I swallowed it down like I needed it to live. She tasted as good as I remembered, and I kissed every inch of her face, learning her all over again and in a new way at the same time, leaving soft, wet traces with my lips that I rubbed into her skin with my thumbs, and she moaned softly.

"I want you, Frannie. I've wanted you all this time, and I thought there was somethin' keepin' us apart—I thought you *wanted* to be married to him—but that's gone now."

I couldn't believe I was saying the words. They'd been burning a hole in my tongue for years, and now, I couldn't stop them. It was the wrong time, the wrong situation, the wrong everything, but I still listened while they escaped my mouth.

She stopped kissing me, her body going stiff and her lips turning to stone beneath mine. "Why?"

"What?"

She took a step back and a deep breath, and when she opened her eyes, she said, "I'm not the same person I used to be. I'm not the same girl you used to love."

Taking one step in her direction slowly, I said, "I know that."

"So why do you want me? I've already told you, I'm not good for you. This mess I'm in, it's—I won't put that on you."

"You think I care about what people say?"

"No, you probably don't, but you will care, Carey, if it costs you the job you love. You've had to deal with Doug professionally. You really want him meddlin' in your personal life? He'll threaten you. He'll do anything he can think of to mess with you just 'cause he won't want me to have you. And I have no idea what my father's up to. You'll have to ask him that question. I want nothin' to do with him either."

"Frannie—"

"No." She backed another step away from me. "Please, just let me go."

Nodding, I stepped back, too, till my back touched the wall, and something clattered to the floor behind me, but my eyes wouldn't stray from hers. "Okay, Fran. If that's what you really want." I wasn't her jailer, and I didn't want to be another man who forced her to do something she didn't want.

"It is," she said, but it was just a whisper before she

turned, unlocked the door, threw it open, and ran away from me.

WHEN EVVIE HAD TAKEN Grace and Frannie home, I slumped in a chair on my friends' porch, and Jack sat next to me.

It wasn't like him to stop for a chat, and I couldn't even hear him breathe before he said, "You know what that man does to her, right? You've heard the gossip in town? Seen how scared she is?"

We both faced forward, neither of us wanting to admit out loud how bad we both suspected things had gotten for Frannie. "I hadn't heard it. Nobody tells me anything. But I know now."

"It's gotta stop. That little girl don't deserve that kinda life. Neither of 'em do."

"I know that too."

"How can I help?"

"I WANT you to visit all the farms on this list. Bob wrote it up for me. Take Evvie and Jack Jr. with you so it don't look suspicious. Maybe act like you're stoppin' 'cause your kid wants to pet some cows and goats, but ask Marvin and the other owners how things have been goin'. Get the gossip. They won't talk to me, but you're a ranch owner. One of their own. They'll complain to you."

"You got it," Jack said the next morning before I sent him off to do my investigating. I had bigger fish to fry at the moment. "Anything specific you want me to ask about?"

"Anything. Bad luck, dead animals, sicknesses, issues in town or with their ranch hands. They won't bring up money, but see if anyone mentions cash offers for their land. I'm appointing you a Special Deputy Sheriff for this if anybody asks. Hopefully they won't, but be professional, and don't let anyone know unless you absolutely have to. That'll just cause more gossip, and it'll make this harder. I need to know what these ranchers have in common, but if I ask outright, it'll spread through Wisper like an STD. Then, when I get back to town, I can start makin' my rounds and filin' reports."

"Where you goin'?"

"I'm headin' to the big city. I got some slimy politicians to interrogate."

I HADN'T BEEN to the capital in a while, not since I won my first election, the youngest man from Teton County to accomplish that particular feat, but when I got there, Cheyenne, Wyoming was the same.

It was almost a seven-hour drive from Wisper, so I made sure my deputies had Teton County under control and rented a motel for the night, and when I checked in, I spoke to a few locals, trying to get a feel for how they thought the local government and their elected officials were working out for them.

No one had anything bad to say about SA McKinnon, if they even knew who he was, and nobody knew who Jillian McKinnon was. They knew Governor Buchanan, though, and most people liked her. She'd gotten a few infrastructure initiatives passed, and the roads and bridges, at least around Cheyenne, were much improved since she'd been elected.

But really, that was all I was going to be able to glean

from local residents and business owners. Now, I needed to go straight to the top. I needed to speak to SA McKinnon, Frannie's dad.

I promised myself I wouldn't get emotional and I wouldn't ask him personal questions about his daughter, but I'd grown up around the man, so surely we could connect on that fact. At least, I'd hoped we could.

When I arrived at his office the next morning and checked in with the receptionist for my appointment, I expected to have to wait a while to meet with the SA, but instead, I was whisked into Jill's office by the woman Billie had mentioned from her searches—Vera—like my ass was on fire and she had the only fire extinguisher in the whole state of Wyoming. She didn't introduce herself, but her name was printed on her coffee tumbler. She looked so much like Jill from behind, that when I first walked in, I thought it was Jill on the phone behind the front desk.

"Good morning, Sheriff Michaels," she said when she noticed me waiting for her.

Funny, I hadn't introduced myself yet.

Flashing her my "sheriff's smile," I said, "How do you do?"

She didn't answer. "Come with me."

Vera was a thin, middle-aged, no-nonsense kind of woman, with dirty-blond hair to her shoulders and a scowl permanently fixed to her face. She announced my presence to Jill with a cough, and when she left us alone in Jill's office, she slammed the door shut behind her.

Nice to meet you too, jeez.

But Vera was no matter. What I'd found out from Billie's overachieving hacking skills was at the forefront of my mind, and it was maybe the hardest thing I'd ever had to do to keep my composure while Jillian talked circles around me about absolutely nothing at all.

Removing my hat, I held onto it, gripping the sides of the brim hard while she started in on a string of irrelevant platitudes. "Oh. Sheriff Michaels, how nice to see you. Vera told me you had an appointment, but I wasn't expecting you this early. Are you early? What time is it?" She looked at her phone for a second, then set it on the desk between us, looked up, and smiled. "Have a seat." She motioned to the chair opposite her desk, and I sat. "I apologize in advance. I have meetings all afternoon, so I'll need to keep this brief. Are you in Cheyenne visiting?"

"No. I'm here to speak to your dad."

I wanted to know what he knew about Carl Aberforth and the land offer he'd received, if anything, but now that I was in Jill's office, the questions I had about why she'd gone down to Texas after the 911 calls were boring a hole in my head. It was nearly impossible not to interrogate her. And seeing her, seeing how hard she was trying to distract me—or maybe she was trying to bulldoze me too—it made me more suspicious. It put a bee in my bonnet, but it wasn't the right time, and I somehow managed to keep my mouth shut and my composure intact. At least in the beginning.

"Well, since you're here, I wanted to tell you how much Daddy and I appreciate your service to the people of Wyoming. Daddy just loves his constituents, and we're both so grateful for your support."

"No need to thank me, Jill. Just doin' my job."

"Right. Of course you're humble, which just makes you all the more respected. You know, Fran told me you're the youngest sheriff in the history of the state or something like that. That's really impressive. Congratulations."

That stopped me for a second. Fran had followed my career? I'd had no idea.

All of this Jill said with a smile on her face, but it felt ungenuine, and she was rude and dismissive, checking her phone or laptop every other minute, which surprised me. Fran and Jill's parents had instilled good manners in their girls. I remembered that specifically because it was the thing Frannie was always fighting against when we were kids. She hated to wear dresses or makeup, and she more than disdained being a "lady." And if Frannie was made to take shit from someone simply because they were in a position of power or they were her elder, she fought the hardest then.

Frannie had always rooted for the underdog, and she never stood by while someone with no power was railroaded by someone who had more than their fair share. Like a battered wife.

"So, it was nice of you to stop by, Sheriff Michaels," Jillian was saying, closing her laptop. She stood from her chair behind her overly ornate desk. "But like I said, we've got a really busy day today, so if you don't mind, I'll cut this—"

"I do mind, actually," I said, and her eyes flicked to mine. I stood too. I felt like she was trying to use her physical position standing above me to gain a little power over me, but even with her fancy high heels, she was no match for my six-two frame. Placing the hat in my hands back on my head—manners be damned, apparently—I straightened my posture. "I came here to speak to SA McKinnon. I understand you're his—what are you exactly? Fran told me you're a lawyer, but from what I've seen, that's not what you do here in your job with your dad."

She cocked an eyebrow, surprised at my brazenness, if I had to guess. "I am a lawyer, a very successful one, but I've taken a leave of absence from my firm to work with Daddy in his capacity as the State's Attorney of Wyoming, but it's really none of your business what I do, and I can't imagine what you could need this information for, so what are you really doing here?"

"Well, now, see, that's none of *your* business. I'm an elected official and part of the chain of command here in Wyoming, so if I need to speak to SA McKinnon, that's what I'll do. You ain't gonna stop me, even though that's what you're tryin' to do here. I have no idea why you'd try, and I thought you and I were on friendly terms, but if this is how you wanna play it, more power to you. I'll just go around you, as is my right."

Jillian forced a small laugh, and her demeanor changed in a millisecond. "There's no need to get upset, Carey," she said, and I could've sworn she'd changed the tone of her voice to be a little more… seductive? It was lower and it felt heavy, like syrup.

"So now it's Carey, not Sheriff Michaels?"

"C'mon, we grew up together. You ate dinner at my house more than you did at your own. I thought we liked each other." She touched the collar of her black silk blouse with one painted fingernail, dipping her chin a bit. "I know you were Fran's friend, but I always kinda wondered—"

"You wondered what? What is this?" I motioned to her, noticing a little too late how she'd cocked her hip and the fake smile on her lips that I was guessing she'd hoped would woo me somehow. "I have an appointment with your dad, and I ain't leavin' till I see him."

She sighed and straightened. "Daddy is out to lunch with Senator Osprey. He won't be back for hours. You can reschedule if you'd like, but there isn't an opening in his calendar for weeks."

"If that's the case, then why did his office make this appointment today?"

"I take the appointments Daddy doesn't have time for. He assumed I could handle whatever it was that you needed, which, by the way, you haven't yet said."

"What I need is to talk to SA McKinnon. Can you help me with that? If not, we're done here."

"Then we're done," she said flippantly, the rude and inconsiderate Jillian returning just as fast as she'd disappeared, and I turned to go as she rolled her eyes and opened her laptop again.

"You know," I said when I was at the door, "I was hopin' you'd prove me wrong today. But I gotta tell you, Jill, my suspicions were spot on about you, and now I'm wonderin' if you have your dad's best interest at heart. I know you don't care about your sister or your niece, and I dunno what that's about, but I think from the attitude you're givin' me, you know that I know there's somethin' goin' on here, and I figured you'd like to know that I'm gonna figure it out."

Anger burned in her eyes, and she gripped the desk phone in her hand, not even waiting until her office door was shut to start yelling into it.

CHAPTER SEVENTEEN

FRANNIE

DOUG SHOVED his way through my front door the next night. "You're *fuckin'* the sheriff now?" He pushed me, but I was prepared for it and stood my ground.

"Doug, Grace is sleepin'. It's midnight."

"I don't give a fuck."

"Well, I do. Please keep your voice down." It was always a struggle, trying to stand up for Grace without flat-out defying him. I knew what that would get me.

"You don't tell me what to do." He laughed. "That mouth of yours is only good for one thing, and it ain't talkin'."

I followed him to the kitchen, hoping I could convince him to leave if I gave him the little cash I had. He hadn't yet found my hidey hole in the hall closet, thank God.

"Mama?" Grace's voice was so soft behind me, but I heard it, and Doug's head popped up from behind the fridge door. He was ransacking it, tossing our food on the floor. He had a bandage on his arm, and it was dirty and covered in dried blood. It grossed me out being so close to our food. All I could do was pray that he wouldn't mess with Grace's insulin in the fridge door. He'd thrown it on the floor before when he was mad about something, breaking the glass vials, and it had resulted in Grace ending up in the hospital for two days.

Looking at her over my shoulder, I pleaded with her silently, my eyes begging her to go to her room. If this was going to get bad, I didn't want her anywhere near it. When she didn't move, I said aloud, "Go back to bed, Grace Mae, please. Everything's okay."

"She looks like a hobo's kid," he said. "Can't you do somethin' 'bout that? She didn't inherit that mop of hair from my side of the family." He kicked the fridge closed. "No beer?"

"I don't drink beer," I said, hatred dripping from my mouth. "I don't like how it makes certain *people* act." I didn't mean to talk back, but it was so damn hard not to, and becoming harder every day. I was waking up, and the part of me who'd always argued in the past was getting more diffi-cult to ignore.

He dropped the package of baby carrots he was holding and stomped over to me. "What was that?" Angling my body in front of Grace, I pushed into his space. He'd never hurt her before, not physically, but I didn't trust him any farther than I could throw him.

"Nothin'," I said, even though I wanted nothing more than to punch him.

With his mouth right next to my ear, he said, "That's what I thought." But then, quick as lightning, he grabbed a fistful of my hair, yanking my face to his mouth. "What kinda mother are you? There ain't a goddamn thing to eat in this house."

Grace screamed.

In my ear, he warned, "Make the kid shut up."

"It's okay, Grace," I said quickly. My breath was erratic

from the pain, but I tried to make my voice sound steady so she'd believe it was true. "I'm okay. Please, baby, go back to your room."

"Stop hurtin' her," she begged. I couldn't see her, but I heard the terror in her voice.

Doug pushed my head with the heel of his hand, but he didn't let go of my hair so a clump of it was ripped out when he shoved me. He grabbed more and forced me backward. Trying not to trip, I used the momentum of our movement to steer him away from Grace, but he trapped me between the kitchen door and an old wooden cabinet we used as a pantry.

Looking over his shoulder, he slurred a little. Of course he was drunk. "Your mama'd be fine if she could learn to keep her smart mouth shut. Looks like you might need to learn that lesson too. Get your ass back to bed," he ordered, but Grace didn't move.

He turned back to me, pulling me against the side of his body, crushing his mouth against my cheek, and I had to stop myself from gagging. I could smell the beer and chew on his breath. "Oh, I almost forgot. Tell your new boyfriend that if he can't keep his hands off my wife, I'll break 'em."

"My life is none of your business."

"Oh no? How's that divorce comin'? You get the papers yet?"

"No." My eyes snapped to his. "What do you know about that? What did you do?"

"I ain't done nothin'. Just pointin' out how stupid you are if you're still waitin' on that shit. You're never gettin' rid of me."

He let go and pushed me again, and I tried to move between him and Grace, but he kicked a kitchen chair between us. It skidded across the floor, knocking into the folding table we'd been using to eat on. She jumped out of the way, but still, she stood her ground, glaring at Doug. A part of me was proud of her, but a bigger part just wanted her to run and hide. He didn't seem drunk enough to really cause trouble—I hoped—but she was safer if she was out of sight.

"I see you been teachin' our daughter how to be a bitch just like her mama." Shaking his head, he clicked his tongue. "Guess I'll have to go get my own beer since my *wife* is useless. Gimme my money."

When I didn't immediately jump to get the money Terre had paid me from my purse, he ripped it off the counter, dumped the contents on the floor, and kicked around till he found the two twenties and a ten.

From the clothes he was wearing and the smell of old hay and animals, I could tell he'd been working at a farm or ranch, probably at the Johnson cattle farm since it was next door to his mama's house, so he shouldn't have needed my money, but he'd take it anyway, 'cause he could. It always surprised me when he actually worked for a living. He could never hold down a permanent job, though, or he just didn't want to. That was the real reason he stayed with his mama, even though we were technically still married. He ran out of money often, and he knew she'd pay for his beer and cigarettes. She was an asshole just like her son.

I was furious with myself. What could I have been thinking? How did I ever end up with a man like him? Had I been that desperate to get away from my father?

He scooped up the money and turned to face Grace. "Quit lookin' at me like that," he spat, but when Grace disobeyed him and stared harder, narrowing her eyes, he pushed her with one hand to her chest, and she fell backwards onto her bottom.

The look of heartbreak on her face nearly broke me in two, and the anger inside my body became so big, I thought I would explode from the force of it. Anger at myself, at my father, my mother, and flat-out rage at Doug. "Seeing red" was an expression, but I know knew what it meant.

He laughed and walked out of the house, slamming the open screen door behind him, knocking it loose from its hinges.

"Mama!" Jumping up, Grace ran to me, and we crumpled back to the floor. I was shaking. Everything inside me wanted to kill that man. How dare he hurt Grace?

He could lay hands on me, push me, pull me, hit me, he could drag me down a flight of stairs, smash my face in the dirt, he could do whatever he wanted to me. It was bad enough that Grace had had to be a witness to some of that, but he would not get away with putting his hands on her.

Ever.

<hr>

IT WAS SO hot in my car the next morning, I thought I might be hallucinating. I'd been waiting for Manny Perez to show up at his bar for over an hour. I'd never done it before, but I called Evvie and asked her to watch Grace for me. She came right away and picked Grace up, no questions asked, and they'd gone back to the ranch. It still terrified me to be away from her, but Grace couldn't go where I needed to, and I knew from the look on Jack Cade's face when he promised she'd be safe there that she would be.

It was pure luck that my car started when I turned the key in the ignition, and I was afraid to turn it off in case it wouldn't start again, so I sat there in the running car in Manny's empty parking lot with no air conditioning, waiting and remembering what my life used to be like, and suddenly, I was exhausted.

Tired of so many things. Tired of myself.

I closed my eyes because I couldn't fight the weight pulling on my eyelids and felt my head roll toward the window, and the heat lulled me into some kind of dream-like state…

Sometimes I walked in the shadow of my own shadow.

This big looming vision of who I used to be walked ahead of me, and I lagged behind, peeking around myself occasionally, if the nerve built up enough, but it usually didn't. Sometimes I couldn't see who I was anymore because the other me was blocking the sun. I couldn't feel it on my face or in my heart.

Except for when Grace smiled.

Nothing made me feel as full and warm as she could. My daughter made me feel like I was the most important person in the world, and maybe, someday, I would grow bigger than my shadow, like it was never there. Like it had been me the whole time, not this poor excuse for a woman, a mama, a daughter. A person.

I wondered when I'd disappeared. I couldn't remember doing it, and the only memories I had from before and after, besides those of Grace, were of Carey.

Before Grace, he was the one to make me smile and shine.

I wasn't complaining. My life was shit, but it was mine and Grace's, and I wouldn't have changed much of it if I could have because it made Grace and me close. Like when you hear people say they wonder how their lives would've turned out if they'd never had kids? Not me. I'd never had that thought.

But many nights, lying awake alone even though there was another human being right next to me, I wondered, what if I had stayed in Wisper and married Carey, and what if Carey was Grace's dad? What if I had let him love me?

Would her hair be even more red? Would she speak with strength in her voice? Would she sing really loudly when she was happy and dance around, not caring what anyone thought of her, instead of the quiet, scared ten-year-old girl she was now, the one who was afraid to breathe for fear that it would make her dad mad or make me sad?

Would she shine like I used to?

That Francesca was so far away, but I remembered shining brighter than any sun, and when Carey kissed me with his innocent teenage lips, that sunlight radiated through my whole body, to the tips of my fingernails, even to the ends of every strand of my hair, and now, as I fell in and out of dreams, I remembered thinking Carey had been able to feel the sunlight filling me back then. I wondered why he didn't yell out in pain because it burned his skin when he touched mine.

Now, when he touched me the way he used to, it surprised me that he didn't freeze to death—

"Fran?"

Jerking awake, I started when the looming presence standing over my car knocked on the windshield.

"You okay in there?" Manny asked.

Slumping forward in my seat, my head hit the steering wheel, and relief poured out of me. "You scared me, Manny."

"Sorry, but whatcha doin' takin' a nap in my parkin' lot at eight in the mornin'?"

"I need to talk to you," I said, and I opened my car door and stepped out. The shaking still hadn't stopped, and Manny looked me over when he noticed.

"What's goin' on, Fran? How can I help you?" His voice was soft, but he was probably confused. I didn't make a habit of hanging out at his bar. In fact, the only times I'd ever been inside of it was when I had to pick Doug up 'cause he was drunk and passed out or because he'd gotten in yet another fight and had been kicked out. I was surprised Manny hadn't permanently banned him by now.

"Um, can we go inside? I-I—" Looking behind me, I made sure no one was out walking their dog or spying from a window. "I don't want anyone to see me here."

"Okay," he said, chuckling, "I'll try not to take offense."

"Oh, no! That's not what I meant. It's just, what I need to talk to you about is… sensitive. And my husband…"

Manny was well aware of what kind of man Doug was even without knowing how physical things had gotten. He could probably guess. "Say no more. C'mon. You hungry? I'll make us some eggs."

AN HOUR LATER, when I walked into the sparsely decorated lawyer's office on Main Street in downtown Wisper and saw the man standing behind an old, weathered desk in the waiting room, more memories came flashing back. I remembered Brady Douglas from school, but he looked so different now. He used to be this thin, scrawny kid, with deep dark-brown eyes and perfect skin. Our senior year, he'd played football, and I thought I remembered he was even the quarterback.

Now, he was a man. A tall, dark, and very handsome man. His hair was a lot longer than I remembered, though still above his collar, but it made his native heritage easy to see, and it made him beautiful. His eyes were the same, and they were kind when he spotted me standing in the doorway.

"Fran McKinnon? That you? Oh, sorry, Morris. I always forget you married Doug."

Probably because it was the thing people had least expected of me. No one knew why I'd really done it.

I nodded, straightening and slinging my purse over my shoulder, noticing how the sun coming in the big glass windows was shining on him. The two rectangular windows were framed with what looked like homemade green-and-white gingham curtains, and they faced Main Street. For a second, I worried who might see me in a lawyer's office, but I worked hard to tamp down my anxiety. This was too important for me to chicken out. Again.

"That's okay," I said. Hopefully, I wouldn't be Fran Morris much longer. I took a quick, deep breath and smiled. "Hi, Brady. Long time no see."

"Do we have an appointment? I don't remember seein' anything on my schedule."

"Oh, no, I have an appointment with"—I pulled the sticky note I'd written the lawyer's name on from my back pocket—"with a Jeanine?"

"That's my mom. Don't you remember from our soccer games? The ones we always lost." He laughed. "She used to bring fruit snacks and Kool-Aid. This is her practice. I'm just here workin' while my family—you know what," he said when he noticed my fidgeting hands. I couldn't decide where to put them. Should I hide them in my jeans pockets, or should I hold onto my purse strap? Either way, he wouldn't notice them shaking. "It's not important. Uh, well, my mom was called into court this mornin', so you're stuck with me, but the lucky part is, I got nothin' else to do, so I'm all yours."

"Oh. Um, I-I could just reschedule. I don't wanna take up your time."

"Fran?" he said, leaning a little, trying to put himself in my line of sight when I looked down at my shoes. God, when

I was younger, I would've walked into this office and demanded what I needed. "It's no trouble. Unless you'd be more comfortable with a woman, but I promise, I'm professional and confidential, and I'm licensed in the state of Wyoming and have plenty of experience, if that's what you're worried about."

"O-okay." I kind of did want to reschedule, but I didn't want to wait. It felt like I was running out of time, and Grace was more important than my comfort, so I needed to make sure her future was taken care of in case mine ended. Doug was getting physical again, and I was worried it wouldn't be long before he put me in the hospital. Or worse.

I needed to prepare for that. The truth was that I should've done this a long time ago, but I'd been stupidly waiting for my sister to get back to me about my divorce. Well, no more. I wasn't waiting on anybody else to do anything for me anymore.

"C'mon back," he said, turning and motioning for me to follow. When we were seated in his tiny, sweltering office that was oddly overflowing with dark green, vining plants, he said, "Aren't your dad and sister both lawyers? I'm kinda surprised to see you here."

Shit. "Yes, but I don't wanna bother them. They're really busy, and, well, this is… I'd rather keep this, like you said, confidential." That was the truth, kind of, but I still felt like a liar.

There was a ruckus outside when the glass door to the law office banged against a wall, and then a man appeared in the hallway outside Brady's office. We both turned in our chairs.

"Mr. Burroughs?" Brady asked. His eyebrows were raised, and he looked confused.

The man spoke slowly, like he wasn't sure what he wanted to say. "I, uh… Well, I'm sorry. You're busy. I—shit."

"It's okay. If you wanna wait, I can see you in a bit."

"I can go," I said, dismissing myself before Brady even had a chance to.

"No, Fran. Wait right here. Please, just excuse me for a minute." Brady rose, the look on his face full of pity for this man who was swaying in the doorway. Was he drunk? He looked awful. He was sweaty, and he had dark circles under his eyes. The thought that they were haunted crossed my mind, but it wasn't my business. His face was unshaven, and though the stubble on his strong jaw normally would've been attractive, his unkempt clothing and the lack of respect he seemed to have for his appearance was not.

I'd never seen Mr. Burroughs before. He wasn't from Wisper, but Brady seemed to know him.

"Come with me, Theo. This way," he said, trying to lead Mr. Burroughs down the hall, but Mr. Burroughs paused and stopped to look back at me.

"I'm sorry," he said, and there was so much more than just those two little words in his voice. I felt sad for him. He was clearly in pain. I had no clue what it was about, but sadness and regret had settled over him like a damp blanket.

"Excuse us, Fran. I'll be right back." Brady shut the door, and when I couldn't see or hear them anymore, I calmed my nerves by imagining what could be tormenting the man so badly.

My imagination wasn't that inventive, though, and when Brady reappeared, he looked a little disheveled, like maybe he'd tried to wrangle the man. They'd had some kind of exchange. That was clear.

"I apologize," Brady said. "That was… unexpected." Pushing his messed hair away from his forehead, it formed a neat wave again, the way he'd most likely styled it this morning before he came to work, completely unaware of the weird happenings he was about to experience. First me showing up in his office, a school friend he hadn't spoken to in over a decade, and now this odd Burroughs man who seemed to have some kind of effect on Brady.

"Uh, where were we? What can I help you with?" he asked, lowering himself into his chair again. He leaned back, crossing his ankle over his knee. His desk seemed too small for him, but he looked a picture of success in his sharp gray suit and brown loafers, and I was happy he'd found a life that fulfilled him. At least, I assumed he had, but just like me, he could be a wreck on the inside and no one would ever know. Not like Theo though. His disaster was written all over him.

"Do you need to deal with that?" I asked, nodding over my shoulder toward the door.

"No. Please go ahead," he said, adjusting his tie. His eyes flashed to the door for a second, but then they settled on me, and he waited patiently for me to continue.

"Okay. Well, I need a will, and then I need some legal advice."

"Sure. That's easy enough. Have you made up a list of your assets?"

"I don't have any of those."

"No house, car, money in the bank?"

"No. I-I can't pay you. Your mama said she'd do this pro-bono. It was a favor for a friend." A very large, protective, bar-owning friend.

"I'm not worried about the money, Fran, but what is it you wanna put in your will if you don't have any assets to list?"

"My daughter. I need to be sure she'll be taken care of if anything were ever to happen to me. Can you help me do that?" I didn't yet mention that I'd be naming the town sheriff as Grace's guardian even though Carey had no idea I'd be doing it. But if I couldn't be here for Grace—if anything did ever happen to me—I didn't want her ending up in Doug's or his mama's care. And Carey was the safest and kindest man I'd ever known, so unless he wanted to dump her into foster care, which I knew he'd never do, then Carey would get custody of Grace. At least, I hoped Brady could help me figure out how to make that happen.

Understanding dawned on his face. "Yeah," he said softly, and the look in his eyes, the pity he was trying unsuccessfully to hide, told me he knew about me. He could guess what I was afraid of. "Of course. Don't worry. I think I can help."

CHAPTER EIGHTEEN

CAREY

"GRACE IS HERE," Evvie said when I knocked and she opened her front door. I'd gone to the farmhouse first to meet with Billie again, but she sent me over to see Evvie at her and Jack's cottage down the way. "I was gonna take her to play with the twins and Jack at the big house, but she seemed a little bit… upset this morning when I picked her up, and I just wanted to give her a chance to calm down before she gets bombarded by the whole family and all that craziness."

"Fran asked you to watch Grace? She never leaves that kid."

"Yeah. I was surprised, too, but she called first thing this morning. She wouldn't say why she needed me to watch Grace, and I didn't ask. But, Carey, things weren't right over there."

My heart kicked into a sprint behind my ribs. "Was she— did Fran look like…"

Evvie peeked over her shoulder at Grace sitting on her couch, flipping through one of Jack Jr.'s picture books, then looked back at me. She shook her head a little and whispered, "No. She looked okay, physically."

Relief filled my body, and I hung my head. But that didn't mean Doug hadn't hurt Grace or Fran in some other way.

"Okay," I said, trying to slow the pounding. It was so loud, I could hear my heartbeat outside my body. "Would you mind if I talked to Grace for a minute?"

"You can, but don't upset her, Carey. I know you won't mean to, but she's terrified, and I don't know why, but that little girl is heartbroken."

Nodding, I tried to reassure Evvie that I'd be delicate. I'd left my gun in my truck, but I removed my vest and handed it to her for safekeeping while I tried to compose myself before I spoke to Grace. I'd questioned plenty of people in my line of work, many of them kids, but nothing could've prepared me for my next conversation.

Grace didn't seem to notice me at the door or when I walked into the house, 'cause when I sat next to her on the couch, she started and jumped, but when she realized it was me, she threw herself into my arms, latching on like nothing I'd ever felt, her little fingernails digging into my shoulders, and she cried. She sobbed, and Evvie excused herself to the bathroom. I suspected she was crying too. The sorrow in Grace's voice was the saddest thing I'd ever heard.

I held her against me, cradling her head to my chest, hiding my own tears and hoping she could feel that I was a safe place—that when she was in my arms, nothing would touch her.

Her hair was a mess, a ginger wildfire around her face, and she looked up, placing her hands on my cheeks, holding me captive with her tiny fingers. She swiped a tear away from my cheek, and the gray eyes looking back at me reminded me so much of her mama's, and all the pain I saw in her was doubled. "Please make him stop hurtin' her. You can do that. You're the police. Please," she begged. "Please!"

Maybe it wasn't a good idea to promise such a thing. I could lose my job. I could go to jail if I went to the lengths I wanted to go to keep Grace and Frannie safe, but none of that stuff mattered when that innocent little girl looked in my eyes and begged me. I would've done anything to keep my promise, and it occurred to me then that there was nothing in the whole world I wouldn't do for her.

"I will, Gracie. I'll make it stop. I promise."

GRACE DIDN'T SAY MUCH ELSE, but she didn't need to. She stayed with Evvie, and though she seemed happy to see the Cade kids when I drove her over to the ranch house, I could still see the storm cloud over her head. She was too damn young to have to know the kind of pain she did, too young and too innocent to have to live through what she'd had to.

Jack, Dean, and Kevin were all working in the barn, and Jay and Finn were in the house with Evvie and Billie, so I knew she'd be safe when I left. It was hard to go, though, with Grace attached to my side like a starfish suckers itself to a rock.

When I'd convinced her that I would come back, she let me go, and I drove to Fran's house, but she wasn't there. She didn't pick up her phone when I called, and she didn't text back. I was worried about where she might be, and I drove around a bit more, looking for her car or for any sign of Doug, but I didn't find one.

Frank was on patrol, and he reported Doug's truck being parked in his mama's front yard. Frank had been keeping an eye on Doug Morris for me, but so far as he could tell, Doug hadn't done anything too exciting, and Frank still had a job to do, so it wasn't like he could park outside the asshole's house 24/7. Without an official reason for an arrest or surveillance, there wasn't much either one of us could do. But I was working on that.

"Hey, man," Jack said when I answered his call. "You left before I could tell you what I found out."

Damn, it was hot in my cruiser. Not even ten a.m. yet, and already ninety-five degrees? It felt like we were living in Hell. My hat was on the dash, already damp with sweat.

Swiping beads of it away from my forehead, I said, "Sorry. There was somethin' I needed to do."

"I know. Evvie filled me in. Have you found her yet?"

"Not yet."

"Want me to send Finn to look too?"

"No. Grace said Doug left their house last night and that Fran was okay, and I know he was at home after that. I have a feelin' she just needed some time alone. I think they were both pretty shook-up."

"What happened?"

"I'm not entirely sure. Grace said he didn't hit Fran, but somethin' happened to make 'em both so upset."

"Alright, well, lemme know if you need help lookin'. In the meantime, though, it seems the McCluskies, Don Headstrom, Jerry Moyer, and Carl Aberforth have all been offered money for their land. And every one of 'em have had some kinda accident or weird thing happen on their property lately, somethin' that turned out to be expensive to fix or was a big loss financially. I made a list for you of all the ranch hands working at more than one farm. It's a small list, like you thought.

"I also talked to Phil Beasley. She had a fire in her barn, too, but she's convinced it started accidentally. Some guys were up at her place as a favor to old man Milson. Phil's barn needed some work so some hands went up to patch a few holes in the roof. That place is a dump, unfortunately, and it's fallin' down around her, so I dunno if she's right that the fire was an accident, but it's worth lookin' into. Actually, I was thinkin' we should have a good, old-fashioned barn raisin' and build her a new one."

I felt like doing anything else at the moment, but I laughed. My friend was the grump of all grumps, but he reminded me often how soft he was inside. "Okay. Thanks for doin' that for me."

"Anytime, brother. You let me know if there's anything else I can do."

"I will."

So four land offers and maybe a fifth on the way? Phil's place was up in the mountains pretty far, unlike the other farms Jack had mentioned. But there'd been talk of a ski resort some rich banker types had been trying to build up there for years, so it wouldn't have surprised me if that was what was going on. Phil was a staple in the Wisper community, but she'd fallen on some hard times over the last several years, so it also wouldn't have surprised me if she at least considered taking any money she might be offered. She wouldn't like to do it, but she'd been struggling up there all alone on the mountain since her husband, Rand, had died.

But what could Fran's dad have to do with any of this? Sure, he could easily facilitate the transactions, give dirt on the landowners to the developers since he was from Wisper and knew the area and people, but Billie had already dug into his financials, and there wasn't anything resembling a payoff anywhere near his bank account, and he was busy in Cheyenne with his court cases and political business. If he had time to meddle in Wisper affairs, we couldn't find proof of it.

Jill didn't have any money. They both lived pretty mediocre lives, financially at least. Jillian had made a good amount of money in her job as a lawyer, but she'd given that up, and she made less than I did now. Billie'd had a hard time getting into the governor's private finances—her current information was made public because she was the governor, but her past financials had been a little harder to hack, but when Billie finally cracked the code, Buchanan seemed clean too.

My tech who'd taken a cast of the tires from Carl's place hadn't found anything specific, except that Frank had been right and the tracks were ordinary, everyday, six-year-old truck tire tracks made by a generic brand anybody could buy off the street, which led me to the conclusion that if the SA, his daughter, or the governor were involved in this, whatever this was, they were working hard to conceal it, and that meant that I would need to work even harder to—

The shrill sound of my phone ringing again nearly made me jump through my cruiser's roof. I answered, hoping to God it was Fran, even though the number flashing on my screen was unknown to me. "Sheriff Michaels."

A gruff male voice cleared his throat, right in my ear. Yanking the phone away from my eardrum, I heard the voice mumble, "This is SA McKinnon. I was told you were in my office, but I missed you?"

About fucking time. I'd been trying to get a hold of this guy for days. The meeting I'd had with his youngest daughter hadn't gone so well, and now, after talking to Frannie, hearing what she'd said about her family growing apart, which I knew wasn't quite the truth, I needed to know what this man knew about what his daughter and granddaughter had been going through and why he allowed it to continue, and I needed to know what, if anything, he might have to do with Carl's property being targeted.

"Yessir," I said, sitting up a little straighter. I was parked in front of the flower shop downtown, and the heat rising up from the street was unbearable. I had the window rolled down for air flow and the air conditioning on high. Like that was doing me any good. "I spoke to Jillian when I was there, but she wasn't able to give me the information I need."

"I apologize for missing our meeting, Carey. My receptionist must have confused your appointment with another. I had no idea you'd be in Cheyenne."

"You were unaware that we had an appointment?"

"Yes. Unfortunately, I think you may have fallen victim to my assistant's failing memory. I know I should probably find someone more efficient, but Gladys has worked for me for years, and I just can't seem to let her go even though she seems to botch at least one appointment a week. You should see the state of my calendar. Anyway, I was invited to a last-minute lunch meeting when you were here, but she assured me there were no pressing appointments I'd be missing."

"Gladys? I spoke to a Vera when I was there."

"Yes," he said. "Vera is Jillian's assistant, but she sometimes handles things when Gladys gets overwhelmed."

Just as I'd hoped the other day, Fran's dad relaxed while he was talking to me. He'd seemed uptight at the meeting with the governor, but this was the Bradley McKinnon I remembered. Friendly and accessible. Well, except for when Frannie was in trouble for her many and various teenage antics, but when we were young, he was a great dad. I remembered looking up to him since my own dad was barely there and worthless when he was.

But now Mr. McKinnon sounded like the same guy Frannie used to worship. And if my instincts weren't wrong, he sounded like he truly had no idea we were supposed to have a meeting.

"Well, what did you come all the way out here for? That sure is a long drive."

"It is, sir, but I've been wantin' to speak with you, and I haven't been able to get you on the phone."

"I apologize again, Carey. Is it something serious? It must be for you to make the drive, so why don't you tell me now?"

"Your daughter's… husband is the issue. Or one of the issues," I said, and McKinnon's friendly accessibility disappeared as soon as I mentioned Doug Morris.

His tone changed in a nanosecond. It was closed and guarded, and I pictured a mask made out of wood falling down over his face. Impenetrable. "I don't involve myself in my daughter's domestic issues. I've long since resigned myself to Francesca's bad decisions, Carey, as you would be smart to do. She made her choice. What good can come of you getting involved? You haven't mentioned that you've charged Mr. Morris with anything, so I'm assuming this is a personal issue for you? You and Fran used to be friends."

"Sir, I do realize this is unusual. And I'm not workin' a case, officially. At least not one concernin' Fran, but it was clear to me that somethin' was goin' on at the diner when you met with the governor. You, sir, were not actin' like yourself. Jillian was actin' weird, and the governor, though I don't know her well, seemed off to me too."

"Well, that's just—it's absurd. It was a meeting. Nothing more, nothing less. I can't control how the governor behaves, or Jillian, for that matter."

"The man who showed up, Carl Aberforth, have you dealt with him before?"

"No. Never seen the man before in my life."

It was a weird thing for him to say since he'd lived in Wisper for years, and Carl was born and raised here. It wasn't like Wisper was some huge bustling metropolis. Everybody knew everybody. I couldn't throw a rock in the town without hitting someone I went to school with or who knew my mama.

"Okay, and what about Doug Morris? You have nothin' to say about him? Were you aware that he was outside the whole time, watchin' you?" I hadn't told Frannie that I'd noticed Doug loitering outside the diner, but I suspected she'd known. I had a feeling she was used to him creeping behind her everywhere she went.

"No."

"Okay, well, he was. I spotted him as soon as you pulled up."

"Morris is of no consequence to me."

"Morris? That's what you call your son-in-law?"

"We aren't close. Never have been. There aren't many occasions when I need to refer to him at all, so I'm not worried about being on a first-name basis with the man."

"Alright, so you aren't close with your daughter or her family. That's fine enough, but you don't have an opinion on the… *state* of their marriage?" I wasn't sure why I was beating around the bush. Maybe it was my training, the knowledge that if I came right out and accused him of not caring that his daughter was in danger, and that he knew and hadn't lifted a finger to help her, he'd end our conversation, and I'd get nothing further from him.

"No," he said. Just like that. How in the world did he think I'd buy that?

Fuck it. "No? Even though it's common knowledge around here that Doug Morris is verbally and emotionally abusive to your daughter? That's not concernin' to you? It doesn't bother you that Gracie has to live in that kinda envi-ronment every day?"

"It's…" He stuttered, seeming to not know what to say, or maybe he was trying not to say what he really wanted to. "P-people in small towns talk and gossip, Sheriff," he said, like maybe he was trying to convince himself of what he was saying. "You know that." He cleared his throat again. "If that's all you have for me, I'm late for a meeting."

"That's really all you have to say on the matter? Would your opinion on the subject change if I told you that wasn't *all* he's been doin' to them? You know he hurts her? He *hits* Fran."

His sharp intake of breath told me he hadn't known it, not for certain, but he paused, and I waited. I really couldn't believe the conversation had gone in this direction. If this was really the guy's opinion on Fran's marriage, it was no wonder why Fran had grown apart from her dad.

As it was, I was having a hard time not screaming into my cell phone. Better yet, I wanted to drive the seven hours back to Cheyenne to wrap my hands around the SA's throat to choke some emotion out of him.

"Stay out of it, Sheriff Michaels," he said. "Good day to you." And he hung up.

What the hell?

Well, if that was the way he wanted to play this game, I could muster up a good shot or two.

Picking up my dash radio, I called Abey.

"Yeah, boss."

"I need to speak with the governor, Abey. See if you can figure out how to make that happen, would you please?"

I PROMISED Grace I'd come back to Cade Ranch, and as weird as it was for me to admit, the pull to see her again was just as strong as the pull I'd been feeling toward Fran. For different reasons, obviously, but she wasn't my kid. It wasn't my job to take care of her, so why then was she all I could think about?

After only two hours away from her, I was almost in a panic to get back to Grace. And maybe I was hoping her mama would be with her at the ranch by now too.

Not knowing where Fran was or what was going on with her made me feel uncomfortable, like I was itching to get out of my own skin. I needed to know she was safe and okay. And I needed it now.

So that was where I headed. Never mind that it was the middle of a workday or that I had a whole list of calls I needed to attend to. Until I knew Fran and Grace were safe and whole, all that would have to wait.

My phone rang again before I got there, though, and I pulled off to the side of the road to take the call.

"Manny? What's up?" I asked when I answered. "Everything okay? Kinda early for bar brawls."

"The bar's fine, Carey, but I wonder if you got a minute."

"Might have two for you." If Manny was calling, it was important. He rarely did.

"That's good." He sighed. "Now, I been debatin' callin' you 'cause the person I'm callin' you about begged me not to. The thing is, I think she might be in danger, and so I couldn't sit on my hands this time, and it ain't somethin' I feel comfortable handlin' myself."

"Who's in danger, Manny?"

"Fran Morris. She came to me, and I helped her best I could, but—Carey, she asked me for a gun. I didn't give her one, but that don't mean she won't find one somewhere else. And she asked for legal help."

Sudden anxiety was making my stomach clench and cramp. "A gun?"

"Yeah. You know about her husband, right? About what he…"

"I do."

"Well," he said in his deep voice, almost in a growl, "seems he put his hands on their daughter last night, and it was the last straw for Fran."

WHEN I PULLED up to the barn because I'd spotted Grace atop a horse in the Cade's front paddock, the relief I felt seeing the back of Frannie's red head was overwhelming. She was standing and talking to Evvie and Billie, and from her movements, I could tell she was unharmed.

Sitting in my cruiser a little longer than I should've, I let that sink in, let it calm my nerves, and I tried to decipher what this was. Why was I suddenly so engrossed in Grace and Fran's lives? They'd been back in Wisper now for a while. So why had it taken this long for me to see that there was more going on with them than they let on?

It occurred to me then that it was Frannie. She was the reason.

There was something different about her, like the beautiful, strong, and radiant woman she used to be was fighting to get out, like she'd been dormant inside an imposter Fran all these years, but now, *my* Frannie was ready to shine again.

And that bright light drew me back to her like a moth to a flame. I just had to make sure she didn't singe my wings off when I got close.

"S'up, Red," Billie quipped when I approached.

I smiled best as I could, removing my hat and running my fingers through my sweaty hair, and Fran turned.

"I need to talk to you," she said, and I felt like I'd been summoned to the warden's office. She turned to face Evvie, asking without saying the words for Evvie to watch Grace while she was gone, but she hadn't needed to ask. I knew Evvie, and Billie for that matter, would rather die than let any harm come to Gracie, and there was no safer place for her than with Jack and Dean, who were both currently leading her and Gertie around the worn down dirt path in the paddock.

The smile on Grace's face was brilliant and huge, and I wondered if her cheeks were cramping. When she saw me, she dropped her reins and waved.

Evvie nodded silently, too, and Fran took off toward the barn again—maybe stomping was a better word—this time expecting me to follow her.

When we got there, though, Kevin and Jay were in the tack room, and Fran looked a little panicked. She wanted to talk to me, but it seemed Gracie wasn't the only one she didn't want to overhear.

"C'mon," I said. "I know a place."

I led her to the last barn aisle and up the stairs to a small room the guys used as a place to crash when they were waiting for a foal to be born. They used it for other, less productive things too, but I tried not to think about that.

Fran was living in hell, and it wouldn't be appropriate for me to try to engage her in, well, affairs of the heart and maybe some other body parts. It wouldn't be right, even though when she was mad like she seemed to be now, she reminded of my old feisty Frannie, and I wanted her.

The moment we stepped into the room and I shut the door, she rounded on me. "How could you do that?"

"Do what?"

"How could you promise Grace you'd fix everything?"

"I-I…" I was at a loss for words.

"Carey, she believed what you told her. She thinks everything's gonna be okay."

"It will be, Frannie."

"How can you know that? How can you promise that?"

She backed up and sat on the little bed in the middle of the room with her elbows on her knees, and her head fell into her hands. She was wearing a knee-length dress, and her legs were bare beneath it. Her skin was the rosy-peach color I remembered, dotted with so many freckles, they had to number more than the stars in the night sky.

"What? Like you think you're our savior? That's bullshit and you know it."

"Fran—"

"No, Carey." She stood, marching over to me with more purpose in her steps than I'd seen since we were seventeen. I backed up 'cause, if I was honest, she was worrying me a little. And she was more than turning me on.

This was my Frannie.

My back hit the wall, and I held my hands in front of me. "I'm sorry, but you didn't see the look on Gracie's face this mornin'. It broke my heart. What happened last night? Don't lie to me again. I know you went to Manny for a gun."

"Wha— How do you know that?"

"Fran, c'mon. You didn't think he'd let you put yourself in that kinda danger, did you?"

She shook her head. "Well, whatever happened, it's none of your business, and that look on Grace's face breaks my heart every day, but I still manage not to promise her things that'll never come true." She stopped one foot away from me, the sweet scent of her hair and the heat from her body between us. "Tell me what you thought you were accomplishin' by makin' promises to my little girl that you can't keep. You do this for all your voters? Is it some kinda political tactic?"

"Now, that ain't fair."

Her cheeks turned red, and she hung her head. "I know. I'm sorry." When she looked up again, there were tears in her eyes that she tried to blink away, but I saw them, and they broke my heart too. "I shouldn't have said that, but you can't know what it's like to have another life dependent on your every decision. Look what I've done to her. Look at how I've ruined my child's life, Carey. How can that ever be okay? How can we ever be okay if he's in this world? He won't let us be okay. Every time she smiles, he finds a way to wipe it off her face.

"And you comin' in, the big, bad sheriff who she sees as the good guy, a strong man like the father she's always wanted, you're just settin' her up to be disappointed again. I've disappointed her enough. I won't let you do it too."

"I don't plan to disappoint her, Frannie," I said, tucking little wisps of hair behind her ear. Her closeness made it impossible for me not to touch her somehow, however I could that wouldn't hurt her. "I don't plan on disappointin' you either. I meant what I said. I'm gonna make this stop."

"How?"

"I dunno. I thought first you could promise me you won't try to kill your husband."

"I should never have asked Manny. I wouldn't even know what to do with a gun if I had one, but I'm desperate, Carey." She was trembling, shaking her head back and forth, and she was right; desperation was pouring out of her whole body.

"I think we need to go see your dad. I think there's somethin' goin' on with him. I don't have it all worked out, and it makes no sense that he'd involve you, but I can't shake the feelin' that that's what's happenin'. I spoke to him earlier today on the phone, and he seemed oblivious to anything goin' on, but when I mentioned Doug, he changed. His voice changed, and he became angry and withdrawn. Do you have any idea what that's about?"

"No. I mean, he never liked Doug. Can you blame him? But I don't know how Doug could be involved with anything my father's into."

"Unfortunately, I think I might have an idea."

"What is it?"

"I can't say yet. I'm waitin' on a call back from someone, and then, I promise, I'll fill you in. In the meantime, I think we should take a trip out—"

"No."

"No? You don't wanna find out what—"

"I'm goin' alone."

No, not again. "Why you always gotta make helpin' you so damn difficult? There's a river between us, Frannie. I'm on one bank and you're on the other, and no matter what I do or say, I can't get to you."

She stared at me for the longest time, just breathing, and I couldn't figure what she was thinking—

All of a sudden, her lips smacked against mine so hard that I bit the inside of my lip, and all hell broke loose from there.

Her hands were everywhere, stroking my face and down my arms. She moaned and tilted her head when my tongue traced the top of her lip. Lifting up on her tiptoes, she swallowed it, thrusting her tongue in and out, matching the rhythm with her hips against mine.

"Fran, I don't—"

"What? You don't want me?" she asked, but she didn't

believe it 'cause her fingers were already unbuckling my belt. She popped my fly open, and then her hands were inside my pants, and when she gripped my dick and looked in my eyes, it was all I could do not to come right then.

I'd wanted this for so long—forever, it felt like—but as much as I wanted her, I wouldn't put her in a position she'd regret later.

"Frannie," I breathed when she kissed me again. Now my hips were pumping with hers, my hardness against her soft driving me crazy, making the need grow bigger, until she planted her hands on my shoulders and jumped up, wrapping her legs around my back, and her shoes hit the wall. She kicked them off.

The yellow sundress was bunched around her hips, but she yanked it up and reached back in my pants. I was pissed at the stupid polyester getup I had to wear for work 'cause the fabric was stiff and there wasn't enough room for her to maneuver. It didn't matter though. She pushed my pants down around my hips, and the weight from the gun in my thigh holster dragged them down to my feet.

The gun thudded on the floor, and she dropped her legs, whisked her underwear off, and jumped back up. "Please, Carey. I need this. I need to feel alive again. Dreams and promises don't come true, but we can have this. Right now. Just this once. Just this once, can you make me feel like you used to?"

"How did I make you feel?"

"Like I was loved. Make me feel like I haven't been forgotten."

I groaned when she aligned the wet heat of her sex with my hard-on. I was an inch away from ecstasy.

"Please?" she whispered. "I need you."

We stayed like that, staring at one another, me holding her

up with my hands on her beautiful ass, my thumbs massaging the soft skin beneath her dress, and then all logic and reason left my mind. I groaned when her lips met mine again, and I took her mouth with my own.

She was warm and soft, and I thought I'd die from the pleasure touching her like this made me feel.

I spun on my foot, turning us, holding her back to the wall, and I pushed into her body slowly. It was a tight fit since I was harder than I'd probably ever been, and we both moaned loudly. In any other circumstance, I would've been embarrassed by the noises I was making, but I was too far gone to care.

"Yes!" she tried to whisper. "Oh God, Carey, make me come."

"Shit, Frannie. What are we doin'? You can't talk like that, or we ain't makin' it much further than this wall."

"Take me against the wall. I want you to."

Her eyes were burning through mine. All the looks she'd given me these last few years, filled with shyness and shame, they were gone, and in their place was the charcoal fire I'd fallen in love with so long ago.

I gave her what she wanted, pounding into her, 'cause I was lost to move any other way. I needed this too.

I needed her.

She was my home, and I'd been aimless for so long without her that now, we were like a lock fitting into place. She held the key to my dreams. Maybe she and Gracie both did. But either way, right then and there, I vowed to never lock my dreams away again.

CHAPTER NINETEEN

FRANNIE

CAREY ROCKED INTO ME, and the inside of my body gripped him like a fist. It was a wonder he could move at all, but that didn't stop him from trying. Over and over, again and again, he snapped his hips, and my body devoured the force of his desire with abandon.

It was hot and hurried, and sweat was dripping from the both of us, my hair wet with it, and I could feel it sticking to our faces.

It had been a long time since I'd felt this good. Years. Thirteen to be exact, but I'd only had sex with one man, and calling him a man was being generous.

I'd had no idea what I was missing.

Carey's body was strong and sexy, hard and unyielding in the daylight. It was streaming in through the window in this secret room above a barn, of all places, and the light allowed me to see him clearly. I wanted to devour him, to have all of him all at once, to make up for these long years without him. I was furious with myself for never giving him the chance I should have, and the regret was controlling my every move now.

I couldn't get enough.

Unbuttoning his shirt as quickly as I could and lifting his white cotton undershirt, I watched his arm and chest muscles flex and release while he fucked me against the wall, and they made the need I was feeling so much worse. The strength in them made me feel safe, knowing those arms were holding me up and that I wouldn't fall 'cause he would never let me.

Somewhere in the back of my mind, the fact that we weren't using a condom was flashing like a neon sign, but nothing could've made me stop. I needed his body to fortify mine. I needed him to make me feel whole.

I wanted to taste him, so I did. My mouth was hot on his skin, and a rough grumble escaped his throat when I tucked my head in his neck, licking and sucking and scraping my teeth below his ear while my hands roamed his back and ass. I squeezed and pulled, using my legs wrapped around his waist, too, to try and push his body into mine as hard as I could, my muscles shaking with the effort.

It was oppressively hot in the room, and it made everything feel thick and heavy, even the air, but it made what he was doing to me even better. He had to work harder, breathe harder, push harder, strain harder, and he was beautiful like that.

This was a stupid mistake, I knew. Being with Carey could only come back to cause me pain later. Many kinds of pain, but we were too far gone to stop it, and I didn't want to.

I wanted him. I'd always wanted him, and I'd spent years denying us both. My reasons had always felt solid, but now they seemed to be crumbling down around me, like a house of cards, and I wanted so badly to believe that we could have this. We could keep this one thing between us, and it would be okay, like he'd promised.

I wanted to believe him so badly that I was becoming desperate for him to prove me wrong.

That was dangerous too. I wasn't sure what my future would hold, but I knew the outcomes of my choices and decisions were on an accelerated race toward some kind of ending. I was terrified that ending wouldn't include Carey—when had what I wanted ever mattered to anyone? So I held onto him for now, riding him like a wave that would eventually roll away from me and never come back.

Second chances didn't come around a third time, and dreams never came true.

His breathing became heavier when I lifted up and let my body fall back down on his, and his sharp, erratic breath was all I could hear.

He was on the edge, speaking through clenched teeth. "Frannie."

"Please, Carey," I panted, "don't stop."

He groaned loudly, pulling me against him, and the sweat on our bodies connected us. It was slick and warm, and it turned me on more than I already was, which was really saying something because I'd never felt like this before. I'd never wanted anyone like this. It was visceral and all-consuming, and I was moving my body and grasping at his in ways I'd never even imagined before.

He turned and shuffled to the bed. His feet were trapped by his pants caught on his boots, his gun holster dragging behind, but we finally made it there, and he lowered us and sat on the bed, his hands beneath my dress, pushing me harder on his cock, and my head fell back because he felt so good.

I couldn't catch my breath, and I dug my nails into his shoulders, trying to find a way to ground myself in this moment so I wouldn't float away. It was that good, and the thought crossed my mind that I never wanted to come down from his high. I wanted him to do what he'd promised and make everything okay.

But that wasn't real life, and it was a stupid thing to wish for. I'd been there before, and look where that had gotten me.

His hand left my ass while the other stayed clutching one cheek, and when he sucked his fingers into his mouth, wetting them, and pressed them between my legs to rub my clit, a sound came out of me so illicit that, for a split second, I worried who might hear, but it felt too good to care.

I rolled my hips over and over, taking him as far inside me as he would go.

"Frannie," he said again, breathless, his head falling back to watch me ride him, and I swore, if he said my name like that again, I was done for.

His fingers formed fast circles around my clit, making just enough pressure while my body sucked his in and out greedily with every push up and down on my knees. Looking between us, I watched our bodies joined together for a moment, letting the thought that this was what I had wanted for the longest time wash over me. I let it fill me up, like he was.

"Frannie, please," he begged. "I-I need… I can't hold out much longer. This is too much. You feel so good."

"Yeah," was all I could say. My voice was shaking and stuck in my throat, locked behind the scream I was trying not to let out.

He pulled me closer with one hand while his other increased pressure where he was still rubbing me, and changing our pace, he punched up inside me when I came down on him, and silently, my entire body locked into place on top of him, and my whole world broke apart in tiny, crystalline pieces. I opened my mouth to let out the scream, but no sound came out.

I was flying. Soaring. I was so high in the sky, nothing could touch me, but he flipped us, and I was on my back on the bed, my legs spread wide, and Carey was manic, fucking into me like an animal. He kissed me, and I held his face in my hands, looking in his brown eyes, telling him without any words between us that it was okay to let go. That this was what I wanted, and he wasn't doing anything wrong.

His arms were caging me between them, shaking from the strength it was taking to hold his body above mine, and I wrapped my legs around him again, pulling him closer, but it felt like we couldn't get close enough. I kissed him back, and his eyes rolled back in his head when he pushed inside me for the last time, and a shout was torn from his throat when he came.

AT MIDNIGHT, I was warring with myself. I couldn't decide whether to be happy that, finally, I knew what it felt like to be really touched by Carey, or to be freaked out that we hadn't used a condom. Clearly, another child right now would be a problem.

He hadn't mentioned it after, when we redressed in silence, watching each other for any sign of what the other was thinking, and neither had I.

It felt like it was all part of this runaway train my life had become, but I couldn't obsess too hard about it because it led me back to remembering Carey's hands all over me, his body inside mine, his mouth on mine, and his love wrapped around me.

It wasn't helping me figure out what to do, and I was lost

in the memory until I heard a noise outside. I peeked around the kitchen wall, worried that Doug had come back again, but Carey appeared on the front porch, and he smiled behind my screen door. "Is this okay? I don't wanna wake Gracie."

I nodded, and he stepped inside, noticing how the door hung from the hinges a little, but he didn't mention it.

For once, he wasn't wearing his uniform. His red hair was wavy and thick and looked messy without his brown cowboy hat to tame it, and he was wearing faded jeans, worn brown boots, and a T-shirt that said, "Fish Wyoming". The fitted cut of the shirt accentuated his wide shoulders, and thoughts about what we'd done earlier, with my nails digging into those shoulders, flooded my brain again. *Right.* Like I hadn't been thinking about it since the second it was over. I fanned my face with my hand, hoping he wouldn't notice and poke fun at me. Living without air conditioning in this heat was hard for more than one reason when he was around.

He turned in a circle, looking all around, and when I got a look at his tight ass in those jeans, I nearly melted right then and there. To distract myself, I pulled the lemon-blueberry tarts I was making out of the oven and set them on a trivet on the stove to cool. I was wearing an old Wisper High Wardogs T-shirt that hung down to my thighs, underwear, and nothing else, and that was too much clothing for the unwavering summertime heat, especially because I was baking, but it always helped me think.

When he joined me in the kitchen, Carey stood next to me, and placing his hand on my hip, he bent to inhale the aroma wafting up in heated, lemon-blueberry waves of air. "Damn, they smell good. Who you makin' 'em for?"

"They're for you. I remember your favorites."

He stood and leaned over to kiss me quickly. "For me?" His smile was boy-like and delicious.

"Yeah. C'mon. It's too hot in here. Will you switch off the oven?" I asked, and I heard the dial click as I headed to the living room.

Grace and I had planted cut-offs and shoots that Terre had given us in little pots and old butter tubs that we'd poked drainage holes in the bottom of with a screwdriver, and they were growing wildly around the house. They were the only decoration in it besides pictures Grace had drawn that I'd tacked along the walls. I tried to make "gardening" fun for her. We covered the tubs with stickers from the dollar store, and we named each plant.

Carey looked around, taking in eyefuls of our meager home, touching the leaf of a plant here and there while he followed me through the living room. He'd been here before, but I doubted he'd noticed anything other than my beat-up face that night.

His presence in my house was commanding. It was just his natural aura, and he took up a lot of space. Normally, having a man in my house was something I'd come to dread, but now, I wanted to lose myself in the feeling. In him. Again. But I had no idea what to say. I didn't know how to talk to him and had no clue how we could get from here to there.

I was still technically married. I still had a douchebag for a husband, and I still needed my father's support to pay for Grace's health insurance. None of that was going to change any time soon.

I sat on the arm of my faded and torn sofa, wondering what to say, and my eyes raised up to his when he spoke again. "Would you c'mere a minute?" He held his hand out for me, and I took it.

When we were outside, standing side by side on my front lawn, he said softly, "Look up. See all those stars?"

Taking a deep breath, I closed my eyes and turned my head away from him. When I opened them again, dark sky and shiny stars were all I saw. "Yeah. They're beautiful out here, away from the city."

"Yeah," he said, but he wasn't looking at the sky. He was looking at me, and I turned to face him. "When you were gone, when I'd look up at night, all those tiny dots reminded me of your freckles. This is the way I could see your face even though you were so far away."

"You thought about me?" I touched my fingers to his jaw, feeling his short beard tickle them.

"You kiddin'? Every damn day. And it's been worse since you moved home, but Frannie, I had no idea what life was like for you. You never said. You hid it well, and you were so closed off that I thought we'd never know each other again. Not like we used to. Not like this. I'm sorry I didn't fight harder for you. Maybe if I had…"

"Maybe what?" I dropped my hands to my sides. "You could've made Doug not be a monster to his daughter? You could've made it so he didn't hurt me?" I breathed a laugh, listening to the hollow sound of it when out of the corner of my eye, I noticed something green glinting in the moonlight in the corner of Mrs. Quinn's front porch. It was my missing broom. I hadn't noticed it before tonight, but now, there it was, plain as day. She was the mysterious house cleaner? The same Mrs. Quinn who scowled at me every morning?

Carey's voice brought my attention back to him. "Yeah, I coulda made it stop."

"You aren't that powerful, Carey."

"I think you've forgotten who I am in this town, Fran. What happened last night? Gracie was almost hysterical this mornin'. Will you tell me the truth? Please?"

Taking another deep breath, my shoulders dropped when I

let it out. I didn't want to tell him what had happened. I didn't want to admit how weak I'd become to this man I'd loved since we were twelve. But I would because he deserved the truth.

The past was catching up to me, and I wanted him to know me before he lost me again. That was what was happening, and when I realized it, I wanted to scream. What we'd done together was a goodbye. Hurting him was the last thing I wanted to do, but he deserved better than I could ever give him, and he needed to know that too. He was still in love with the girl I used to be, and it was too much to hope that he could love me for who I was now. How could he when I didn't know how to love myself?

"Doug showed up lookin' for money, and he… he *pushed* Grace. He knocked me around like he always does, but it was the first time he'd ever put his hands on her like that." Kicking my flip-flops off, I wiggled my toes into the over-grown grass, feeling its coolness and trying not to feel the rage making me want to commit murder, but then I turned and sat on the porch step. I didn't want him to see the defeat on my face, and I looked at the step. The cement was old, and it was shifting with the cottage's foundation as it aged. Weeds grew in the crack, and I picked at them.

I'd accused Carey of not being powerful, but it was me who was powerless. Nothing had changed.

When I looked up, Carey was still standing in the yard, facing away from me. He was silent, but I could feel the anger seeping out of his every pore. The air was so heavy and still, even the crickets weren't chirping, but I could almost hear his anger crackling in the night.

He was angry at himself for not knowing all the things I'd never said, he was murderously rageful at Doug, and he was angry with me. He didn't have to say it for me to feel it.

Those words would never cross his lips, and he wasn't mad that I'd stayed with Doug—he dealt with domestic abuse victims in his work, so he probably knew all the reasons a person could get stuck in that kind of life and all the ways it was hard to get out—but he was angry all the same. He didn't blame me, of course not, but he was still mad I'd left Wisper in the first place. He was still mourning all the time we'd lost, all the love he'd lost, wasting it on a woman who never deserved it in the first place.

It took a minute, but he finally turned and said, "I want you to come stay at my house. Grace can have my old room. You can stay in there with her if you want. This ain't about sex, Fran. It's about safety. And then we'll file a protective order, and I'll help you press charges."

He wanted to make it all okay, the same way he'd tried before I left home, but I couldn't let him do that. It wasn't just Grace's hopes that were up, hopes that everything would work out, that we could be together, Grace, Carey, and me, and I didn't think I'd survive it when they fell again.

"Thank you. That's really nice of you, but no. It'll only make things worse with Doug, and I don't want his stupidity messin' with your job. No, we're better off here. I can handle him." I didn't mention my father's support, but that was a huge obstacle too. If I moved in with another man when I was still married to a different one, well, that wouldn't look good for my father, no matter the reasons. He wouldn't stand for it.

"Fran, it's kinda startin' to offend me that you won't let me help you and Grace. It's my job."

"Oh really? You let all your cases move in with you?"

"You're not a case, and of course not, but this is different."

"How's it different?" I asked, leaning forward on the

stoop and shrugging. "I'm just like every other battered wife you've come across. I'm… well, you know."

"You're what? Tell me what's goin' through your head. That's all I've ever wanted from you, but you block me every damn time like a fuckin' linebacker."

Did he really not get it? After all these years? "Can't you see? Do you really not see it when you look at me?"

"See *what*, Fran? All I see is you."

Finally, I looked at him. "The weak, pathetic, *stupid* girl who left home and ruined her life! She's not good enough. She was never good enough, Carey. Don't you get that? Why do you think I left you in the first place? Why do you think he knows he can treat me that way?"

He staggered back a step. "Not good enough? For who? For you or for me? You've always been good enough for me, and I think I've been pretty clear that you're all I want. Or is that some excuse? Is this really about you pushin' me away again when things don't go your way? You wanted a bigger life back then, so what? This life, here with me, it ain't big enough?"

"That's not what I'm sayin'. You're gettin' it wrong."

"I don't think I am," he said, and he took another step away. "My life is what's not good enough, or me. Yeah, maybe it's just me, 'cause you've left me twice now." He shook his head, and I watched as the pain I was causing him cracked him in half. "You'd rather stay with a man who hurts you than be with me."

"No!" I jumped up. How could he think that? "Carey, no." I was begging him to hear me. I couldn't let that be what he believed, but he was right. I was trying to leave him again.

"You're doin' it as we speak. You're talkin' yourself into it right now. And I'll tell you what, that's what's stupid, Fran. It was stupid the first time you did it, but you were young, and you made a mistake, like all people do. But now you *know* better. You deserve better. And Gracie? She deserves the fuckin' world, and if you do this again and run away 'cause you're scared… Well then, I feel sorry for you."

"And there it is."

"There what is?" He planted his hands on his hips. It was the first time he'd dared to show anger toward me.

I didn't want to say the thing that was about to cross my lips, but I did, because he deserved *more*. It was up to me to make him see that, whether he wanted to or not. "Pity. That's what this all boils down to, right? It's what I've been afraid of all this time. You're good and kind, and you'll tether yourself to me and Grace 'cause you think it's the right thing to do, and you *always* do the right thing. You always have. Unlike me."

He laughed under his breath and shook his head, and I tried not to cry.

He breathed, "Fuck you, Frannie," and he walked away.

My heart broke in two right then, and I knew I'd made another mistake.

ANOTHER MISTAKE.

I'd known it the second he walked away. Why did it always take doing the worst thing for me to realize the best?

My heart was broken, and I cried myself to sleep, hoping I'd have the courage to go to him and apologize for what I'd said—that I wasn't leaving him, that I never would again— but instead, in the morning, Grace and I dressed and ate, and I drove her back to Cade Ranch. She was excited to spend the next two days with Fiona, Mitch, and little Jack, and Evvie had a water slide for the kids and a kiddie pool set up. I loaded Grace up with more sunscreen than any kid had ever worn, plopped an old gardening hat on her head, and kissed her cheeks.

Instead of only asking for his forgiveness, I was going to prove to Carey that I deserved it. I wanted to deserve him, and I hoped by the end of the day, I would have the resources to get us out of the mess I'd put us in. There was no guarantee, but I was prepared to go to any length to get what we needed.

Grace loved living in Wisper. She was making friends, and so was I. I didn't want to have to run or leave, and my father had the power to make that a reality while, at the same time, getting rid of our biggest obstacle.

He'd never seen the need to help me with my divorce before. Jillian always told me that he hadn't wanted to be involved and that I shouldn't ask because it would put our father in a difficult position—he couldn't use his influence to get me out of my mess—but I wasn't planning to ask today. Today, I would be demanding action from my father.

I needed to prove to myself that I wasn't powerless, and I needed Carey to be proud of me for doing something brave so that I wouldn't be the awful, insecure woman I'd been to him last night. I needed to make it right, and I needed to prove to myself that I was what Carey had said—good enough. Good enough for Grace, for him, and for me, because we were all that mattered.

The mess I'd made for myself and my daughter was getting bigger, even though, for the longest time, I'd tried to make it seem small enough that no one would notice, but now it was time to end it.

Carey was right that this hell Grace and I had been living in needed to end, but it wouldn't be him doing the ending.

It was gonna be me.

CHAPTER TWENTY

CAREY

BILLIE WASN'T KNOWN for leaving her hacker dungeon—a.k.a. the dinner table at Cade Ranch—so I was surprised when she pushed through my office door, knocking it against the wall. She was wearing all black, as usual, like a damn ninja.

She plopped into the chair across from me at my desk and sighed. "I don't like when you're right."

"Well, then you're gonna be perpetually unhappy," I joked. I wasn't really in a joking mood after last night, but Billie's quippy comments were easy to laugh at. "What was I right about this time?"

"I was really hoping Fran's dad was just elitist and douchey, but turns out, he is up to something shady. I don't know what yet, but he's got someone spying on your Fran."

"What?" I was so caught off guard by that bit of information, I didn't react to the "your Fran" comment. Fran wasn't mine. If she were, she'd let me in. And I hadn't noticed anything suspicious like someone following her or Grace. Were my instincts off, or was the "spy" that good? "Who is it? Why would anyone be watchin' Fran?"

"Okay, so I know you didn't ask me to do this, and maybe it's a little creepy, but I hacked into the SA's home computer. I may or may not have done a few illegal things to get access that I will *never* tell you about, but..." She looked at me, unusual vulnerability on her face, and she swiped her thick dark bangs away from her eyes. "You know how much I can't fucking stand it when someone's being abused. Especially a woman. And if that kid is being—" Taking an exaggerated breath, she tried to relax back into her chair. "Anyway, I took it upon myself to dig a little deeper than you might've intended. Sue me." She shrugged with indifference. "Somebody might actually sue me after this, but I won't apologize."

"Billie, get on with it." I appreciated her help, but I was irritable. And I wasn't sure this whole thing wasn't a waste of time. I mean, if Fran's family was doing something criminal, I wanted to know what it was, and I wanted to kill Doug Morris, literally, but I was pretty sure I needed to get over the delusion I had in my mind of me, Fran, and Grace being the perfect family. Fran had made it clear she didn't want that.

"What's up your butt today?" When I didn't answer and the impatient scowl on my face didn't change, Billie said, "Fine. Whatever. So I overheard a conversation SA McKinnon was having with someone over the phone."

"About Fran and Gracie?"

"Yep. Whoever he was talking to seemed to be asking for orders. The SA said—wait. Hold on, I recorded it on my phone." She pulled her cell from her back pocket, clicked it on, and we heard Fran's dad say, "Keep watching them. Keep your distance, but I want to know who she speaks to, where she goes, and I need to know where my granddaughter is at all times. If that means you have to use some kind of tracking device or you need to install cameras somewhere, do it. Just don't let anyone *know* you're doing it."

I was stunned. Why would it matter to the SA what Fran was up to? She seemed to be in the dark about his ambitions, other than in a general sense. She was angry at her father, but it all felt personal to me. I didn't think Fran knew anything about her dad's job.

But it strengthened the feeling in my gut that whatever Bradley McKinnon was up to had to do with Wisper. Why else would Fran's activities matter to him? He'd made it clear her personal life wasn't something he cared much about.

"You haven't found any evidence of a payout, have you? Any proof that he's hired someone to do this?"

Billie shook her head. "Nope, and I already asked the guys. No one's noticed weird people hanging around the ranch when Fran and Grace were there. You'd think after what they've all been through, they'd notice that kind of thing."

"True." *I* should've noticed that kind of thing, but I didn't say that.

"I tried to trace the call, but it came from an actual payphone. Did you know they still exist? Anyway, I got the feeling it wasn't the first time the SA was speaking to whoever was on the other end of the line, but maybe this is a new thing?" She shrugged. "I don't know. But McKinnon didn't give me dangerous or psycho vibes, so maybe he's having his daughter and granddaughter watched out of some kind of precaution. Did you ever get ahold of him?"

"Yeah, he finally called me back, but I didn't get anything useful from him. He says he's never met Carl Aberforth before, which isn't true—they were practically neighbors when Fran's family lived in Wisper—and when I asked about Fran and Doug, he shut me down. He don't like the guy, but McKinnon couldn't give two shits about his son-in-law, and he tried to make it seem like he wasn't concerned about the abuse. Though, there was somethin' in his voice. Almost like maybe… like maybe he didn't know about it. I don't know how in the world that could be possible though."

"All right, well, we know Grace is safe for the next two days at least. Did Fran tell you where she was going?"

"What? She left?" Seriously, did no one think to call me anymore? The fucking sheriff?

"Yeah," Billie said cautiously as I erupted out of my chair, and it hit the wall behind me. "She asked Evvie to keep Grace overnight tonight. She didn't tell you? I thought you two were all hot and heavy the other day?"

"No." I hung my head, anger and frustration making me want to scream at Frannie. "She didn't say a word." Unfortunately, my intuition was telling me there was a reason for her silence, but I doubted it was a good one.

A string of bottle rockets going off outside the station had me practically screaming, "Sonofabitch!" I stomped to my office window, and when I looked outside, I saw a man's back as he was running away. I couldn't be positive, but it looked a lot like Doug Morris's back, and I was sure of it when the guy following behind him tripped over his own feet and fell in the middle of Main Street. I got a good look at Vern Wexler's face then.

"Hold that thought. I'm about to arrest a moron."

"IT WAS JUST A JOKE, SHERIFF," Vern slurred, drunk already at ten in the morning. His dirty T-shirt was on inside-out and backwards, and I could smell the beer on his breath. He didn't ask for a lawyer when I told him he had a right to one, and I sure as hell wasn't going to remind him. I hadn't found any fireworks on him, not even a lighter, so I didn't plan on actually arresting him, but he didn't know that, and I hoped I might get some information out of him before he passed out. He'd sleep off his morning buzz, and I'd let him go. Rinse and repeat. We'd been here before.

Shaking my head, I slammed the cell door shut in his face. "Where's Doug, Vern?" If Fran was MIA, where was Doug? She'd promised she wouldn't do anything drastic, and I believed her, but… something was happening.

We had two jail cells at the station in a small room at the end of the hall, and Vern was a regular visitor to Wisper, Wyoming's old-west accommodations. The cells had been there since the days of Butch Cassidy, and they were dark and dingy and lacking any kind of modern convenience, so it was the perfect place to stick Vern since the idiot couldn't seem to walk two steps without hurting himself or causing some kind of trouble.

He tried to focus on my face but blinked instead when he couldn't. "Who?"

"Man, I swear, you get dumber every time I see you. Your buddy. Your cohort. The moron who just lit and aimed illegal fireworks at a government buildin', that's who. I woulda thought after you blew up your own hand"—I nodded to the almost black-with-dirt bandage unravelling from Vern's hand —"you might've learned your lesson."

He looked down, turning his hand this way and that, like he'd forgotten he almost lost a finger. "Dunno what you're talkin' about," he mumbled, shaking his head and shrugging at the same time, but he was too unsteady for either action to be convincing. He stumbled backward, landing on his ass on the cot behind him.

"Alright, well, let's see. Public intoxication, attempted destruction of government property, threatenin' government employees, the purchase and use of illegal fireworks. You know all fireworks are illegal in Teton County, right, Vern? And I'm guessin' you pissed somewhere outside. You're too drunk not to have, so that's public indecency, public urination. We can go ahead and add dumbassery to those charges, maybe tomfoolery."

Vern's eyes grew bigger and bigger, even though the last two charges were bullshit. Apparently, his idiocy knew no bounds. "No, no, c'mon, Carey. I was just fuckin' around."

"Yeah, well, this time you fucked too close to my job and my employees. I take my job seriously, Vern. Since you've never had a real job before, maybe you can't understand that, but you can't pull this kinda stunt and expect to walk away from it. Unless…"

"What? Unless what?" He jumped up but fell forward and, at the last minute, latched onto the cell bars. He was too drunk to stop his momentum, though, and he slid down to the floor with the most ridiculous wince on his face. His reattached finger had to be throbbing by now, if he still had any feeling in it. Distantly, I wondered if it would affect his ability to give me the finger like he usually did.

I crouched in front of him. "Unless you're willin' to… Naw, you'd never do that. Doug would be mad at you, and we both know you'd *never* go against Doug. He's the boss of you, right? Is Doug your daddy, Vern? Wait, there ain't somethin'… *sexual* goin' on between you two, is there?"

Doug and Vern's intolerance was widely known through Wisper. They spent half their time hassling the few LGBTQ folks we had residing in our community, so I knew this would get under his skin.

"Aw, God. Why'd you go and say a thing like that? Now I'll never get that picture outta my head."

"Just sayin'." I shrugged, all nonchalant-like. "It ain't normal the way you follow him around like a puppy. Maybe he's got you on a leash. A leather leash with metal studs. Maybe you like when he—"

"Damn, man, shut up." Vern slapped his hands to his face, like that guy in that old painting, *The Scream*. "Whatever you wanna know, I'll tell ya. Please just stop." He grabbed the cell bars again but released them so he could hold himself up off the floor when he dry heaved, and he fell onto his back, smacking his head against the cold hard floor. "Ohh, I feel sick."

"The feelin's mutual," I said. "Where's Doug?"

"I dunno, man. I really, truly don't. He's probably holed up at his mama's house by now. There's a fort in the woods back there."

"A fort? Like the kind you make with fallen tree limbs when you're eight?"

"Yeah. How'd you know?"

"Oh my God, Vern," I said, squeezing the bridge of my nose between my thumb and finger.

He sighed. "If he ain't there, I got no idea. We were just supposed to distract you. That's all. I didn't mean any harm."

Distract me? From what? But I didn't let on that I'd caught that slip.

"What's goin' on between Doug and Fran's dad?"

"Huh?"

"SA McKinnon. You know anything about somethin' Doug might have goin' on with the guy?"

"No. Doug didn't say nothin' 'bout that. I mean, I guess the dad might know the sister owes Doug money, but Doug didn't *say* that. The bitch better pay up, too, or shit's gonna get intense. That bronco she promised him's gonna win him a buckle next year, you'll see."

"What's Fran's sister payin' Doug for, Vern?"

His eyes popped open when he realized he'd spilled the beans. "Who?"

Grinning like a wolf in a henhouse, I reached for a bottle of water on the table behind me and handed it to him through the cell bars. "Thanks, Vern. You've been super helpful. Sleep it off, and if you're lucky, I'll let you outta here 'round dinnertime, deal?"

"Aw, man. I didn't mean that," he yelled after me when I left the room. "Wait, will you tell Shelly to bring me some crackers? I feel sick to my tummy."

I snort-laughed and kicked the door shut with my boot. Oh, Vern. Never a dull moment with the guy, that was for sure, but he'd just confirmed what I'd been suspecting was true.

Doug Morris was the tether tying Jillian McKinnon's feet to the fire, and her shit was about to go up in flames.

ARRESTING Vern hadn't taken long—he was way too easy to catch—so Billie was still in my office when I got back, typing away on her laptop. She was perched in my chair behind my desk, and she had my office fan aimed at the side of her face.

"I caught all that. I'm looking into Jillian McKinnon's finances again, but I'm telling you, Carey, there's nothing to find. Oh, here," she said and held out a folded piece of paper. "I forgot earlier, but Grace wanted me to give that to you."

Taking the paper from her, I flipped it over in my hand. It was a piece of folded notebook paper, like a kid might use for her math homework, and when I opened it, I noticed Frannie's messy scrawl, but the paper looked old. It was wrinkled and soft, like it'd been opened and folded a bunch of times.

"Grace gave this to you?"

"Yep," Billie said. "I didn't read it. She said it was from Fran and for your eyes only. The kid's pretty persistent when she wants something. You'd never guess it, though, since she barely speaks."

"She talks to me," I said, and I sat, straightening the paper. I looked up at Billie, but she was busy on her computer, and I knew she wouldn't interrupt till I was done…

Dear Carey,

I'll probably never send this letter, but I needed to say these words to you. I thought if I wrote them down, it might help.

I wanted to tell you that I miss you.

Do you miss me?

I think about you every day, and I wish I could introduce you to Grace.

Carey, she's amazing. She's everything I'll never be. She's so smart and brave. She walked and spoke for the first time on the same day! The camera on my phone doesn't work anymore, so I couldn't record it, but I couldn't forget that if you paid me to. If you knew her, you'd be so proud of her. You'd laugh at how she forgets words. She inserts a different one that she thinks will fit what she's trying to say, and then she just keeps talking, as if "butterfly" means the same thing as "buttered bread," or maybe that it's close enough and I'll just automatically know what she meant.

I know you're not proud of me, and you're probably angry with me. I'm not proud of me either, but when I left, I truly thought it was the only choice. It's funny, isn't it? The things we convince ourselves of when we're young.

I <u>was</u> young and stupid, and you tried to stop me from ruining my life, but I wouldn't listen. I never did, did I? And now Grace and I are stuck here. The world went on without *us, and it's my fault. It's my fault that when she looks out the window in the morning, everything she sees is barren, dirty, dry, and lonely. I wish she could see the mountains around Wisper. I wish she could play in the creek where you taught me to fish.*

Sometimes I sit here wondering if the earth has stopped spinning. We wouldn't know. We're stuck down here, and I think so much about what it would be like if I'd never left Wisper.

If I'd never left you.

I thought that I should tell you. I should explain why I left, but now it seems like a waste of breath. Would it even matter to you that I loved you with my whole heart? It was so big, you know? It scared me, and by then, my dad already had me believing I wasn't worth it.

I'm sure you have a wonderful life. I wonder if you're married or if you have kids of your own. I'll admit, just the thought makes me jealous. From the day I found out I was pregnant, I wished you were Grace's dad. That's pretty selfish of me, I know, but it's just a silly wish. Another dream that will never come true.

Anyway, I wanted you to know that you didn't do anything wrong. I left because I was wrong. I wasn't good enough. Not for you, for my family, and not even for myself.

I didn't always think that, but if the decisions I've made since I was seventeen have taught me anything, it's that I was right to leave you. It was the right thing to do because it gave you a chance to find something more. Someone more.

For a long time, I thought that person might be me, but I'm convinced now that I was wrong.

Besides, I've forgotten who I used to be. I hope someone remembers. I hope you do.

I miss you. Did I say that already?

I still love you, and I hope someday you can forgive me for letting you believe I didn't.

YOURS ALWAYS,
Frannie

MY HEAD WAS SPINNING. That was what Fran had meant when she said she wasn't good enough? I'd been so angry last night that maybe I hadn't heard what she was really saying. It wasn't about me at all, about my life not being big enough for her.

The letter looked old enough to have been written when Grace was little, so maybe seven or eight years ago, and Fran had kept it all this time?

Now I needed to see her again. I needed to tell her she was wrong. She was good enough. There was no one better, and I loved her. I always had and I always would.

I stood. "Okay," I said, and Billie looked up at me. "The rodeo avenue might lead somewhere. If we can't find a direct payout, Jillian might've paid him some other way, or maybe she had someone else pay him. I doubt she'd really buy Doug a horse, but you never know."

"Only in Wyoming," Billie said, clicking away on her laptop. "Wanna tell me what was in that letter?"

"No."

She twisted her lips in a pout. "Okay," she said, looking me over with one squinted eye. "So then maybe whatever's going on with Jillian and good ol' Dougie was started back in Texas. Did you confront her about what I told you, about why she was always lurking around after he'd hit Fran? I mean, maybe she just went to check on her sister—what kind of person wouldn't if her sister was being abused—but if that were the case, why wouldn't she help Fran? There's no evidence of Jillian ever doing anything to improve Fran and Grace's situation, which, with her considerable resources, you'd think there would be."

"No, I didn't bring it up. It wasn't the right time, but you were right that Jillian's behavior isn't normal, and she's not to be trusted. She was rude and, I dunno… weird when I was in Cheyenne, and I didn't even mention Doug Morris. And I'm pretty sure she's the reason her dad had no idea I'd be there. You were also right that she runs the show in that office. I don't think anything gets done without her say so."

"Okay, so where do we go from here?" Billie finally stopped typing and looked at me, waiting for me to give her somewhere new to go with her investigation.

Planting my hands on my hips, I took a deep breath. It was unusual for me not to have a clear direction when working a case, but the ball of anxiety in my gut and my emotions were muddying everything up.

"Carey, I know Fran means something to you. Grace does too. I can see it when you're around them. But don't let that get in the way of your instincts, because it's your instincts that have helped so many people. It's why this town, hell, this whole county, trusts you and depends on you—because you trust yourself. Don't stop now."

Closing my eyes, I released the breath and tried to focus. Images of Fran and Grace all alone down in Texas were blinding me from thinking straight, but I needed to figure this out for them. She hadn't left because she loved Doug Morris. She'd left because she loved *me*, and she believed she didn't deserve to be loved back.

She was wrong.

"You're right," I told Billie.

"I know," she said without hesitation, trying to lighten the mood.

"Okay. I want you to work on one thing: Jillian McKinnon. She's gotta have money somewhere if she's payin' Doug or buyin' him shit. Find it. I *know* she has somethin' to do with what's been goin' on around here with the farms and ranches. She's got other people doin' the dirty work for her, and it's startin' to be glaringly obvious that one of those idiots is Doug Morris. Look for friends, former co-workers. What are they up to? The answer's right there. I know it."

"What are you gonna do?"

"I'm gonna go pick up Doug Morris at his mommy's house."

CHAPTER TWENTY-ONE

FRANNIE

MANNY'S CAR was a lot nicer than mine.

Growing up, he had been like a community dad to all us Wisper kids, so I knew if I asked, he'd help me. Asking wasn't as hard as I'd thought it would be, and I felt a little silly that I'd insisted on going it alone for so long. That was what Wisper community was all about. How had I forgotten that?

I apologized for putting him in the position I had when I asked him for a gun. I couldn't do that to Grace any more than I could do it to myself, though the urge to shoot my "loving" husband was always there. Manny had been more than willing to let me borrow his car instead, and he also offered to beat the cuss out of Doug, but I declined that offer.

I would do this the right way, the legal way, and the non-violent way because that was what Grace deserved.

Besides, if Carey had to arrest me for murder after what I'd said to him last night, there was no way we'd ever come back from that.

The air conditioning stayed on the whole seven-hour drive to Cheyenne. I made it in six, and the radio even worked. Listening to music was a luxury I hadn't had while driving a car in years, not since my little Kia's AM/FM radio died, and I loved it. Manny had really good speakers, and I sang the whole way, scream-singing for two hours at least. I sang so loud for so long that my voice was threatening to disappear. The mainstream pop songs that came on the local channels as I drove through the high plains in the southeastern part of Wyoming weren't really my style—I was more of a country girl—but I didn't even care. I knew some of the words, and belting them out in the car was therapeutic.

It was like I was releasing the last thirteen years of the shit my life had become so I could make room for a better future for Grace and me.

And that future was going to start today, and I hoped with all my heart that it would include Carey.

I wasn't above begging for forgiveness.

I'd left Grace with Evvie and the Cades, and I'd written out a two-page instruction sheet about what she could and couldn't eat, how to administer her insulin injections, which Oly assured me she was comfortable giving, and the signs and symptoms to look out for in case Grace became hypoglycemic, and what to do if she did. They all promised me Doc Whitley was on speed dial, and that I could feel comfortable to go and do what I'd needed to do for years.

I trusted them, so I did.

And now, as I climbed the stairs to the statehouse in Cheyenne, I went over my list in my head. I was going to demand the truth from my father.

I wanted him to tell me what I had ever done that was so bad that he couldn't love Grace and me. I wanted him to tell me why he was holding us captive, dragging out my divorce and withholding the money my mama had left me. That money could set Grace and me up for years. I could go back to school to finally get my degree, maybe even start my own bakery, and Grace wouldn't have to live in fear. My mother wouldn't have wanted that. She would've wanted her only grandchild to feel free and happy.

I knew my father was behind all of it. I wasn't stupid. A divorce shouldn't have taken five years. Jilly had all but admitted it, and so had Doug when he mentioned it the other night. He didn't come right out and say it, but what he had said and the way he'd said it told me what I needed to know.

I had a legal right to the money my mama had left me. Brady had confirmed it, and he'd offered to help me get access to it, but I wanted to give my father a chance to do the right thing first. I guess maybe there was still a part of me that hoped he was redeemable. I doubted it, but I still wanted it to be true.

Shame for embarrassing my father had been stopping me this whole time, but I was an adult, a mother. It wasn't up to him what I did or didn't do with that money, so why had I allowed him to use it to control me all these years? I was going to demand that he admit to what he'd done and to give me what was left of the money, and then I was going straight back to Wisper, to Carey's office, to file a restraining order against Doug, because I trusted that, unlike Doug's cop buddies in Texas, Carey and his deputies would make sure it would stick. And if my father refused to relent and push my divorce paperwork through, then I would report him. I'd go to the goddamned governor herself if he didn't give me what I was owed. He had to be breaking laws to withhold my divorce petition. Brady had confirmed that too.

When I reached the top of the steps, I was still pumped up with confidence from my drive, but the heat was sweltering. Surely, a storm would be breaking through this wall of wet, hot misery sometime soon. It had been weeks since I felt like I could breathe.

I wanted to appear in control and strong, but the sweat making my hair wet, dripping down my spine, and wetting the back of my tank top wasn't helping with that illusion. The damp spot on the ass of my skirt probably wouldn't either, but it was no matter. I was here. I knew what I wanted to say, and by God, I was going to say it.

I wished Carey could see me now, and I was hit with a wave of regret that I'd pushed him away again, wanting to do this on my own. I wanted him to see his old Frannie make her comeback. Finally, I was doing something he could be proud of me for. Grace would be proud of me too.

But I had to do this by myself and for myself, and no one could stop me.

Except they did.

As soon as I walked into the cavernous state building with its dark wood staircases and black-and-white tiled floors, two men approached. They were dressed in plain clothes, but there was a holstered gun on one of the men's hips. It was too hot for jackets, so the gun was just hanging there for all the world to see. Did they allow weapons inside the statehouse? I wasn't sure, but this guy had one. One of the men rested his hand on the back of my arm, and I looked up into his eyes.

Quietly, he said, "Mrs. Morris, I apologize for this, but we need you to come with us. Quickly, please."

Oh no. No man was going to stop me today. Nuh uh. "I'm sorry, gentlemen. I have no idea what this is about, but there's somethin' I need to do."

Unfortunately, they were twice my size and loaded with muscles. It was infuriating, knowing no matter how determined I was, they could stop me. I vowed right then and there to take a self-defense class as soon as I could afford it. Or maybe Manny could teach me. He was ex-military and a total badass. I bet he had some moves.

"Not right now, there isn't," the other man said, and they steered me to a door at the back of the first floor.

I'd dressed up a little, hoping to appear polished. Most of my clothes were secondhand, but I refused to wear anything Jilly had sent me because my father wanted to control how I dressed, so now, my too-big dress shoes clacked against the tile, making a loud echoing noise throughout the hall, and even my feet were sweating.

Nerves were fluttering throughout my body, like anxious hummingbirds, flitting around in there, poking my stomach with their beaks, threatening to make me throw up. What were these guys, like men in black? And how did they know who I was? Did my father hate me so much that he wouldn't even allow me to walk into his office building? It was a public building, for pete's sake, the seat of the Wyoming legislature. Surely, I had every right to be there, just like every other citizen of the state, but the voice in the back of my mind was trying to make me believe that I *didn't* have that right. I was a failure. A dropout. A shitty mom and a man's punching bag and doormat. I'd made so many mistakes. Maybe I didn't deserve what everyone else did.

Looking around at all the lawyers and politicians loitering in the building, that insecurity grew. They all had their lives together. They knew what they wanted, and they knew how to get it. I didn't. At least, for the last thirteen years I hadn't.

But at the same time, a power was growing inside me. I recognized it. It was me, the real me, and she was growing stronger every minute. She might need a little time to get her bearings, but the old Francesca McKinnon was back for good.

One man opened the door, and they led me through it, and when the other closed it behind me, a new man spoke. He was tall, skinny, and pale, with dark, scraggly hair and a thin nose and even thinner chin. It was pointed, and it reminded me of a cartoon character from one of the shows Grace used to watch on PBS. The only thing missing was a handlebar mustache and an evil laugh.

"Francesca Morris?"

I mustered up all the courage I could and stood tall. "Yeah? What's goin' on? Where's my father? I need to speak to him right now."

"Never mind that," pointy-chin man said. "Have a seat." He motioned to a lone wooden chair in a corner, but I didn't move a muscle, and he wasn't looking at me. Instead, he was focused on the stack of papers in his hand.

"I'll stand, thank you. And you can tell my father that I'm not leavin' till I say my peace."

Revealing herself, the governor stepped around this man. "Agent Jeffries, I think an explanation might help Mrs. Morris cooperate."

Whoa. Okay, maybe they were men in black. It registered, though, somewhere in my mind, that it was convenient for her to be there in case my father refused my demands. I wasn't kidding. I'd report his ass.

"Governor Buchanan? What's goin' on here?" I blinked at least ten times, trying to reconcile the scene in front of me. Granted, I'd never been in the state building or my father's office within it before, but I was pretty sure this wasn't what it usually looked like.

Scanning the poorly lit room, I finally noticed that there were several people in it besides Agent Jefferies, the men in black, the governor, and me. There were two long tables, and seated along each one was half a dozen women and men dressed in business clothing, working on computers with headphones over their ears. There was a map and various papers covering one wall, and a bank of desktop computers lining another, cords and wires running everywhere, covering the floor like vines. It was intimidating and a little scary.

"Look, I just want to talk to my father. It'll only take a minute. I can see y'all are busy, but I'm sorry, I'm not leav—"

Governor Buchanan interrupted me, "When was the last time you spoke to your father?"

I couldn't understand what I was seeing. It was like some bad undercover cop TV show, and now I knew—felt in my gut—that my father was up to no good. I'd guessed at it before, but it had to be why these people were all here, why they were staking out my father's office.

"Francesca?" the governor asked, bringing my attention back to her and Agent Jeffries.

"I'm sorry. What was the question?"

"Come on. Let's sit down and I'll explain."

When we were seated at the far end of one table, the governor right next to me with her chair angled toward mine, someone offered me a cup of hot coffee, which was absurd since it was a thousand degrees outside, but I guessed that was probably normal for all these super-professional types.

"No, thank you," I said, waving them away, and then I stared at the governor, waiting for her or someone, anyone, to start talking.

She smiled politely. "Your father and sister are… under investigation. What you have—quite untimely, I might add—walked in on is a sort of sting operation. These FBI agents have been investigating a string of crimes they believe your family to be mixed up in. So you see, we can't allow you to barge into your father's office right now because we're currently trying to ascertain what he's doing. The problem is, we haven't seen him yet today. Your sister is upstairs in her office, but your father hasn't shown up for work, which is odd. So can you tell us when the last time you spoke to him was?"

"Uh…" I moved my head from side to side. Maybe the weird words she'd just said would fall out if I shook it hard enough. The FBI? Investigation? I'd suspected my father of being untrustworthy for a long time, since the day I caught him with his slimy tongue down the throat of a woman who was not my mother, but Jilly? Were they saying my sister had done something wrong?

I couldn't believe that. Sure, she was ambitious, but Jilly was honest. Wasn't she?

"Do you remember what you talked about?"

"I-I…" Wait. The last time I'd seen my father was at the diner weeks ago. "The same time you saw him. In Wisper at José's Diner. Remember? You were there."

"I've spoken to him since then, but that was the day the FBI informed me of the situation, and they urged me to accept his request for the meeting. They were listening to our conversation."

"Wait, if y'all are trackin' him"—I looked around at all the computers again with their silent operators who kept peeking at me—"then wouldn't you know when I last saw him?"

Agent Jeffries sighed. "It's not like it's portrayed in the movies, Mrs. Morris. Yes, we're investigating your father, but there are other players involved, and we have to spread our resources to cover all of them. Like your sister. When did you last speak to her?"

"Jilly? I dunno. Last week? I think. But you can't mean that Jill had anything to do with whatever my father's mixed up in. He's the one you want, right?" He was the jerk. The lying, cheating, worthless father who'd basically disowned his own daughter and granddaughter.

"Actually, no. Your father is a secondary target in this investigation," Agent Jeffries said. "It's your sister we need. And since you're here, you can help us. You could get closer to her than we—"

The door flew open, and my father stormed in with his own man in black. They both stopped when they saw me, and the room went still.

"Jesus Christ." Jeffries tossed the papers in his hands into the air and they floated to the floor in a silent flurry, and then he turned to stare down each of his employees, one by one. "No one had eyes on the damn door?"

"What is this?" my father demanded of the room at large, but his eyes stayed on me. "Francesca, what are you doing here? How did you get here?"

"Uh, nice to see you, too, *Daddy*. I drove here."

My father whipped his head to glare at his... well, whatever the guy was. Whoever he was, he was built like an ogre, and his deep, furrowed brow was a little disconcerting.

The man shrank back a little at my father's accusing stare. "My guy said her car's still parked in front of her house. He sent pictures, I swear."

Huh? How would he know that?

"You are utterly incompetent," my father said to the man, and then he turned back to me. "I need to speak to my daughter. Give us the room." He'd always acted like he was in charge, whether he was or not, and I hated that about him.

Jeffries stuttered, but my father shut him down. "Yes, yes, I know. You've been investigating my office. My daughter, Jillian, in particular. I will cooperate to the fullest, but first, I *need* to speak to Francesca."

Jeffries's head fell forward, and he let out the biggest sigh of frustration I'd ever heard. "I hate this fucking job."

"Governor, I apologize, I'm sure you're quite ready for me to explain, and I will, but—"

"You can talk to your daughter, SA McKinnon," Jeffries allowed, "but I'm not leaving this room. And your man"—he nodded to my father's security man—"can wait outside."

"Fine."

The men in black escorted the ogre out to the hall, and then one returned to pat my father down. When he was satisfied my father didn't have any weapons, he stepped back against a wall, crossed his arms over his chest, and became a statue, and my father pulled a chair out at the table and sat next to me.

"Is Grace safe?" he asked, and I could've sworn there was urgency in his voice.

"What? Why would you ask that, and why do you care?"

"Francesca. Please."

"She's safe. She's with my friends."

"Are you certain? Obviously, my PI is worthless if you could make it all the way to Cheyenne without him noticing."

"I-I… Why?"

"Can you check?"

He was making me panic. Did he know something I didn't? Of course he did. Everyone did.

I pulled my phone from my purse and called Evvie, but she assured me over and over that Grace was fine. She was happy, playing with the kids. There hadn't been any trouble at the ranch. I knew my daughter was in good hands.

"Everything's okay," Evvie said again.

"Thank you. I have to go, but I'll call back as soon as I'm done here," I said, and I hung up.

"Grace is safe," I repeated.

My father sighed, his whole body slumping forward. "Thank God."

Jeffries tried to chime in. "Do you know something that we d—"

My father interrupted him, but he wouldn't take his eyes off mine. "I think if you look closely, sir, you'll see that the woman in Jillian's office who is dressed like her is, in fact, not Jillian. It's her assistant. I just received a phone call from Jillian, and she has fled." He held his phone out toward Jeffries, and Jeffries took it, clicking it on and swiping furiously.

"What?" I was dumbfounded. Jill ran away? To where?

A slew of curses fell from Jeffries's mouth, and he called several of his people back into the room. They got to work, their fingers flying across their keyboards, but my father took my hands in his and the whole room faded away—like at the beginning of an episode of *The Twilight Zone*.

CHAPTER TWENTY-TWO

FRANNIE

MY FATHER HADN'T TOUCHED me on purpose since I was probably fifteen years old, so it felt weird. The look on his face now was softening, almost apologetic, and I was more than a little confused.

"Your sister knows that she's under investigation. She discovered it this morning, and she has quite literally freaked out. It's my fault."

"How is it your fault?" Jeffries demanded.

"Francesca, I am so sorry."

My eyebrows hit the roof. "For…?"

"I was demanding the truth from her, and I guess she figured it out. She wanted to know how I'd found out about your marriage, what's been happening to you and Grace. Francesca, I didn't know. I swear. Jillian kept it from me. She kept *a lot* of things from me. I was aware that she was… doing dishonest things. I've known that for a while now. I allowed her to run my life, and in doing so, I've opened myself up to a world of trouble. But I swear to you, I had no idea what you'd been going through."

"But-but when we saw you... You're always so angry with Grace and me."

"Not angry, I was... sad, disappointed maybe. But the last time we saw each other, I was worried about you. I saw the bruise. I didn't know what to make of it."

My head snapped back like I'd been slapped. "Okay, let's say I believe you." I laughed out loud, the sound like a weird ringing in my ears. "I mean, never mind that all you had to do was *look at me* to know, but then again, I s'pose you weren't lookin', were you? But what's all this got to do with me or Grace right now? What does Jilly bein' under investigation have to do with me?"

"So much, and I don't know where to start."

"At the beginning," I offered. "That would be nice."

My father inhaled deeply and sat up straight. "When you left home, I was so angry with you. I couldn't accept that you would throw your life away like that."

"Not really feelin' an apology in any of this."

"You were such a vibrant young woman, but you were so stubborn. Then you married that... *man*. I was irate. I wanted to disown you. I suppose I did, and then I did what I'd always done. I focused on my career, and I chose to cut you out of my life. There are no words that could convey how much I regret that decision, but all I can offer you is that I'm sorry. I was wrong. I know that now."

He reached his hand toward my face, and I flinched back. "How dare you? You think some lame apology can make up for what you put Grace and me through?" I scoffed. "It can't. Let's just get that straight. And if you were so sorry, why is this the first I'm hearin' of it?"

"I was angry for a long time. It took your mother dying for me to see how wrong I'd been. But by then, Jillian had come to work for me, and I was too much of a coward to face you myself. I sent her, and that was the decision that has caused this whole mess. And Jillian has spent the last five years convincing me that you hated me and were actively trying to hurt me or embarrass me."

I didn't believe that, but there were more important things at the moment. "I'm surprised you even remember Mama. You treated her worse than you treated me."

"That's not untrue, and it's something I'll have to live with for the rest of my life."

"Good," I said. I crossed my arms. "But none of this explains the FBI or why Jillian is in so much trouble."

"Oh, Francesca, you ran away from home to escape me, but Jillian, she ran toward me. She became indispensable to me. But the whole time I thought I was working and bonding with my daughter, she was using my position to get us further and, I suspect, to make herself wealthy. She has lied, cheated, stolen, blackmailed, and schemed, and I am so ashamed that all I've done is sat here, watching her do it."

"Jilly?" I looked at Jeffries, and he confirmed it all with a nod. To the guy's credit, he actually looked like he felt a little sorry for me. The governor was still next to me, but she was silent. Everyone was silent, watching this moment between my father and me, like we were a matinee movie.

"I... I just don't understand. Why? Why would she do that?"

"That's my fault too," my father said. "My behavior when you were teenagers has impacted both your lives. Jill thought she had to prove her worth to me, and I suppose, over the years, she became obsessed with it, always working some angle to make me need her more, love her more.

"I've been doing a little investigating on my own lately. I had a meeting with a Senator friend of mine recently, and something he said to me raised an alarm in my mind about

Jillian. I hired someone to look into it and to keep an eye on you and Grace because I found that Jill was involved in some kind of land grab in and around Wisper. I'm ashamed of all the things she got away with right under my nose. But the thing I will regret until the day I die is that I allowed her to affect my relationship with you."

My father hung his head. "The money I was sending you ended up in Jill's hands, for the most part. I believe she was stringing you along with small amounts, but not the amounts I had intended. I trusted her to take care of you and Grace, and I was wrong to do so. And I found paperwork in her office pertaining to your divorce. It seems Jillian has been delaying it. I suspect it has something to do with whatever she's involved with in Wisper. She's pulled Douglas into it too. That's why I wanted to make sure Grace was safe. Jillian mentioned Grace when I spoke with her earlier, and I was worried she might do something drastic." He looked up, right into my eyes, and his next words were like a plea. He was hoping I'd feel some compassion for him. "I was there when Grace was born, in the hospital in Texas. I saw her. I held her when you were asleep.

"I knew that I should've been speaking with you directly, but by the time I… got over myself, I was so ashamed of how I'd acted, and I couldn't face you. And I didn't know if Jillian had involved you in her mess. For what it's worth, since I found out what she's been doing, I've been trying to protect you by continuing to keep my distance. I couldn't be sure that she or Douglas hadn't involved you somehow."

Shaking my head, I jumped out of my chair, wondering if I was somehow asleep and didn't know it. I knocked into the governor, and she steadied me with a gentle hand on the small of my back. "Mama left that money to me! You shouldn't have had any control over it at all. And if you loved your granddaughter so much, how could you allow her to live like that? If you were there, you had to have seen how bad it was for me, even then. You didn't notice the bruise across my face when you spied on me in the maternity ward? He hit me when I was nine months pregnant with his child. Did you know Grace almost died twice because of that man? And you did nothin'!"

Every single person in the room was holding their breath. No one moved or spoke, and my father was shaking his head furiously. "No, Francesca. I didn't know. The nurses told me you'd fallen, that you were clumsy because of the pregnancy. I believed it—maybe I wanted to believe it—but Jillian hid everything from me. She hid the police reports, the divorce, the… the medical reports. I didn't know. I swear I didn't. Not until Carey Michaels called me a few days ago. That was when I finally accepted that my daughter was doing the awful things I knew people were whispering behind our backs, and that was when I knew what you'd been going through."

I backed away from him. "So that's your excuse? That you were too weak to admit the truth? That you were too much of a coward to admit what you'd done, so you let your other child handle it for you, and 'oops, so sorry, she mucked that up'?

"I ruined my life because of you. I failed so many times trying to live up to your impossible standards. Nothin' I ever did was good enough for you. Don't you get that? Why do you think I ran off? Did you think I was that stupid? Did you really think I loved that man?" I laughed, but it came out sounding strangled. "No, you didn't think about it at all, did you? So, here's the truth. I ran away from you because all you ever did was make me feel worthless and useless.

"Well, ol' man, the joke's on you, 'cause if I hadn't left, I wouldn't have had Grace, and she's made me see that you were wrong. I'm a good person. I'm a great mother, and now that I don't believe your bullshit anymore, I'm gonna be strong. I don't care if you think my dreams are stupid. They're mine, and I'm gonna make 'em all come true. I don't need your approval. I never did. *We* never did."

I turned to Jeffries, trying so hard not to cry, but the tears were welling up in my eyes anyway while my father called my name over and over, trying to explain himself, but I didn't want to hear any more. "I want out of this room right now. If you don't let me out, I will scream so fucking loud that every media outlet in the state of Wyoming will hear me, and I won't stop until yours, my father's, and my sister's faces are plastered across the nightly news, and your investigation will be ruined."

Jeffries nodded and led me to the door himself.

Unfettered rage was making me shake from head to toe. I could barely control my body, and it took all of my concentration to walk the ten feet to the door. When I got there, Jeffries opened it, and I walked out.

I didn't look back. I didn't wonder what would happen to my father or my sister. I didn't care.

I just wanted to go home to hold my daughter.

All the pain and the shame I'd felt for disappointing my father had been a lie. I was never the disappointment. They were. It was all a lie.

Our entire life had been a lie for so long, and I was done with both of them.

There were still so many questions, most having to do with Jill, but in the moment, none of it mattered.

The governor and her team of men followed after me, but I made it back to Manny's car just as they caught up, and when I opened the door to get in, she held it, not letting me pull it closed until I looked at her.

"What!"

"I just wanted to let you know that the FBI will continue to investigate. Your friend, Sheriff Michaels, is arresting your husband, probably as we speak, back in Wisper. I spoke to him myself. And Mrs. Morris?"

"Stop callin' me that. I'm *not* that man's wife anymore. My name is Frannie McKinnon."

"Frannie," she said softly, "I will personally walk your divorce petition to the appropriate judge and wait in front of him or her until they sign it. I promise you that."

The breath rushed out of me, and I sobbed. I couldn't stop it.

Just like that, it was over. The relief I felt was indescribable. It was big and it descended down on my body like a drug. Doug had no right to be in my life anymore. If he fought for custody, which he never would 'cause he couldn't care less about Grace, but if he did, from the look in her eye, I'd bet Governor Buchanan would support me. Maybe she'd even help me somehow. Her men all looked uncomfortable as I blubbered, my eyes becoming swollen and snot leaking out of my nose, looking all around. I was looking for...

I needed him.

I needed Carey.

CHAPTER TWENTY-THREE

CAREY

GOVERNOR BUCHANAN CALLED to fill me in and asked me to personally go after Doug Morris, which I had already been planning to do after I'd checked on Grace, and the governor said she was expecting a report on his arrest right away. When I spoke to her, she told me Fran was okay and on her way back to Wisper, but that she was pretty upset. After learning about all the messed-up stuff her sister had been up to and her betrayal, I didn't doubt it, but I resisted the urge to commandeer a helicopter to go get her. I knew she needed time to deal with the information, and I knew she'd need to come to terms with it on her own.

She was struggling with herself, trying to find herself again, but she wasn't a damsel in distress, even though I wanted to carry her on my shoulders and protect her for the rest of time.

Besides, I had official county and state business to attend to and, I suspected, there might be a few federal charges thrown in there when the FBI got ahold of Doug Morris.

Plus, I wanted to be the guy to bring down that worthless,

abusive, neglectful piece of shit. For Frannie and Gracie, but I wanted it for me too. Badly.

When we arrived at his mama's house, good ol' Dougie was holed up in his little-boy fort, just like Vern had said, dressed in dirty khaki shorts, a Miller Lite T-shirt, and what looked to be women's running shoes that were too small for his feet. He had a shotgun, but he didn't have the balls to shoot me, though he threatened to.

"Don't come any closer," he warned, his gun waving like a flag in the wind in one hand while he climbed out of his ridiculous hiding place on his knees. When he stood, he pointed the gun at me, but his aim was a little off 'cause his hands were shaking.

"Or what?" I couldn't help laughing. "You gonna shoot the air five feet away from me? 'Cause that's where you're aimin' your gun. Drop it, Doug. You're not as tough as you wanna believe, and I'm wearin' a bulletproof vest. Are you?" He lowered his gun, but I didn't lower mine, and I stepped forward. "You're under arrest, and if you try to run, you won't get far. Deputies Lee and Sims have my position covered, and the state police are on their way. FBI too. We know you've been workin' with Jillian McKinnon. You're up to your elbows in charges. The governor of Wyoming is involved now. There's no gettin' outta this."

He looked around, searching the woods to see if I was telling the truth, and when his eyes landed back on me, gun still out and aimed at his chest, and my eyes murdering him but my heartbeat slow and steady, he tried to run, but he didn't get far.

Finding an old length of rope by his fort next to a pink children's backpack, I holstered my weapon and picked it up, then circled it round my head the way I'd learned to rope a horse working all those summers at the ranch, and I lassoed that motherfucker on my first try. He hit the ground face first, and I rushed forward and climbed over him, letting the weight of my legs hold him down. He was bigger than me by an inch or two, and he had twenty pounds on me at least, but my satisfaction was heavier.

"Is that backpack meant for Grace, Doug?" Searching behind my shoulder for Abey, when I caught a quick glimpse of her, I nodded toward the backpack, and she approached from behind a tree fifty yards away. "Abey, look in the bag. What's in it?"

After holstering her gun, she lifted the backpack and looked inside. "There's a sealed package of needles in here, three children's shirts, a pair of shorts, and… a banana? You're not a very efficient packer, Mr. Morris," she said, and she snorted.

Leaning down close, I pinned Doug's arms to the ground with my knees and spoke right next to his ear. His nose was gushing blood. "You were gonna try and kidnap your kid, weren't you? Thought you could use her to leverage yourself right outta trouble. Bet you thought the SA would trade his granddaughter for your freedom. The needles were for Grace's insulin, weren't they? But, Doug, you know you need the actual insulin too. Where were you gonna get that?"

He struggled against me, but I dug my knees into his sides while I brought his arms behind his back and pulled at the set of handcuffs Velcroed to my vest. When they detached, I snapped the cuffs on him and yanked them into place. "You'll *never* touch her again. Either of them. And what's more, you'll come to realize not havin' Frannie and Gracie in your life is a loss, the biggest fuckin' loss you'll ever know, but lucky for them, the feelin' won't be mutual.

"No one will care that you're gone, Doug. No one will miss you, and their lives will be so good without you.

Because you're not there. However many years you spend in jail won't be your punishment. Losin' Frannie and Gracie will be the death of you, and you don't even know it. It might be slow. Might take twenty years for you to realize what you've done, but it'll come to you. And when it does, it's gonna hurt so goddamn bad, you'll wanna die.

"It ain't gonna mean shit to you now, but someday down the road, you're gonna wake up. All the stupid things you've done are gonna come rushin' at you like a runaway train, and when that happens, I want you to remember this: What you gave up is mine. The life you gave up is mine. *They* were always mine, and you been layin' hands on what's mine for far too long. I will not forget that.

"And now, I get their love. I get those looks from my woman in the mornin's, those looks full of trust, friendship, lust, and forever." I laughed low and close to his ear. I could feel the heat from it on my lip, and normally, being this close to the douchebag would've made me gag, but this time, it made me happy 'cause I knew he'd hear every single word coming out of my mouth next.

"But the thing that will hurt the most, the thing that will make you cry yourself to sleep like a baby every night for the rest of your pathetic life is this: When Gracie's sad and she cries, it'll be *me* she hugs, not you. I'll be there for everything. When she laughs, when she's nervous, when she dreams—she'll share it all with me 'cause I love her and 'cause she already knows I won't *ever* let her down. She'll forget you exist"—he pulled at the cuffs, testing their strength, and he winced when they pinched his wrists, and I was glad it hurt— "and it won't even cross her mind to call you or write to tell you about her life 'cause lettin' her down's all you've ever known how to do."

I climbed off him, and Frank appeared, reaching down to

help me lift the asshole, but I held my hand up, signaling to Frank that I wanted to do it on my own. I gripped the handcuffs and pulled, but anger was making my hands shake, and Doug cried out in pain. I wanted to keep pulling till his arms detached from his body and he bled to death, but Frank stepped around me and lifted Doug the proper way. He knew I wouldn't want to risk giving him some loophole he could exploit or use to get out of the mess he'd made, which meant I needed to accept Frank's help so the rage I was feeling didn't cause me to make a mistake.

When he was standing in front of me with a smirk on his cocky face and my deputy's big hand around the back of his neck, Doug only had one thing to say. "You're the one who's gonna be sorry. You think that bitch is worth that big ol' speech you just gave, but she ain't. You can have her. All she does is talk back anyway. And the kid's nothin' but a pain in my ass. Have fun payin' for her medical shit."

"I knew you were stupid, Doug, but someday you'll realize that Frannie talkin' back is the best thing about her, and you just gave it away for free. And takin' care of Gracie will be my honor, whatever she needs."

I laughed at him, and he spat in my face, but I'd dealt with the idiot too many times not to expect it, so I scooped his nastiness off my chin with a sterile container I'd put in my pocket for just such an occasion and sealed it with its cap.

"Thanks for the DNA, Doug. I gotta say, I wasn't expectin' you to be so cooperative. And now we can connect you to the crimes committed out at Carl Aberforth's ranch. Those won't get you a life sentence, but I'm guessin' Carl's ain't the only place we're gonna find your DNA, a stray hair, or some of your blood. Don't you worry, I got all the time in the world, and you know everybody in town's gonna be talkin' about you, so they'll all call me to report any crimes you've committed against 'em. I think you know how much I love my job, so it'll be my pleasure to attend to all those calls."

"Load him up," I told Frank, and he yanked Doug toward Abey's cruiser.

Abey was almost excited at the prospect of such a big to-do going down in our county, and I watched her Mirandize him and stuff him into the back of her cruiser. When he was locked in, she hopped up and down a few times, turned, and saluted me, then drove off with a pissed-off Dumbass Doug Morris glaring at me out the back passenger-side window. She made sure to blare her siren all the way through town so there wouldn't be one resident of Wisper who didn't know Doug was on his way probably to federal prison.

All the farmers and ranchers who were being targeted had one particular thing in common: They had all hired Doug as a day worker, just like I'd thought, and I suspected he was behind the fires, the busted fences, the dead animals, and all kinds of other cruel crimes. Carl Aberforth didn't hire ranch hands, preferring to do the work himself so he didn't have to pay anybody, so Doug had no choice but to break into his barn, though what he thought he was accomplishing by stealing a tent was lost on me. But then again, no one had ever accused Doug of being a genius.

He'd been doing Jillian McKinnon's bidding because she'd promised him money. In fact, there was an envelope stuffed full of five-thousand big ones in the backpack, which I logged as evidence of a payoff.

They'd been working together for years, which was why Jillian had gone down so often to "visit" her sister in Texas. She hadn't cared at all about the abuse Grace and Fran had been subjected to. She only went there to make certain her arrangement was still intact and that Doug wasn't going back on his word. The feds were already looking into it. Looked like she'd been up to the same shady shit down near El Paso. That was where it had all started.

Doug had a list of contacts on his phone, and Jillian and her secretary's numbers were on that list, along with someone named Anna Maldonado, who, after some quick back-hacking, Billie told me was a woman who'd gone to college with Jillian. She was the dark-haired lady who'd been driving around my county, trying to talk everyone into selling their land and lifeblood. The feds were already onto her, and she was later found and arrested in Grand Junction, Colorado.

Apparently, she and Jillian had been on the take for several years. Jillian had used some of her schemes to further her dad's career, sure, but at some point, she'd decided to use them to get rich.

She and Ms. Maldonado had all kinds of money tied up in illegal businesses and properties from the Pacific Ocean to the Mississippi River. They were all in Maldonado's name, of course, and the two women had kept a proper distance from one another, which was why Billie had a hard time finding them and why Maldonado was currently in handcuffs, but Jillian was tied to her like a noose once investigators knew where to look, so she ran, and the FBI was on her like a dog with a bone.

This thing was so far out of my jurisdiction, so after Doug was booked and locked up, and after I brushed my teeth and scrubbed my face clean in the restroom at the station, I made my report while I waited for Frannie to get home.

WHEN SHE GOT to my office after checking on Grace out at the ranch, Frannie came right for me. She dropped her purse on the floor, kicked off her shoes, and climbed over me in my desk chair.

"I love you," she said. "I've loved you from the day you moved into the house next to mine, and nothin's gonna stop me anymore from lovin' you till the day we die."

"Oh yeah? Well, that's good news 'cause I love you too."

"Will you tell me why? I've treated you so badly. I left you. I denied you. I want you to love me, but how can you?"

"When the universe hands you back the key to everything you've ever wanted, you don't ignore it. It sucked waitin' for you to come back to me, but I did 'cause the light in your eyes right now, the way you fight so hard for people who can't fight for themselves, and the sound of your laugh have me hooked. I knew it the minute I heard it, when I saw you, dirty and barefoot on the side of your house when we were twelve."

I reached my head forward to kiss her nose. "You were made for me, my Frannie."

"I'm a different person now, you know that, right?"

"How are you different?"

She scoffed. "I've been hidin' for so long. The real me disappeared."

"Maybe she had to do that to survive," I said. "And she ain't hidin' anymore." The biggest smile erupted on my face. "It's good to have you back, my Frannie. Man, I missed you."

She smiled, too, and it lit up her eyes, and I couldn't stop myself from kissing her. "I missed me too," she mumbled against my lips. "I'm sorry for what I said last night."

Wrapping my arms around her, I pushed into my knees and stood. "C'mon. We got a lot to talk about."

"Where we goin'?" she asked while I carried her out past Abey at the receptionist's desk.

"Later, boss," Abey said with a smirk and a wink.

The smile on my face, like the cat who ate the canary, had her laughing at me, then I kicked open the front door and carried Frannie into the sunshine. "We need somewhere private. I was thinkin' my house. Maybe you can decide what color you wanna paint the bedroom."

"Carey, don't joke."

"I ain't jokin'. I want you with me, Frannie. Forever. You and Gracie. We're gonna have the life we always shoulda had. And not 'cause I feel sorry for you, but because it's what we deserve."

She locked her legs behind my back. "That sounds really good."

"Alright then, I need to make love to you—not sittin' up or against a wall," I said, and she blushed, her millions of freckles quickly disappearing under her red cheeks while she scanned Main Street in case anybody was watching us. They were. C'mon, this was Wisper. "We need to talk, and then we can go get Gracie and take her home."

"Deal," she said, and she kissed me.

LOOKING UP AT THE CEILING, Fran said, "I can't believe Grace gave you that letter."

When Fran called her, Evvie said she'd bring Grace to my house in the morning—Finn and the kids had turned Evvie's living room into a fairy house using couch cushions and sheets strung up everywhere, complete with twinkle lights—so we had hours, just me and Frannie. We'd been talking and exploring each other. Well, we'd done other things too. My old Serta Sleeper had never seen so much action, but I was just happy to have Frannie back in my arms for good.

"Why didn't *you* give it to me?"

A little abashed, she said, "I dunno. I was afraid to, I guess."

"Afraid of what?"

"Scared that maybe you wouldn't feel the same... or, worse, that you would. I was terrified of the person I'd turned into. And ashamed. What if you were ashamed of me too? I couldn't have handled that." She closed her eyes. "I have a whole notebook full of letters I wrote you."

"Really?"

"Yeah."

"Will you let me read 'em?"

She squealed and giggled when I wrapped my hands around her hips. They were warm, and I wanted to flex my fingers and pull her to me, but she squirmed away. "No! They're embarrassin'."

"After all the things we've done in this bedroom, a few words are gonna embarrass you?"

"Yeah. 'Cause those words are my heart on a page."

"Well, good then, 'cause I wanna know all of you. Every body part, heart included."

She smiled shyly but closed her eyes again. "How could I not know Jillian was involved with Doug? That just doesn't sit right with me. She came to Texas every time we had a fight, and I thought it was to check on me, to make sure Grace and I were okay, but now I think she came to make sure Doug was still willin' to do whatever she wanted. She was afraid I'd make him angry and he'd stop helpin' her."

"I think you're right," I said, and I moved over her naked body, kissing her breasts and her ribs, one by one, on my way lower. Goosebumps rose all over her, and I smoothed them away from her thighs with my fingertips.

"Maybe I shouldn't say this to you, you know, considerin' you're the sheriff and all," she said, tangling her fingers in my hair, "but I'm so mad at her. If she were standin' in front of me, I'd kill her."

"No, you wouldn't. You're better than that."

"Fine, maybe I wouldn't, but not because she doesn't deserve it."

Crawling between her legs, I spread them wide, trailing my fingers between them, and she sighed.

"The FBI will find her, and she'll go to prison. Sounds like she was into some pretty serious stuff. She tried to black-mail Governor Buchanan. That's how this whole thing got started."

"God, I just can't reconcile this criminal Jillian with my little sister Jilly. Who is she? Why did she do all those things?"

"I dunno, Frannie," I said, and I lowered my head. My lips were an inch away from heaven, and I breathed her in.

"Carey, I've been sweatin' all day," she complained, and when I spread her wet lips apart with my fingers, she wiggled a little.

"You smell good." I growled like a caveman and licked a path from her entrance all the way to her clit, swallowing and savoring the taste of her on my tongue.

Her back arched off the bed, and she gasped. Her fingers tightened in my hair when I pressed the tip of my tongue to the little nub, and I flicked it, pushing two fingers inside her. Driving her wild with my fingers slowly, I watched her. Her eyes were closed while she undulated her hips on the bed, seeking more pressure, seeking release, and I wanted to give it to her, but I couldn't stop watching her.

I'd waited so long for this. It had been my wish since I was probably fifteen years old, maybe longer.

So then, maybe dreams did come true.

Her messy red waves were spread across my pillow, her

skin wet with sweat, and I pressed my mouth to her hip to taste her again, but I was overwhelmed, and I stayed there, breathing her in.

"Don't stop," she begged, and she opened her eyes to watch me, too, when I stilled. "Carey, what's wrong?"

"Nothin's wrong," I said, and she brushed her fingers over the worry lines on my forehead. "It's just that I've wanted this for so long, and I can't believe I get to have you like this." I paused, removing my hands from her body, and she sat up.

"You look so serious right now. Please tell me what you're thinkin'."

"I will never hurt you, Frannie. I'll never hurt Gracie. I won't ever cause you pain."

"You can't promise that, Carey. Life will happen, and sometimes it'll hurt, but I know I can get through anything if I have you and Grace. And I know you'll always be there to see us through it."

"Damn straight I will," I promised. "And if I don't, you can ask Abey to throw me in jail. She'll be glad to do it."

"Deal," she said again, and she pulled me down on top of her. "Now, show me what I've been missin' all this time. Make love to me again, and don't stop till I'm screamin' your name."

Chuckling, I did just that. Spreading her legs wider, I pushed into her body as far as I could, and we both moaned. It felt like coming home, and I couldn't figure how I'd lived so long without her.

HOURS LATER, after we were spent and stupid from making love to each other in all the ways we'd both dreamed about, I pulled on a pair of sweats and dressed Fran in one of my T-shirts and a pair of my boxers and dragged her to my kitchen. I wanted to feed her, but she took over omelet-making duties when I couldn't stop staring at the side of her face while she washed my dirty dishes at the sink, and I burned the eggs.

Standing behind her, I was growing hard again, and I kissed the back of her neck, watching the dull, stormy light from the window make shadows across her skin, when my front door was thrown open.

I pulled a t-shirt over my head when I heard Evvie yell, "Grace, wait! Shoot. Please, God, let them have clothes on," and then Grace appeared in my kitchen doorway. She stopped running when she saw her mama and me by the stove pressed together, and she pumped her fist in the air. "Yes!"

"I'm so sorry," Evvie said, appearing in the doorway, too, completely out of breath. "I parked the truck out front, and she took off like a bandit. I tried to stop her."

"It's okay." Frannie laughed and held her arm out for Grace, and Grace walked over, tucked herself against Fran, and looked up at me. She smiled so big, and she wrapped her arms around us both and buried her head between us to hide it.

Mumbling against my side, she said, "I don't wanna catch actual fish, but will you take me fishin'? Foam is home, right?"

"Foam is what?" Fran said, looking back and forth between Grace and me, her face confused, and she looked a little bit grossed out.

"Nothin'," I said, smiling down at Grace. "That's a fisherman's secret only me and Gracie can know."

"Fisher*person*," Grace said, "and I get to pick out the bows."

"Bows?"

"Yeah, those pink and yellow frilly things you tie on the ribbon to catch the fish."

"Child, we do not use *bows and ribbons* to catch fish. Those are flies and lines. That's your first fishin' lesson," I said, and I lifted her into my arms. "And you can choose whichever flies you want." Kissing her cheek, I carried her to my old childhood bedroom to show her where she'd be sleeping from now on.

Frannie said it was a little possessive that I wanted them to move in so quickly and probably technically too soon, but she'd smiled when she said it and kissed me.

So it was settled. I was never letting either of my girls out of my sight again.

CHAPTER TWENTY-FOUR

FRANNIE

A WEEK OF BLISS.

Our lives were halfway settled already. I'd changed my mailing address at the post office, and we'd moved all our possessions over to Carey's house... Our house. It hadn't taken long. We didn't have much, and after the old cottage had been emptied, I left a strawberry pie in a box on Mrs. Quinn's porch to show her how much it had meant that she'd helped us. I knew she wouldn't want to be thanked in person, so I left the pie with a note that simply said, "Thank you."

Grace loved our new house, and Carey took her to the hardware store to pick a paint color for her bedroom walls. Of course she chose pink, and he painted it the next day.

She was overcoming her shyness more every day, and it was a beautiful thing to see. And Carey was adorable, figuring out how to care for a child on a daily basis. Some of it scared the crap out of him, like Grace's medication and when I made the mistake of telling him she'd probably start her period in a few years. The look on his face then was abject horror and anger, and he vowed to arrest any boy who tried to touch her.

But with other things, he was a natural. Like connecting with her. They already had their own inside jokes, and he seemed genuinely interested in everything she was. She spent an hour one day explaining the game she liked to play on my phone, which was just a memory game with dragons, unicorns, and jackelopes, but he listened the whole time, ooo'ing and ahh'ing at all the right times, and then they'd played it.

Carey had bought Grace and me new phones, and when I said she was too young, he begged me to let her have it, saying it was for safety purposes only. But I saw the smile on both their faces, and they downloaded her game as soon as they turned the new phone on, and now, they texted more than Carey and I did. The phone was useful for more than just games though, because the insulin pump Doc Whitley had ordered for Grace would connect to it, and we'd be able to send the results to my phone, too, so we'd always know what her levels were. I was amazed at just how easy it was, and so damn thankful. I could barely imagine what it would be like not having to carry needles and insulin around in a refrigerated bag.

School registration paperwork had come, so Grace was enrolled at Wisper Elementary School for her fifth grade year, and she was excited. School didn't start till late August, though, so we had almost two months left of summer to enjoy.

My divorce from Doug came through within a week from when the governor promised to see it through, and she personally delivered the papers to me. She had been in an abusive marriage, too, before she became governor, and we sat in my new kitchen, discussing all the ways my life could change now that I was a free woman.

I explained what the divorce meant to Grace on the back

porch one afternoon while we watched a huge storm spreading its dark clouds over Wisper, its wind already starting to whip. By now, we were desperate for the rain.

Grace was fine with the divorce and with Doug being locked up. She even said she felt "relayed," and when I asked what she'd meant, she said, "You know, when somethin' happens but you're not sad about it. You're happy, and you go 'whew!'"

"Relieved?"

"That's what I said, Mama."

I laughed, and we'd gone inside to make toasted marshmallow macarons in our new kitchen. Grace chose the flavor 'cause she said Carey liked to fish and camp, so he'd love them. He'd bought out the entire freaking grocery store for us because he said he didn't know what Grace could eat, and he begged me to bake for him. So that was what we did, and it felt like we were in a queen's kitchen, we had so many ingredients to choose from.

He came home from work that night with a brand-new laptop still in its box, and when he handed it to me, he also handed me a manila folder.

"Open it."

I did, tentatively, and there was a mountain of brochures inside for online culinary and pastry schools. There was also a pamphlet for a month-long intensive program in Paris, and he said we could make a family trip of it when I was ready. I wasn't so confident that I thought I could get in, but I knew I'd try because it looked amazing. I'd been dreaming about all the French pastry techniques I could learn since that day, and I'd been teaching myself French in secret with an app on my new phone.

I wasn't being secretive on purpose, but I supposed it was

a habit I'd have to learn to break. For so long, I had to hide anything that made me smile.

My father hadn't been arrested, though he was being sued by many people and businesses. Jillian had used his name and his clout to further her evil schemes, and he was left to clean up after her. The FBI hadn't yet found her, but they said they'd keep looking.

He called every night to check on us and to try to talk to me, but I finally told him I wasn't ready. I needed more time. I wasn't sure if I'd ever be ready, but he was Grace's grandfather, and since everything had happened, she'd been asking about him, so I hoped for her sake the forgiveness, or at least partial forgiveness, would come in time.

But I wasn't in a hurry. It was time for us to live. We weren't sad and scared anymore, and that meant there was a whole world out there for Grace and me, and we were both more than ready to take it by storm.

The actual storm, the one howling outside, was finally here, the thunder shaking our home in the middle of the night, when Carey got a call on his radio. Wisper had cancelled its Fourth of July celebration and fireworks because of the storm, and it seemed anticlimactic to such a degree that I felt like I was mourning the loss just a little. I'd been waiting for it like it was a celebration for the end of a really sucky era.

"Sorry, babe. I gotta go into the station. Abey said there's an accident down Route 20, and there's been some kinda vandalism near the station. A broken window and a small fire. I gotta check it out."

"Okay. Be careful. It's really nuts out there," I said, pulling the covers up around my ears when the thunder boomed so loud, they started ringing.

"I will," he said, and he leaned over me on the bed to kiss me when he pulled his pants up.

I looked in his eyes, watching how the light from the bedside lamp made them less brown and more cinnamon.

"Why you lookin' at me like that?"

"Oh, no reason."

He looked down at his legs. "What?"

His uniform pants hugged his strong thighs in just the right way, and when he strapped his holster to one of those thighs, my belly fluttered, and I imagined him trapping my legs between his own. Shrugging, I said, "I just never thought I'd find polyester sexy."

"Oh, really?" He kissed me again, tugging the blanket down to my waist, and he slipped his arm under my back and lifted me to meet his lips again. "Abey says we oughta cut the legs off our pants to make bootie shorts. Think that'd do it for ya?"

"Oh yeah," I said, giggling, and he tucked me back under the blanket and turned, smacking his ass cheeks with both hands.

"I'll do it tomorrow. Gotta go. I love you."

"I love you too. Get outta here, sexy Sheriff Michaels."

He grabbed his hat from a hook on the wall and plopped it on his head. "Bye, my Frannie."

But he poked his head back in the door. "You girls gonna be okay?"

"Yes," I said, smiling when his worry over leaving us warmed my whole body. "Go. We'll be fine. It's just a little thunderstorm."

"'Kay," he said, "call if you need me," and he knocked on the door frame and left.

After wandering into the kitchen for a glass of water, I checked on Grace. She was blissfully oblivious to the storm and sleeping like a rock, so I watched the rain pummel the street in thick sheets from the dark living room window for a while. I couldn't believe how different our lives were now, and I remembered being afraid of the dark. Now, I welcomed it 'cause I knew I could handle it.

I kept thinking I was living a dream, but it was the past that was the dream, hazy and see-through now that it was over, and I was glad for that. I felt like myself again, like nothing and no one would get in Grace's and my way ever again. I wouldn't let them.

Finally, I went back to bed, snuggling into the down comforter, feeling overly happy that, for once, I wasn't sweating and hot in the middle of the night. We had air conditioning now, and Carey kept it at a low sixty-seven degrees, but when I was seconds away from falling into sleep, Grace screamed, and sudden terror had me ripping my blanket away to get to her.

CHAPTER TWENTY-FIVE

FRANNIE

THUNDER BOOMED AGAIN and lightning cracked while I raced to Grace's room, trying not to freak out. The fear was just a knee-jerk reaction, but we were safe from Doug now. Her night-light was probably out again, or the storm had finally woken her. I was amazed she'd been able to sleep through it this long.

"It's okay, baby, it's just the storm," I called to her, but when I got to her door, I skidded to a stop, my bare feet squeaking on the cold wood floor. Someone was standing in front of her bed.

Doug was in jail. It couldn't be him. And the person seemed slighter than a man, so I took a step closer, squinting my eyes, trying to see in the dark.

"Jillian?"

My sister turned toward me when I flicked the switch on the wall beside me and light filled the room. She'd dyed her hair black and chopped it to her chin, and she was wearing a black tank top and cutoff jean shorts. She looked like the "gothy teenager" now.

She glanced back at Grace, and Grace scrambled up to her

headboard, pulling her covers to her chin, but when Jill turned back to me, she fixed her eyes on mine. "I need my money, Fran."

"W-what? Money? I don't have your money. How did you even know we were here?" I smiled at Grace when she peeked around my sister, trying to reassure her everything was okay, and I held my arm out. "Grace, c'mere."

"Please. Like I couldn't guess you'd go running straight to your sheriff. Really, Fran? It's a little soon, don't you think? And Grace, you stay right where you are."

Grace's eyes grew large with fear. It wasn't what Jill had said that was scaring Grace but how she said it, with a threat in her voice.

"Jillian, you're scarin' her. Whatever this is, let Grace go downstairs, and you and I can talk here."

"Why would she be afraid of me? I'm her aunt."

"Because you snuck in here. It's the middle of the night, and you don't look so good." I motioned toward her, and she looked down at herself for a second, but then she straightened.

"I need that money, Fran, and we're not going anywhere until you get it for me. Grace and I will wait for you here, but if you tell Carey I'm here, this is the last time you'll see your daughter."

I couldn't believe what was coming out of her mouth. "You're threatenin' us? Are you serious right now?" She couldn't be serious, but if she was, she'd find out really quickly what lengths I'd go to for my daughter. Weak Fran was gone, and in her place was Wonder Woman.

Jillian looked around Grace's room, at all the pink stuffed animals and pictures of puppies, horses, and kittens adorning the walls. "Looks like things worked out for you just fine. So go get me my money, and I'll get out of your way."

"What money! I don't have your damn money."

"No, but your boyfriend has it at the station. I gave Doug five thousand dollars in cash, but they took it when they arrested the buffoon. Go get it."

"I don't have access to that. I wouldn't even know where to start lookin'. There is no money, Jill. Get used to it. Grace and I had to."

She scoffed and rolled her eyes. Really? Our tortured existence was annoying to her?

"What is the matter with you? Who are you? Have you always been this way? I feel like I never even knew the person I shared a room with all my life."

Anger exploded out of her, and her accent returned in a flash. High-powered Jillian McKinnon, the lawyer, was gone, and in her place was little Jilly.

"You have no idea what it was like for me, Fran! Everyone loved you. You were the perfect daughter, and you left! It's all they talked about. Daddy didn't even come to my graduation. Mama was wastin' away, and he couldn't be bothered to care. Nothin' made him happy except for his job. And I was alone. He was always gone, travelin' for work, and on the rare occasion he was home, I had to sit back and watch him with other women. Everybody knew, and everyone in this stupid town was judgin' me!"

"So w-what?" I stammered, disbelief making my brain short circuit. "You thought that was good enough reason to imprison me and Grace? Do you have any idea how bad it got for us? Do you know what he did to us? How we had to live? Don't you care? I went a whole week with nothin' to eat except for a sleeve of crackers. A week, Jillian! Because my husband was off on a bender and I had no car and no money, but I didn't eat even one single morsel of food, because if I did, that was food outta Grace's mouth, and that was unacceptable. And there you sat like a queen on a dais, judgin' me for somethin' I did when I was a teenager, tormentin' me and *fucking* with my life. With my daughter's life. What right did you have? How could you do that to us?

"Are you the reason I couldn't get a job?" I didn't know why it was only just clicking in my mind, but suddenly, I knew it was all her fault. I'd applied to fifty places when Grace was a baby, before we knew about her diabetes, and my helpful, successful sister was my reference on every single application, but they all had some stupid, lame excuse for not hiring me. It had undermined my confidence even more than my own bad decisions had. "That was you, wasn't it? 'Cause if I worked and found a way to dig us outta the hole we were livin' in, then you wouldn't have had leverage over Doug."

"Please, I did you a favor. They were all shit jobs, Fran, and you got to stay at home and play the good little housewife."

"You're delusional. That's what this is, right? You aren't in your right mind. You can't be. Get away from my daughter, or I'm callin' Carey." I was calling him either way, but I'd left my phone in my bedroom, so I had to try to lure her away from Grace so I could get it.

"The money, Fran. You need to go get it."

"Fine," I said, trying to stall. "Grace, stay here." When Grace's eyes met mine, she nodded her little head once behind Jillian. She wanted me to know she was okay. There was something else in her expression, but I didn't know what it could be. My instincts were telling me to get Jill away from her, though, so I turned and motioned for Jill to follow me and was relieved to hear her footsteps behind me. "C'mon. I have to get dressed, and you'll have to help me think of somethin' to tell Carey, 'cause he's not gonna believe that I'd leave Grace alone in the middle of the night durin' this storm."

She was desperate for the money she thought she was owed—the story of her life, apparently—but it was making her careless.

"What are you doin'?" she asked when she followed me down the hall and I went straight to my bed.

"Just gettin' my robe," I said, pulling it from the bed and over my shoulders. My phone was in the pocket. "It's cold in here."

"Hurry up, Fran. I need to get *out* of this town."

"I don't have all my clothes hung up yet. Some are still in a box." I went for the box across the room, faking having a hard time opening it and trying to figure out how to text or call Carey without her noticing.

"It doesn't matter what you wear," she barked. "There." She pointed to a pair of Carey's workout sweats hanging on the back of the closet door. "Just put those on and find some damn shoes."

"Okay." Walking to the closet, I said, "So what would you like me to tell him?"

"I don't care what you tell him! It doesn't matter, just get the money. I have nothin'. They've frozen my bank account, and Daddy locked me out of his."

Pulling Carey's sweats on as slowly as I could, I laughed and said, "Maybe you shoulda thought about that before you—"

"That's enough." She grabbed the back of my neck, and I froze with one leg in the sweats and the other trapped somewhere in the middle. "I'm not stupid, big sister. I know what you're doin'."

"Jillian, let *go* of me." The ice in my voice scared even me, and Jillian stumbled back a step.

When she let go, she pushed me, and I fell forward. But when my knees hit the floor, the bone cracking against the hard wood, I snapped. She was no better than Doug. In fact, she was worse. She'd known all along what he'd been doing to Grace and me, and she allowed it to happen. She'd facilitated it and turned her nose up at it at the same time.

I lost my sister for good in that moment. The anger inside me grew and grew until it couldn't fit inside my body anymore. I lunged at her from the floor, growling or screaming something. I wasn't sure what. The sound was foreign, and somewhere in my mind, a sudden thought registered: if I let myself hurt her the way I wanted to, I was no better then she or Doug either.

The rest of me didn't care, though, because my hands wrapped around her throat. She'd been three inches taller than me since we were in middle school, but the momentum and the force of my anger at her in that moment propelled me forward, like a wild animal, and I took her down to the floor.

She kicked and reached, trying to choke me, too, but I managed to pin her arms with my knees, and she cried that I was hurting her.

"And now you know how it feels."

"Mama?"

Grace appeared in the doorway, and the look of fear on her face stopped me cold. I couldn't hurt my sister. Grace deserved better than that, and so did I. "Call Carey, baby. Where's your phone?"

She held it up, the thing seeming huge in her little hand. The screen was still lit and displaying her messaging app. "Already did."

Our front door slammed open downstairs, and within seconds, Carey, Abey, and Frank Sims were all surrounding Jill and me in the bedroom. Carey lifted me off the person who used to be my sister, and Abey hauled her off the floor. The petite, blonde female deputy was a lot stronger than she looked, and she was smiling like a fool when she handcuffed Jillian.

"Whoowee," Frank said, tipping his hat back on his head. "What a week."

"You have *nothin'* on me," Jillian spat.

"No?" Carey asked. "Then how come you're shakin' in your boots? No matter. Ain't my place to build a case against you. I'm just the guy who gets to haul your ass to jail. Suits me fine." He turned me in his arms to face him while my sister struggled against the handcuffs Abey had just wrapped around her wrists. "Work for you, Frannie?"

"Works for me," I said.

After watching Abey and Frank escort my sister out our front door and through the pouring rain to Abey's patrol car, Carey turned me in his arms, holding my face between his hands, looking in my eyes. "You okay?"

I nodded up at him, my heart beating so fast that I was afraid it would stutter and stop. "Grace?"

"Right here, Mama," she said, and her head popped up behind the couch.

"Oh, my girl. C'mere."

She came to us standing in the doorway, and Carey wrapped us both up in his strong arms. "Told ya. You're better than that." He winked at me.

"It was a close call," I admitted.

"Nope"—he leaned down to kiss my nose—"it wasn't close at all. I know you, Frannie, and you're the best kinda person there is. It's why I love you."

"Me too," Grace said, hugging me harder.

"Can I ask you a question though?" Carey said, and he

wiggled his eyebrows under his hat, rainwater dripping onto Grace and me from the brim.

"What?"

In the most awful French accent, he said, *"Voulez-vous coucher avec moi?"*

"What's that mean?" Grace asked, scrunching her nose in confusion.

I laughed and shook my head. "I can't hide anything from you, can I, Sheriff?"

"Nope. You sure can't, and I hope you never will again."

EPILOGUE
CAREY

"Gracie," Dean asked, "if you don't wanna catch anything, why're you botherin' to fish at all?"

We were standing a few feet away from the girls, three feet deep in the river. Dean and I both wore waders 'cause the water came up to our knees, but Gracie was in her pink and purple striped bathing suit and was wet from head to toe. The fishing hat I'd bought for her was shielding her easily burned skin from the harsh sun, but we'd pinned our favorite flies to it, so it doubled as a display.

"You don't wanna help 'em?" He looked back at his daughters, covered in dirty sand, giggling and knocking over the "sandcastle" they'd built, but it was really more just a sand lump.

I looked down at Gracie, and she smiled up at me. "Nope," she said.

"How come?" His daughters had zero interest in fishing with us, and he couldn't understand why Grace did.

"'Cause Gracie's a master fisherperson. She takes it very seriously," I said, and Dean looked back and forth between us, then shrugged. She refused to attach a hook to her line, and he was stumped by it.

She was still a little shy around my friends sometimes, but it never stopped her from standing by my side in the river all day. She still hadn't caught a fish, and I doubted she'd ever truly try, but being together was the thing. And she didn't get mad anymore if I caught a fish 'cause we took the catch home and cooked it up for supper. Oddly, she loved fish, and she liked to help me grill them on our back porch.

My mama called from the riverbank, "Son, c'mere. Maybe you can decide this disagreement I'm havin' with Fran." She was ecstatic when I told her Fran and I were together, and she'd been up to visit several times since. Her only comments besides jumping for joy that she was finally a grandma was "It's about time," and "I hope you locked that motherfucker up for good."

Which, by the way, wasn't far off the mark. Doug Morris, Frannie's *ex*-husband, was still locked up in jail, and it looked like he'd be headed toward twenty years in the Wyoming State Penitentiary once the courts got through with him. Apparently, he'd dug himself in pretty deep with little Jilly, helping her plot, scheme, steal, and blackmail all kinds of people, starting with court clerks and going all the way up to the attempted bribe of Governor Buchanan and two senators. And that wasn't even mentioning what he'd done to the local farmers here and around El Paso.

We wouldn't be seeing Dumbass Doug Morris any time soon, and that worked out well for all of us. Especially Gracie. Since he'd been arrested, she was a different kid. She wasn't perfect by any means, which was a good thing, and she was finally coming into her own. She'd even been grounded for talking back to her mama, and Frannie told me later that night after she'd sent Gracie to bed early that she was proud of her for it 'cause it meant Gracie was finally free to be a normal kid.

My mama was a fantastic grandma. Since she was a redhead, too, Gracie had dubbed us The Four-Square Red Squad, and they were two peas in a pod. Mama was teachin' her to swing a golf club so Grace would be prepared when we flew down to Arizona for a visit.

"Golfing lessons" had turned out to be code for dating, though she really was learning to golf. My mama had fallen in love again after all these years, but she'd been a little worried to tell me about the guy. Andy was all right, though. He was a retired Tempe detective, so we had plenty to talk about, and he treated my mama with respect and love, and that was all I could ask for. She was happy, and I was happy for her.

When I'd waded back through the water and was standing in front of her and Frannie, both sitting on a blanket in front of the tree Grace had leaned against to read not so long ago, I stuck the end of my rod in the sand. "What's up, ladies?"

"Your mama was just weighin' in on a somewhat… sensitive subject," Frannie said, and she cocked an eyebrow.

"Do I wanna know?"

Mama crossed her arms, like she was preparing to argue. "Well, I think y'all should get pregnant right away. Who says you have to be married first? But apparently, I'm the only one who thinks so."

"Jeez, Mama," I said. "Would you butt out?"

"Sorry, Lynelle," Fran said with a smirk. "You've been outvoted." She held out her hand, and I took it and tugged her up to my side, and she hugged me, hiding her mouth in my neck, whispering, "Think we should put her out of her misery?"

"Nah," I whispered back, pulling my fingers through her

wavy hair. The sunshine made it copper colored, and the shiny strands felt like satin on my skin. "Let's make her wait. She deserves it for being so nosy."

"What are y'all whisperin' about?"

"Nothin', Ma. Don't you worry about it. Besides, I already gave you a granddaughter. Now you just sound greedy."

"I know, thank you. I love bein' a grandma so much. But now I want *more* grandbabies!"

"Dream on," I said, smirking, and I kissed my Frannie.

Later that night, after dinner and after Gracie had fallen asleep between Fran and me on the couch, we tucked her into bed, but I went in for a second tuck and a perimeter check while Fran and Mama made their way to the kitchen.

"Good night, Carey," Gracie said, yawning when she peeked her eyes open.

"Night, my Gracie Mae. You have fun today?"

She nodded, her little head rubbing against her pillow, and static made strands of her hair stand up. Now that the humidity spell we'd had at the beginning of summer was gone, the air was over-dry, and we kept the house so cool, it was like we lived in Alaska half the time.

"I'm glad. I was thinkin' we might try a new spot next time. There's a buncha creeks and smaller rivers we could explore. Whatcha think?"

"Yeah," she said, her eyes lighting up.

"Alright, then. Get some sleep. You can dream about all the fish you'll never catch." I winked and turned to switch her dino night-light on. We'd decorated her bedroom with pink cats and dogs, but when Fran told her we could get her a new night-light to match, she stomped up a fit. Her dino was the friend who'd gotten her through some dark nights, and she said she'd never get rid of him.

"I love you," she said in the smallest voice, and I nearly fell over. Was I the same guy who only months ago was having mild panic attacks at the thought of being a dad? I couldn't even remember who that guy was 'cause it felt like Gracie had always been mine. I wasn't her father or her parent; I was her *dad*, and I was more proud of that fact than I'd ever been of anything. She hadn't called me "daddy" yet, but I had a feeling it was coming, and even if it didn't, it was still who I was.

Swooping down, I scooped her out of bed and hugged her so hard, she giggled and squirmed to get loose. When she did, she wrapped her arms around my neck and kissed my nose. "You should shave this scratchy beard."

"Oh, I see how it is. You're gettin' bossy already? I thought I had a few years till that happened."

She shrugged one shoulder. "Just sayin'."

"I love you, too, Gracie. You can't even know how much." Laying her back on the bed, I covered her with her blanket. "I'm here whenever you need me, okay? Always."

"'Kay," she said, snuggling into her pillow.

I watched from her doorway while she fell asleep—once her eyes were closed, it hadn't taken but a minute—and I could've sworn my heart quadrupled in size in that moment.

When I walked in the kitchen, Fran set down her mug and reached for me, and I wrapped my arms around her and lifted her out of her chair, then sat in the same chair and plopped her on my lap.

"Caveman," she said, but she smiled. "We were just talkin' about my mama."

"I still miss Sophia," my mama said wistfully. "Gosh, we

were the best of friends back then. I remember so many nights sittin' out on your back porch or ours, drinkin' iced tea or coffee. We were a couple of gossips, I tell ya."

"Oh, I remember," I said, chuckling.

"Up until almost the end, we talked every day."

"Did you see her a lot when she was sick?" Fran asked, and I knew she was still beating herself up about not being here when her mama passed.

"Not a lot. They were in Cheyenne by then, and she was tired most days," my mama said. "But we still talked on the phone when she was feelin' up to it."

"What'd you talk about?"

"Oh, all kinds of things, but we talked about you and Grace quite a lot."

"You did?"

"'Course we did, Fran. She missed you both."

"How could she miss a kid she'd never met?"

"She felt awful about that."

"I know. She wouldn't go against my dad's wishes. She never could. She was always tryin' to please him."

"She loved him, honey."

"Why? He never deserved her."

"Who can explain true love?" Mama shrugged. "But she did. She loved him to the end."

"He cheated on her," Frannie said, and she swiped a tear away from her eye with a flick of one finger. "Her death was his fault."

"She forgave him, Fran," Mama said, and she sipped her tea. "It was hard for her at first, but before the end, she found her peace with his infidelity. It didn't help the anorexia, but that wasn't all about him. You have to know that."

"Well, I don't. I can't understand that."

"You should try, 'cause part of the reason she forgave him was you."

"Me?"

"She knew your daddy would come around eventually, and when he did, she didn't want you to still be holdin' onto her anger. She hoped you'd forgive him too."

Frannie snuggled back against my chest, and I wrapped my arms around her tight.

"I'm not sure I can do that. I'm tryin' for Grace's sake, but it's… hard for me."

"I know, sweetie," Mama said. "But you're doin' your best, and that's all anybody can ask for." She got up to pour herself more tea, then sat back down and squeezed a lemon piece over her mug and grabbed one of Fran and Gracie's cookies from a plate in the middle of the table. She tossed it in her mouth, chewing and swiping crumbs off her shirt. "So, how'd that meetin' go with the investor gentleman?"

"Oh, it was fine, I guess," Frannie said. "A little awkward, honestly."

"How so?"

"Um, well, I prepared a bunch of pastries for him, and he seemed excited to try everything and to talk about my ideas, but he was drinkin' whiskey or tequila or somethin'. I could smell it mixed in with whatever else was in his cup, but he seemed to like what I served him, especially the profiteroles. He said that after I do the Paris intensive, we should talk again. Actually," Frannie said, turning to look at me, "did I tell you I ran into him a couple months ago when I went to talk to Brady Douglas at his mama's law office? Mr. Burroughs seemed upset that day. I dunno what that was about, but Brady was flustered by the guy. Do they know each other?"

"Yeah," I said. "Brady is Mr. Burroughs's lawyer here in

town. I dunno how well they know each other, but they're acquainted. I think the guy's been goin' through somethin'. I don't know if you've heard about it, but he was involved in a situation a few years back that landed him in the hospital for a while, and he lost some people close to him. They were murdered back in Boston where he's from."

Mama gasped. "Oh my."

"Yeah. It's been a while, but I'm not sure he ever really recovered. You've met Mr. Burroughs's sister, actually. Aislinn, Finn's girlfriend?"

"Oh yes," Mama said. "The lovely blind girl? She's gorgeous. Finn seems completely smitten with her."

"She is very pretty," Frannie said.

"She ain't got nothin' on you," I told her, and I nuzzled my nose to her cheek to kiss her.

"I think you're biased, Sheriff Michaels."

"I think you're biased about my bias, Mrs. Michaels."

"Wha—? Mrs. Michaels?" Mama stomped her foot beneath the table.

"Yeah, sorry, Mama," I said, chagrin making me blush. Plus, I was hoping my mama wasn't gonna swat my thirty-two-year-old ass. "But we did it. We needed to get hitched quick so Gracie's medicine would be covered by my government insurance, but I promise, we'll do the big ceremony and a party and whatever else y'all want."

"Oh, kids, I'm sad I wasn't there when you were joined together the way you always shoulda been"—she reached for our hands across the table, and we each gave her one—"but I understand why you did it that way. I forgive you both just as long as you promise that when we do the weddin', I get to pick out the flowers. I didn't get to have flowers at my weddin', and I've been waitin' your whole life for it."

"Deal," Frannie said. "I get the final say on the cake, but

you can help me plan and choose my dress, and I'll teach you about Grace's insulin pump and her diet so she and the baby can come stay with you when we go on our honeymoon."

"Aw, I'd love that. You know, Andy would love that too —" She dropped our hands and stood straight up. Her chair fell behind her, and she clasped her hands together like she was praying. "Did you just say… baby?"

"Oops." Frannie giggled. "Guess the cat's outta the bag now. Look out, Wisper. Lynelle Michaels will be on a gossip bender in three… two… one…"

"Oh, thank the sweet baby Jesus! Who should I call first?"

"Aaand she's off," I said. "I guess dreams really do come true." I laughed at my mama walking circles around the kitchen, texting God knew who, and reciting a list of people she'd call just as soon as she could "catch her breath again." Eventually, she'd remember she hadn't hugged us yet, and that would set her to crying, I was sure.

Frannie turned, throwing her leg over mine to straddle me in the middle of the kitchen. "They do. You made my dreams come true, every single one."

"Right back atcha, my Frannie, and some I didn't even know I wanted." Gracie peeked around the kitchen door just then. "Like this little dream right here," I said, and I reached my arm out for her. "Ain't you s'posed to be asleep?"

She shrugged. "I heard somebody screechin'." When she hugged us, she whispered, "You told Grandma about the baby, huh?"

Mama yelped when she saw Grace. "Grace Mae! You're gonna be a big sister!"

She lifted her straight off the ground and twirled her around the kitchen, and I laughed and answered Gracie's question. "How ever could you tell?"

If you liked *Rivers Between Us* (or loved it, I hope), please leave a review—even just a few words would help—wherever you buy your books, Goodreads, or Bookbub. Self-published indie authors rely heavily upon reviews to get our stories out to the masses. And thank you. I know it takes time to do this. I appreciate the time out of your day and the effort.

Dear Reader: I knew when I was writing the Cade Ranch series that there were a lot more HEAs to be found in Wisper, and as readers began to fall in love with the cowboys, more and more of you reached out to me, demanding them. But I had already begun working on them. I love the people of Wisper just as much as you, and if one of them needs a happy ending ;), I'm gonna write it!

Thank you for continuing to read what I write. I can't even explain what that means to me, how it helps me and propels me forward to the next story.

There's a playlist on my website for each book I write. Each couple's love story is told in my head through songs. If you'd like to listen, visit my website, gretarosewest.com

And on that note, here it is. An excerpt from *Storms Inside Us*. Remember Brady and Theo from Kevin's book, *Busted*? Turn the page for a sneak peek into their story.

EXCERPT FROM STORMS INSIDE US
BRADY

He was drunk, but still, he was beautiful.

Theo Burroughs was some kind of enigma. A sad, tortured rich boy, but there was something behind all that, and he didn't want people to see him that way; he wanted to take responsibility for the actions and choices he'd made in the past, but he was struggling with it.

It was true, he'd been through a lot, though that didn't exempt him from behaving like every other responsible adult. But something about this man spoke to me.

No, that wasn't right.

He unnerved me. Knocked me off balance somehow. And I was known for being balanced. The lawyer, always the calmest person in the room.

I dreamt about him at night.

So when he suddenly appeared outside my office door one summer morning, I was more than a little surprised.

"Mr. Burroughs?"

He spoke slowly. "I, uh… Well, I'm sorry. You're busy. I —shit." His shirt was rumpled and he was wearing sweatpants. I'd *never* seen Theodore Burroughs in sweatpants.

"It's okay," I said, trying to hide my confusion, but my face was doing its own thing. I couldn't help that. He looked like a bum. Billionaire to vagrant in 5.6 seconds? Three years was probably a better estimate of the time it had taken the guy to fall from grace. "If you wanna wait, I can see you in a bit."

"I can go," my client, Fran Morris, said.

"No. Please, excuse me for just a minute." Standing from my creaky office chair, I tried not to knock over the fifty potted plants my mom kept leaving in my office because she thought they'd help me better connect to the universe or something. "Come with me, Theo," I said to him, trying to steer him back down the hallway.

"I'm sorry," he said to Fran, and I could smell the alcohol on his breath. Had he started drinking already, or was he still drunk from the night before?

"Excuse us, Fran. I'll be right back."

Leaving her waiting in my office, I closed the door and ushered him toward the empty waiting room in the little law office I shared with my mom.

"I need to talk to you," he said.

"Okay, that's fine, but I'm with a client right now. If you wanna wait, I can see you after I'm done." I winced. "Or maybe you'd like to wait till you're a little more… prepared?"

"Pr-prepared?" he asked, and he blinked and swayed a little.

"Um, yeah, you know, maybe if you got a little rest? Drank some water?" *Dried out?* But I didn't say that. I was trying to be subtle, but it didn't seem to be working, so I took the direct route because Fran was waiting, and she had some real problems, things that could impact her and her daughter's lives. "You need to sober up, Theo. G'on home. Get some sleep, and we can meet tomorrow mornin', okay? Sound good?"

"Yeah, okay," he said. "I'm sorry. I've been waiting to talk to you. I mean, I didn't have an appointment. I just meant, I've been wanting to talk to you, but every time I try, I lose my nerve." He hung his head. "I'm sorry. This isn't me. I-I… I don't know who this is, but it isn't me."

Reaching for his hand at his side, I touched my fingers there, and he looked into my eyes. "It's okay. Is what you want to talk to me about urgent?"

"No. I… No."

"Alright then. Get some rest and we can speak tomorrow. Can you be here at nine?"

"Yes, of course. Thank you."

"Do you need a ride?"

"No," he said. "Don't be absurd. I'm a grown man."

"I didn't mean anything by it. It's just that you live in Jackson and I haven't noticed you driving a car. Do you have one?"

"No. Wait. You've noticed me?"

Smiling, I said, "You aren't hard to miss." Wasn't that the truth.

He hung his head again. "Because I'm a wreck, right?"

No. Because you're a beautiful wreck.

Pre-Order Storms Inside Us Now
Releasing Winter 2022

WANT MORE?

Become a Wisperite!
Join my newsletter for exclusive stories, Wisper news, and
The Cade Ranch Sexcapades—naughty little interludes for
my subscribers ONLY!
Jack and Evvie's wedding scenes are there!
Sign up for your first FREE short story,
Wild Heart: Welcome to Wisper
Sign up on my website!
gretarosewest.com

I would love to hear from you, email me at
greta@gretarosewest.com.
I'll reply.
You can find me on the usual social sites, but I mostly hang
out on Instagram, Facebook, and Goodreads.

Join my Team!
Receive an advanced review copy of my next book. Join my
ARC Team, a wonderful group of people who help get the
word out when I release a new book!
Sign up on my website
gretarosewest.com

ABOUT THE AUTHOR

 Greta Rose West was a floundering artsy flake until cowboy Jack Cade showed up, knocking on the door of her brain, pounding on it, and then he just plain kicked it down. She's a boy mom to a grown freakin' man, and she lives in NW Indiana with her husband and her two precocious kitties, Geoff Trouble and Sally Mae Midnight. When she's not writing, she's reading and devouring music. She enjoys indie films no one else likes, and her favorite food is Aver's Veggie Revival pizza.

You can find her on Instagram @gretarosewest, in her Facebook group, Wisperites Unite!, or on her website.

gretarosewest.com.

www.ingramcontent.com/pod-product-compliance
Lightning Source LLC
Chambersburg PA
CBHW061103190726

48286CB00006B/1868